ALL BETS OFF

Jaime Clevenger

Spinsters Ink
2006

Spinsters Ink, Inc.
PO Box 242
Midway Florida. 32343

Printed in the United States of America on acid-free paper
First Edition

Editor: Cindy Cresap and Catherine Harold
Cover designer: LA Callaghan

ISBN 1-883523-71-0

Acknowledgments

First, I must thank my grandma and great aunts who planted the seed for this little tale. Many years ago, I sat on the piano seat in my great aunt's crowded house in San Francisco and listened in awe as the gray-haired matriarchs shared their accounts of survival during the 1906 Quake and the Great Fire. My mom told me then to learn from the women who had lived our history rather than just the textbooks. The characters in this novel are mere shadows of the strong and intelligent women that persevered through this disaster, and I can only hope that they don't mind the liberties I have taken with their stories.

Thank you to my family and friends for your support in this project and for reminding me to take time to occasionally sleep, laugh and sing out of tune. Thank you to Linda Hill for giving this story a place to grow. Thank you to my editors, Cindy Cresap and Catherine Harold. Special thanks to my readers, advice-givers and some of the smartest women I know: Christine Clevenger, Jackie Murray and Corina McKendry.

About the Author

Born and raised in the San Francisco Bay Area, Jaime Clevenger has a deep-seated love for the people, history and landscape that make Northern California beautiful, engaging and entirely unique. Jaime currently lives in a beach town with her fabulous partner, three cats and lots of plants. She spends her days riding her horse, teaching karate and writing. By night, she works as an emergency veterinarian where she has occasionally been caught scribbling down story ideas on the back side of prescription notes. Jaime has also written The Unknown Mile and Call Shotgun and is currently adding the finishing touches on a fourth novel. She hopes very much that you enjoy this book.

Prologue

A faint sniffling teased me from sleep when the sky was still a hazy black. I pulled the wool blanket over my ears, hoping to muffle the sound, and turned away from the dark window. Fog settled over the city nearly every night, and I hated the damp air that seeped through the thin pane of glass. Someone was crying. Before long, the noise became more irritating than the chill on my back. I plugged my fingers in my ears and swore silently at Mary. Mary, my six-year-old sister, would often wake me in the dead of night having to pee. The darkness frightened her, and she'd whine until I lit a candle. Sometimes I wished she'd just wet the sheets.

When a fresh round of sobs broke loose, I grudgingly eyed the bed opposite mine. Strangely, Mary was sound asleep. Next to her, a trembling form disturbed the even line of the faded purple quilt. It was Caroline, my other sister, but the quilt shook as though a creature much bigger than a four-year-old girl was hiding under it. "Caroline?"

No answer.

"Are you all right, Carol?" I asked.

The sobs grew less frequent, more subdued with the attention. If I ignored her, maybe she'd drift back to sleep. I rolled over and nestled lower in the covers. An intermittent whimper continued for the next few minutes. I finally slipped out of my warm cocoon, cursing the cold floorboards that stung my feet as I padded over to the other bed. Without waking Mary, I tried to make a space under the quilt. Caroline peeked her head up and moved over to make room for me. She leaned against my shoulder and rubbed the tears from her eyes. Her face felt hot, almost feverish, though she shivered with my touch. Mary snored on. The sound seemed almost stubborn now.

"What's the matter, Carol?" I smoothed her hair into place. "You're not the one who's usually up at this time of night. Are you afraid of the dark now, too?"

"The house was shaking." She paused and gazed up at me. "Did you feel it?"

"There wasn't any shaking."

"Yes, there was." Her light blue eyes shifted uneasily, and I half expected some tale of ghosts to come out of her. She continued in a whisper, "It shook so hard that the roof cracked and then everything fell down. I saw the clouds."

I smiled. "You've had a bad dream. That's all."

"No, it wasn't a dream. The house broke. I saw it. First the roof, then the windows . . ." She pointed at the window by my bed and nodded. "Everything broke as loud as thunder."

"Maybe it was thunder. There could be a storm brewing. But nothing's broke, Carol. Look at the ceiling. Do you see clouds when you look up? No, only our old wood rafters. And the window isn't shattered. Maybe you had a dream of an earthquake."

"An earthquake?" She seemed to like the word and repeated it slowly as if she were tasting its newness. "Can that break a house?"

Earthquakes occurred often enough in San Francisco, but it occurred to me that Caroline was too young to have experienced one. Her dream must have been about something else. "Maybe Mary kicked you in her sleep."

"No," Caroline replied obstinately. "The whole house shook. And then a fire started." Her voice sounded distant and older than her four years. I felt a chill steal down my spine. She shot a look across the bed at Mary and then put her finger up to her lips. "Hush. We can't tell Mary. Her dolls burned."

"Caroline, look." I picked up Mary's doll, nestled between the pillows, and patted the red head as button eyes glared back at me. "There was no fire. See, the doll is just fine. She's a bit ugly, but . . ."

She started to climb out of bed. "We should wake everyone."

"No." I caught her arm and held her in place. I couldn't let her unruly imagination run wild. Of all the children, Caroline was the most spirited. And if she weren't the youngest, she would get herself in trouble all the time. Fortunately, everyone in the family kept her on tight reins. "We aren't waking anyone."

Caroline pushed away from me and stuck out her lip. "It's your fault then, Bette." Fresh tears beaded at the corner of her eyes.

I kissed her forehead and wrapped the quilt around her shoulders. "You had a bad dream, Carol, that's all. We'll stay awake and talk of good things."

She turned away and picked up Mary's doll. "Don't be frightened. I'll take care of you." She hugged the doll to her chest and continued, "We'll leave before the fire. Don't worry. I won't let you burn."

Her tone was unsettling. I shook my head firmly. "There won't be any fire."

She gave the doll another squeeze and shifted back on the pillows. "I'm still scared."

"I know." I tucked the blanket under her chin. "But you need to sleep now. Try not to think anymore about your nightmare. I'll be right here."

She closed her eyes, still cradling the doll and humming a nursery rhyme. After a while, I slipped back to my bed and spent the rest of the night listening to every creak of our old house. I didn't know what I was waiting for.

Chapter 1
April 1, 1906

"I married your father when I was seventeen," my mother announced.

For better or worse, mother was as silent as a tomb most of the time. I hadn't decided if it was better or worse. When she had something to say, she would never speak directly. What she really meant was that I should be planning a wedding soon. The bite of potato pancake in my mouth suddenly tasted as flavorless as glue paste when I considered this subject. I swallowed. "I only just turned seventeen this morning."

Mother sighed and waved her hand to dismiss this thought. "Don't try to cause trouble with an argument."

"Trouble? Because I don't want to be married at seventeen?" I had no stomach for a fight at the breakfast table and hoped she'd drop the subject.

Mother let out a long sigh. According to her, I was born causing trouble. I should have been a boy. My parents were only just married when Mother's belly began to swell. Papa worried that it was too soon to have a baby and went to see a gypsy down at the Barbary Coast. The old gypsy told him not to worry and that his wife and new son would be fine. Papa dreamed every night of this child and planned the boy's future. He even set a bet with our neighbors, claiming that Dolores, my mother, was carrying his son. Papa went silent for a month after I was born. I don't know how much money he lost on the bet, but seventeen years later, the first of April, 1906, I knew he still regretted that I turned out to be a girl. Papa named me Bette, not Betty or Beth, just Bette, like when you say "I lost that bet."

After scolding Wesley for wiping his hands on the tablecloth and glaring at Caroline, who had started to sing 'Row, row, row your boat,' Mother attacked the potato pancake on her plate. Mary, who always had to mimic Mother, wagged her finger at Wesley and Caroline and then eyed mother with a smug grin plastered on her face. Charlie had already eaten two pancakes and was wishing for a third. There weren't any more, and I considered giving him mine. Eleven-year-old boys never seemed to get their fill of any food, greens excepted.

Watching Mother fork the pancake into her mouth, I hummed the chorus of the nursery rhyme Caroline had started, just to be bothersome. Mother claimed any songs that weren't hymns were made by the devil's choir. Somehow I couldn't imagine the devil singing along with "Row, Row, Row Your Boat." Mother ignored the humming, yet her frown lines deepened when Caroline started another verse.

"That's enough singing, Carol." Mother folded her napkin and patted her lips. "Bette, your blouse cuffs are filthy."

"The horses never mind," I started, then catching the sharp look in mother's eyes, changed my tone. "I'll wash the blouse after work tonight." My work clothes, a pair of men's trousers that I had hemmed and a light blue blouse with stains on the cuffs, were never truly clean. Staring at the dirty cuffs, I imagined myself in a lacy white gown with long, white satin gloves. I couldn't help but laugh and mother's eyes narrowed at me.

Father folded his newspaper and cleared his throat. "What's this joke about, Bette?"

I stopped laughing. "Nothing."

He turned back to the paper and coughed. Mother didn't look up from her plate. I stared at her dark green dress and the pressed white apron and wondered how different she had looked in a white lace gown. The bodice from Mother's wedding dress was stored in the cedar chest in my parents' room, and I'd run across it at least a dozen times while trying to find bed linens or our one set of fancy napkins. Mother had saved it for her daughters' weddings. As far as I was concerned, the bodice could remain in that cedar chest forever.

"There's a meeting at the pier tomorrow," Papa read to no one in particular. "This newsman says we may have a strike soon."

Mother grumbled something about strikes under her breath. I knew she was worried about a strike. I was too. If the men at the waterfront didn't work, we wouldn't have any deliveries to make. Missing even a couple delivery days meant we'd be hard pressed for cash at the grocer, and Charlie's stomach wouldn't take credit.

"I want to marry when I'm sixteen," Mary said. "I don't want to wait until I'm as old as Bette and have to wear trousers."

Mary often annoyed me as much as Mother. This morning it was all I could do to ignore her comments and not start an argument. "Someone has to ask you to marry them first, you know."

"I don't want to marry at all," Charlie countered. "I'd rather be a ship clerk."

"I thought you were going to be a fireman," Wes said, his mouth full of pancakes. "Do firemen have to get married?"

Charlie nodded.

"What about ship clerks?"

"No." For some reason, Charlie had decided ship clerks didn't have to marry anyone. He was adamant about this, and the two boys fell into a discussion over which professions allowed a bachelor.

"Are you almost ready, Papa?" I asked. Papa looked as if he were lost in thought and he'd only had a few bites of his pancake. "I thought you wanted an early start today." I was anxious to escape the breakfast table and Mother's hawk-like eyes.

"My coffee's still hot." He took a sip of his coffee and nodded at my plate. "And you're not finished eating."

Mother patted her lips with a napkin and glared at me. "Charlie, go get Cousin Jane's letter from the front room. It's on the desk." Charlie excused himself from the table and reappeared a moment later with the letter in hand.

"Read," Mother decreed in her monosyllabic fashion.

Charlie groaned, as did everyone else at the table, except Mother and Papa. He had poor reading skills, and Mother was always torturing him to practice aloud. Charlie stuttered and stumbled through Jane's letter. The letter was filled with details of Jane's wedding, including the china she'd picked and the red roses on the cake. I pitied Jane, knowing that after her church bells and the handsome groom's kiss under the steeple, she would be doomed to a life filled with children, constant cooking and housework.

"That was fine reading, Charlie," Papa said, cutting Charlie off mid-sentence. No one complained that the letter wasn't finished. Papa set the newspaper on the table, coughed once, and then stood to signal our departure. "Hurry up, Bette. No reason to be late for work."

I excused myself and handed my plate of unfinished pancakes to Charlie. Without a word, he promptly wolfed down the remainder. Mother whispered something in Papa's ear and handed him our lunch sack.

Papa and I grabbed our coats and slipped out into the brisk morning. We had a long walk to the stables and always made our way silently. Later there would be enough noise to fill the day, and we both cherished our half-hour of peace. But this morning I couldn't enjoy our walk. Mother's ugly wedding dress plagued my thoughts. If it weren't for white lace, a wedding might be less onerous. As we passed the edge of Chinatown, the brightly painted gates leading into the Orient world caught my attention. I had seen the wedding parades of the exotic Chinese brides and envied their red silk gowns, but now I wondered if they had as little say in marriage as I had.

I'd been fashioning independence from wedding gowns for well over a year. My grand scheme began when I failed Classical History at St. Anthony. Instead of repeating the semester, I decided to leave two years before graduation to help Papa with his delivery business. Papa ran a two-horse wagon team delivering orders from the ship docks to the businesses in town, and when the delivery season slowed, he could barely afford his one hired man. Mother thought Charlie should help Papa with the business, but he was only ten. She wanted to cage me at home as her personal maid. For weeks I pleaded with Papa to let me help with the horses in the stables or at least loading the wagon, and every night I heard Mother telling Papa that the stableyard was no place for young women. I wouldn't let up though. Soon enough, Papa conceded, much to Mother's chagrin. Once I had wedged my way into the stables and learned to care for the horses, I made every attempt to show Papa I could drive the wagon. After a month, Papa fired the other man, and I traded my long skirts for a pair of trousers.

Mother claimed God would strike me down for wearing men's trousers. She swore she wouldn't talk to me at all, which really wasn't that surprising, but it upset Papa. We came to a compromise when I promised to wear a skirt so long as I wasn't working on the wagon and a dress every Sunday.

After a few months working with Papa, I was convinced I'd never need to marry. As I figured it, I could take over the delivery business when Papa was too old, and I'd hire Charlie to help. Papa didn't know my plan, but he knew he couldn't get along alone anymore, and he seemed to enjoy my company on the wagon. He never made any mention of my trousers, but did suggest that I embroider flowers on my blouses for Mother's sake, if not for God's. I happily embroidered roses on my blouse collar and wore dresses on Sunday, thinking this a blessing compared to spending the week as a servant to my silent mother.

We reached the stables just after seven, and half the horses were already hitched and gone for the day. Papa used to insist we begin work before daybreak, but lately he seemed to need more rest and had taken to sleeping late.

"Hello, Bette," Nathan, one of the stableboys, called to me. "No dress for work today?" He nodded sheepishly when he saw my father and added, "Morning, sir."

Nathan and his family attended our church, and I had bumped into him last Sunday after Mass. His eyes seemed to pop out of his head when he saw me in the blue dress, and I regretted the meeting instantly. The stableboys teased good-naturedly, but I was tired of being the butt of so many jokes. They couldn't understand how a girl could wear a dress one day and trousers the next. Although I looked awkward in dresses, I didn't mind the shape of my body. I was taller than most women I knew and had a broader chest, thin waist and breasts that no one would boast of. This meant that it was easier to pass as a boy when I tucked my hair back and wore trousers.

"Morning, Nathan," Papa returned. "How are your mother and father?"

"Fine, sir."

"Save some of the good grain for Trader and Midge tonight. They'll have a hard pull today." Midge, one of our two horses, whinnied when she heard Papa's voice. Her head popped over the stall gate, and she searched the corridor until she saw Papa approaching her stall. Our other horse, Trader, still had his head buried in the feed trough.

Nathan nodded at my father and then glanced at me. "Bette, I didn't mean anything by the joke about your dress." He kicked one of the tie posts and kept his eyes focused on his mud-caked boots. "You looked nice at church, that's all."

I shrugged. "I prefer my trousers."

"But you look real pretty in a dress. I mean, you look fine in trousers too, but—"

I grinned at him and then made my way over to Trader's stall. "I've got work to do, Nathan." If I had to pick one of the stableboys to bother me, at least Nathan wasn't the worst one there. He was handsome, in a way, and I didn't mind him when he smiled. But after the talk of weddings this morning, I was in a bad mood to deal with any one of the boys.

Nathan followed right behind me. "Seen Frank lately?"

Frank was my best friend and one of Nathan's old pals. "I've seen him around." I unlatched the gate on Trader's stall and slipped a halter on the horse. "Why?"

"Just say hello for me."

With a nod, I led Trader out of the stall, hoping Nathan would find some work to do and leave us alone. Papa already had Midge tied up to our wagon and was picking her hooves. He handed me the hoof pick when he had finished. "Check Trader's feet." Papa was always telling me to check the horses' feet. He was adamant about the health of their soles.

Nathan stood behind me, watching as I started on Trader's hooves. He went over to Papa's side when I glared at him. "Do you want anything else besides the extra grain for the horses, sir?"

"No, that's all. Just mind the horses well tonight."

"Yes, sir, I will. Have a good day." Nathan turned and trudged back to the barn.

When he'd finally disappeared inside, Papa whistled low and said, "I hope he doesn't forget the grain tonight. He'll probably spend all day thinking up another excuse to talk to you."

"He's just bored." I didn't want to think of Nathan trying to get my attention. "The stableboys always pester me." I doubted if I'd befriend any of them after all the teasing I'd endured about working a wagon team.

Papa and I returned from work after dusk, filthy from a muddy delivery on the south side of the city, and exhausted. The line of houses on Harrison Street seemed to stretch for miles, and the walk home always felt longer than our morning walk. You could smell and hear that you were getting close to the waterfront before you could see our home. The waterfront was known for a strange brew of Irish, Portuguese and German immigrants, loud street fights after the pubs closed, a pervasive odor of fish and the city's best apple strudel. We lived in one of the stacked homes, called that because each one was stacked up against another just like a house of cards. Our house had a real front porch with a wrought iron railing that Papa had found at the shipyards and a red door, setting it apart from the others on our side of the street. Otherwise, it was hard to tell one house from the other.

Charlie met us at the door. "You're late."

"We had a long day," Papa answered. He set his hat on Charlie's head and handed him our coats. "Go tell your mother we're home now."

"Where's Frank? I thought he would come with you." Charlie peered out the doorway as if he expected Frank to suddenly jump out from the bushes.

"He's probably still working. Don't worry. He'll be here later to fight over the food with you."

"Do we have to wait dinner for him?" Charlie asked, obviously hoping I'd say no. "There's chocolate cake tonight because it's your birthday."

"Yes, we're waiting dinner for Frank. And I know it's my birthday."

Charlie always had food on his mind, but the other children were just as excited about the cake and could hardly wait for Papa and me to clean up. Caroline and Mary helped Mother ice the cake and begged to lick the chocolate off the spoon. Wes and Charlie organized their toy soldiers' battle around securing extra slices of cake.

After Papa had changed out of his work shirt, he came into the kitchen and went over to the phonograph. It was Papa's prized possession, and none of the children were allowed near it. The sound of a waltz filled the room and Papa closed his eyes briefly and he sighed deeply. I wondered what it was about the music that he loved so much. He went over to Mother's side and laid his hand on hers, "Will you allow one dance before dinner? It's a shame to not dance to such a nice song."

She sighed and set down the dishrag. Papa smiled at her, and the next moment they were spinning about the room. I watched them, thinking that my parents could not be more different. Papa was always joking and telling stories while mother only glared and criticized. The one song ended and Mother let go of Papa's arm, muttering something about all the work she had to do. Papa let her go with his smile half-turned down. He sat down next to me and then coughed a few times as he caught his breath.

"I dance with Papa!" Caroline begged, reaching out to take Papa's thumb in her fist.

Mother quickly scolded her for bothering him. I took Caroline's hand from Papa and stood up. "You need to learn how to dance first. Stand up straight and hold both of my hands."

She looked up at me. "But you're a girl. Girls are supposed to dance with boys."

"It doesn't matter who you dance with when you're learning." I twirled her in a circle like a ballerina and then tried to follow the waltz pattern I had seen Papa dance. "See, now you're a real dancer, Miss Caroline."

She laughed and clapped her hands as I let go of her hand. Papa watched us from his seat, and I could see he wanted another dance. He smiled at me and winked, as if to say, "We can't always fight your mother, but we try."

"Another dance?" Caroline asked.

"Later. Go and help Mary with the napkins."

With a sigh, Caroline trudged over to the table. Mary was folding napkins for each plate and arranging the silverware. Of all my siblings, I believed Caroline and I were most alike. We both had straight blonde hair that wouldn't curl for church, round faces and hazel eyes. As for Mary, she looked most like Mother, with dark, almond eyes, long lashes and curly auburn hair. She also had Mother's reclusive nature. Charlie and Wes both shared Papa's dark features. Wes was little for his age and had a leaning toward gentle things, while Charlie was growing taller every day and acted like a gangly giant.

Just after the children had the table set, a knock came at the door. I ran to answer it, knowing it would be Frank. Mother shot daggers at me as I passed. She hated anyone running in the house.

"Happy Birthday!" Frank smiled and stepped through the doorway. "God, something smells delicious. I haven't missed dinner, have I? I was held up at the Douglas place. They're building a new garage for their horseless carriage."

"Don't worry. We haven't even finished cooking the spätzle," I said. "And we will always hold dinner for our guests. Even you."

"Even me? Dear Bette, how gracious you are," Frank said, faking a highbrow British accent. He grinned. "Well, I'm famished as always."

Frank and I had shared our birthday dinners for as long as I could remember. His family lived across the street from mine, and we'd been friends since we were toddlers. Our families were considered settled, by waterfront standards, meaning the same people had lived there longer than ten years. And in fact, only the grocer's family had lived in the same house for longer than one generation. Although families moved in and out of the waterfront with as much care as the tides, everyone still knew if their neighbor's business was doing well or not. Everyone also knew that Frank and I would marry. The St. Anthony clergy and the Harrison Street Grocer were to blame for propagating most of the gossip. I also blamed our mothers.

According to the rumors, our parents had a wedding planned for us since we were in diapers. For a long time, neither of us wanted any part in this scheme, but lately I'd sensed that Frank's feelings on this changed.

Although I liked Frank, I'd rather poke him in the eye than marry him, even if he was my friend. When I was nine years old and first heard the rumor about a betrothal, I wanted to kill Frank, and tried. Fortunately, he was just as strong as I was and put up a good fight. We both came home with only a few good bruises and thought that was the end of it. One of the St. Anthony nuns saw the scuffle and informed our parents about our boxing match. Neither of us could sit on the wood benches at school the next day from all of the welts that our fathers' belts had left.

"How was your day?" Frank asked.

"Good. Busy."

"Any news about the shoremen striking? I never get any gossip about the waterfront now that I work up on Nob Hill."

"No news." I shook my head, glad that Papa wasn't around to hear Frank's question. The men at the waterfront seemed to talk of nothing other than the impending strike, but I was sick of it.

"So, what are we eating with the spätzle? Is that sausage I smell?" Frank asked.

I waited for him to hang his coat in the hall closet. "Do you think of anything besides food?"

He considered the question while rubbing his stomach. "Not this long after lunch."

"You're impossible."

Frank grinned. "Is that sausage from Mr. O'Connor?"

"Yes. Don't tell me you can smell the difference."

He nodded. "He has the best meats in town. What else?"

"Green beans." I laughed as he cringed at this. Frank avoided all vegetables. "And chocolate cake."

"God, I'm hungry. Lead the way."

Nothing smelled as appetizing as sausage and buttered spätzle noodles. I forgot the strain of the day and relaxed in the warmth of the kitchen as Frank and Papa started up a conversation and Mother sent me back to cooking. Frank and Papa both had no new news on the probability of the shoremen's strike, but their theories were plentiful. After awhile I had to concentrate on the green beans, minding the boiling water, and I lost track of what Frank and Papa were saying. Their voices grew hushed, and I had to struggle to hear what they were secretly discussing. Just as

Mother was moving the sausage off the stove, I heard Frank say something about an engagement. A hiss of grease covered his words.

I couldn't help but stare at Frank. What had he just said to Papa? Suddenly Mary started crying over someone taking her doll's blanket. Caroline blamed both of my brothers. Mother hushed them into silence with chores setting the table. In the cacophony of complaints from my sisters and the rattle of dishes, I missed every word Papa mumbled. He only mumbled when he didn't want someone nearby to hear. Before I'd moved the green beans out of the water, Frank and Papa were done talking.

Papa wouldn't tell me what they'd been discussing, and I knew it couldn't be good news. During dinner, Frank kept smiling at me from across the table rather than focusing on his sausage. I know people are supposed to smile at you on your birthday, but ordinarily Frank has as much interest in eating as a pregnant sow at the feed trough. Every time he looked over at me I wanted to scream. Why would he talk to Papa about an engagement? He hadn't even asked me.

I caught him staring once, and it was almost as if you could hear him thinking, "Someday you'll be my wife." I wanted to stick my tongue out at him. He grinned smugly after complimenting me on the food, and I had to hold my knee to keep from kicking him under the table.

At one point Frank asked me to pass the salt. I realized with dread that Papa used the same tone of voice to order mother to do something. Of course I had to pass him the salt. When our hands touched he grinned again, just like a hyena, and God help me—I had my fork in my hand and nearly stabbed him. Fortunately for Frank, there was grease on the fork and my last bite of spätzle was balanced between the prongs. All his grinning wasn't worth the hell I would catch from Mother, and I didn't want to make a mess that I'd just have to clean later.

Frank had never asked how I felt about marriage. We were not in love. We were only close friends. And although Frank was a few months older, he was none the wiser than me. He was honest and friendly, just as everyone said, and handsome enough in that tall, dark, brooding way. Unfortunately, I couldn't think romantic thoughts about him. Whenever I tried, I pictured the kid who sucked his thumb incessantly, and it was hard to find a man attractive with that image in your mind. But it didn't matter. I wanted to be an independent old maid regardless of my options for a husband.

After our meal, the girls dressed their dolls for bed and the boys fought another battle with their soldiers. Papa and Frank spoke heatedly of unions while Mother and I cleaned the dishes. Charlie and Wes broke away from their battle lines for a few minutes to inhale the allotted fat slice of chocolate cake. Mary and Caroline were entranced with two new doll nightgowns that my mother had sewn. Before long, Wes started fussing from the corner of the kitchen where the one-inch tall metal infantry-men were arranged. The soldiers were splattered with what appeared to be the blood of battle, but in actuality was only chocolate from Charlie's fingers. This chocolate upset Wes so much that he gathered his troops and set them all in the bathroom sink for a bath. Wes was perhaps the cleanest little boy I've ever known.

I tried to listen to Frank and Papa's conversation over the din of the children and the dishwashing. Papa was arguing that the shoremen should strike now, the earlier the better, but Frank thought they should wait until they had more workers guaranteed to strike. Both of them talked about waterfront politics as though it were candy they couldn't get enough of. I challenged them both, "Every time you turn around someone's talking about striking as though it were a good thing, and what good does come of it? Children go hungry, the women work more, and the men drink more."

Frank scoffed at this. "Bette, you don't know the half of it though. Unions are getting the workers rights—rights for a ten-hour workday and rights to be paid on time."

Papa added, "You can't think only about what the strike means to the workers and their families today. We must think about what the workers will gain if the strike succeeds." He continued Frank's list of all the things that the union men had achieved.

I was annoyed. "Strikes mean that we have to turn down delivery jobs, and we can't afford to lose income. Who figures out the cost of a strike? What are we gaining by it?"

Papa ignored my question, and Mother silently chastised me. With one look she could speak multitudes. Now she was saying, "Let the men talk big." Women weren't supposed to make comments about the men's work. I picked up the evening paper and scanned the headlines without reading the articles. Papa finally cleared his throat and announced it was bedtime for the younger ones.

Frank looked over at me and winked once. Our arguments never lasted long, and he hadn't even realized I was upset. The children's bedtime was our cue. He stood up and thanked Mother, then Papa, for inviting him to dinner and shook hands with Charlie and Wes. Little Caroline asked Frank for a goodnight hug, and Mary's eyes nearly popped out of her head. I grabbed my coat and Mother nodded at me.

"Yes, go, but mind the hour, Bette," Papa said.

Ordinarily I would have been held at home at the late hour. But considerations were made for birthdays, and my parents trusted Frank to keep me out of trouble. Frank and I set out toward Market Street, catching a cable car heading to Union Square. We were both feeling antsy for a night on the town. Frank nudged me as we found seats in the car and pointed at the passing buildings. "I'm going to work in that building one day. I'll have a big office with a view of the bay, and I'll spend my days counting gold coins and deciding who deserves a loan."

"You? A banker?" I smiled. We had just passed the financial district, and I was trying to picture Frank wearing an expensive suit with a little watch in his breast pocket, like all the businessmen wore. "Frank, you're miserable at math."

"I don't care. I'll be miserably rich off speculations. Someone else will do my arithmetic." He winked, knowing that I was always the one with higher arithmetic scores. Frank would bite his nails and struggle in agony over an algebra equation for ten minutes before asking for my help. "And where should we live, my dear, when we are rich and famous? A mansion on Van Ness Avenue or Nob Hill? Or shall we leave dear San Fran for Manhattan? Perhaps Paris or London?"

I laughed and pointed at a vagrant curled up on the steps of the Call Building. "I'd rather live there than be rich and famous. The rich on Nob Hill never seem as happy as the tramps fresh off the ferry. And I'd guess it's the same for the gluttons in Manhattan, Paris, and London."

"Well, then we'll be tramps of the world together and spy on all the rich." He smiled grandly. "Shall we head to the Ferry Building tonight and see what passage we might beg for?"

"No. Tonight I want to enjoy our city." I wondered where we could go on our budget of a dollar fifty between the two of us. Frank's family was slightly better off than mine, but we were both saddled neither rich nor poor. Both of our families lived in attached houses, but Frank's house had a fresh coat of paint. Owing more to the fact that Frank's mother had less fertility than my mother, they were able to save more of Jack's income, and Frank's position in the world was much better secured than my own. Frank was an only child, and one mouth costs much less than five to feed. "Let's sneak into the Palace Hotel."

Frank puffed at my suggestion. "Why not go pay a visit to the Douglases themselves? We won't get in that hotel, Bette, you know that."

"No one will deny we have as much right as a nabob to go to the bar for a drink," I suggested. Frank had recently developed a habit of asking for my opinion only to argue against me in a patronizing tone. I hated it, but usually held my tongue. "Frank, when we were kids you would go along with my plans. What happened? Are you too old to be reckless?"

"You know we can't get into that hotel. The Palace only makes accounts for the rich. The nabobs have their place and we have ours. I know the Douglases take their Sunday brunch at the Palace." Frank shook his head. "Trust me, it won't do. We can get a better drink at the Waterfront and still have money for our ride home tonight."

"I have no patience for that." I sighed. "If we have money to buy a drink, then why can't we go in like the Douglas family? I'd like some ginger ale, and I've heard the Palace serves it with a cherry year-round."

"This isn't about going to the Palace Hotel for the worth of the drinks, now is it?" Frank laughed. "You want to go in because I've told you the stories about Miss Sarah Douglas frequenting the Palace. And you have no patience for Miss Douglas or her kind. But you might like her situation."

"I told you, I'd rather be a tramp than jailed away in a mansion with rich folks like Miss Douglas."

"I don't believe that," Frank returned. "We'd both like to have some of the pleasures of the rich. And Miss Douglas seems happy enough with her life."

"Maybe. But she can't work and make her own way in life. She'll always be the daughter of the rich Mr. Douglas."

"As if she'd want to work like us!" Frank lifted the edges of his coat as if it were a dress and curtsied. In a high-pitch voice he said, "Hello, sir and madam, I'm Miss Sarah Douglas and I will be cleaning your horses' stalls this evening. After that, perhaps I'll sing you an operetta?"

I grinned and shoved Frank playfully as he tried to curtsy again. "You make a terrible Sarah Douglas."

"How do you know?"

He had a point. I hadn't ever exchanged words with her or any of the other nabobs. "Well, you never know. Maybe the aristocrats get bored being stuck in mansions and fancy hotels their whole life." I knew Frank was right about wanting a few of the pleasures of the rich, but I wouldn't say he was right about everything. Frank worked for the Douglas family as a stablehand, and he'd had occasion to pull the carriage round for their driver often enough to learn many of the Douglas family goings-on. Frank's job, or at least the airs he held about his position, annoyed me. Still, the Douglases were just like any other family, only they happened to live in a mansion. And what could Frank really know about them? He only mucked out their horse stalls. Frank was just like the stablehands at our barn, and I didn't see how this high-honored job gave him any special knowledge of his employer's family.

Papa had also been employed by Mr. Douglas for several years. He transported building materials for Mr. Douglas's import business. Last year, an explosion at one of the docks started a fire that raced through the warehouse district. Papa was unloading supplies at the Douglas warehouse at the time of the explosion. He was able to rally the other workers into hosing down the buildings until the fire department arrived. Papa should have left then, but he stayed to help the firemen and was injured when another explosion occurred. At first his injuries didn't seem serious—mainly burn wounds on his arms—and he won a promotion for his help in putting out the blaze.

Unfortunately, Papa never claimed the promotion or any grievance after the fire. A few days after the blaze, he began having pains in his chest whenever he tried to work, and he had a cough that kept getting worse. He had to quit his position with Mr Douglas's company, and for several months he could hardly stand to load a full wagon on his own. He began taking smaller delivery jobs then to keep our family afloat.

Papa now accepted small jobs for Mr. Douglas, but we had taken on other customers with small orders to make up for the lost wages. The delivery jobs that we did for Mr. Douglas were always the high spot of the day. He paid Papa well and never asked why there was a girl helping on the delivery wagon. In fact, he always smiled at me as though there was nothing strange about the setup.

Mr. and Mrs. Douglas, their son, Henry, and daughter, Sarah, composed one of San Francisco's wealthiest families. Their mansion on Nob Hill had imported Greek marble columns, French upholstery, Italian chandeliers and ornate, gold-speckled tiles on the indoor swimming pool. At least, that's what Frank had told me. I hadn't actually seen their place yet and didn't really want to. Miss Douglas, the youngest Douglas, was my age. I'd only met her once. Miss Douglas and Mrs. Douglas were shopping on Van Ness Avenue when Papa noticed them. They were just stepping out of a store near where we had stopped to water the horses, and Papa tipped his hat toward the women when they passed our wagon. Mrs. Douglas didn't acknowledge Papa's nod, but Miss Douglas gave a slight tip of her head. The report that Miss Douglas was a beauty did not do her justice. Frank thought she looked like a Greek statue with a better nose, and I couldn't argue with that description. When I saw her on Van Ness Avenue, she was attired in a dark green dress with a full skirt and matching hat. There'd been a recent rain and the roads were thick with mud, but her white gloves were spotless, as were her shoes. I felt filthy in my work clothes, and one long look from her made me feel all of ten inches tall. Thankfully, Mrs. Douglas hurried her daughter quickly toward their waiting carriage.

I tugged Frank's coat sleeve. "The hotel stop is next. I hope you're getting off with me."

He shrugged. "As you wish, my lady. It is, after all, your birthday. I suppose we can always sneak into the hotel through the kitchen's back delivery door."

"No." I was planning on walking into the Palace Hotel just as if I were Mrs. Douglas herself with a cold hundred-dollar bill to drop in any willing hand. "We're walking straight past the bellhop and the doormen. Just watch. They'll scramble to open the door for us."

We jumped off the cable car at the next stop and headed up to the Palace's main entrance. A string of carriages and a few automobiles were parked near the front of the hotel, and Frank recognized the Douglas carriage immediately. He pointed it out smugly. "They've got red velvet seat cushions imported from England in that chaise."

"Why would you care where the Douglases set their bums? Unless you'd like to join them . . . For myself, I wouldn't want a seat in their carriage if it was on velvet, silk or Navajo wool."

Frank laughed and took my arm. "You're exactly who I want to spend my evening with and you know that. I have no interest in Miss Douglas or any of her friends. But tell me, why do you want to go to this Palace dump? There are plenty of other cafes where we can drink well. Or we could even catch a late show down on the waterfront."

I rolled my eyes at him. "The waterfront? What sort of late night show would you have us see, Frank? A little risqué theatre—scantily clad women and vulgar men?" Frank turned red, and I instantly wished I could take back the question. The shows on the Coast were known for the rough men and loose women, but I hated sounding like Mother or one of the nuns.

"No, Bette, well . . ." Frank stammered, "I mean, of course not. There's a vaudeville show at one of the hotels in the North Beach area this month, not the usual fare at all. I've heard it's quite smart. And upright folks go to this show, trust me."

"North Beach? You mean the Barbary Coast?" The last place I wanted to spend my birthday evening was the Barbary Coast with the women of the night, the criminals and the drunkards. Though a few shows that had played in the Barbary Coast had earned a good reputation, my mother would disown me if she heard I'd gone there. "Frank, I only want one ginger ale from the Palace Hotel. Appease me."

He finally acquiesced and we trotted up the steps to the front entrance. The doorman didn't bother to help us with the door, but he didn't bar the way either. He took a look at me, too long, and I could tell Frank was uneasy. But we strode past him anyway, and he turned back to watching the street for approaching patrons. Though we were wearing our best clothes, the doorman could tell we weren't good for a tip. Frank ushered me inside and breathed a sigh of relief. "I don't know if it's a blessing or a curse to have your pretty face, but it got us in the door."

I glared at him. "What do you mean by that?"

"The men notice you, Bette." He shrugged. "I don't mean anything disagreeable. You're pretty, that's all. We wouldn't have gotten in the door without reservations otherwise." He pointed to the right. "The restaurant is this way. We'll have to check the bill to see if we can afford their ginger ale before we order two."

Surprised by his compliment, however badly delivered, I decided to drop the subject. Frank never mentioned my appearance, and I never thought anything of it. Had something changed? We circled our way through the Palace lobby until I felt completely lost. "How do you know your way around here?"

Frank shrugged. "*The Evening Chronicle.*"

Frank had been a newspaper boy for a few years. "You sold copies to the hotel guests?"

"Sold papers on the street out front and snuck inside a few times . . . There's nothing better on an empty stomach than a glimpse of the Palace's famous buffet." Frank smiled.

"And I wouldn't be at all surprised if you hadn't nibbled on a few tidbits here and there."

"Bette, what are you suggesting? That I would steal from the buffet table?" He feigned a look of shock.

"I know you well enough to bet that you'd take more than a good look at a buffet table."

He laughed. "I'd plead innocence but won't speak anymore on the nature of a young boy's hungry stomach."

Frank directed us past the grand stairway leading to the hotel promenade, and I was too distracted by the stately men and done-up women in fancy dress passing through the lobby to think more about Frank's early pursuits. The hotel lobby was immense with marble laid on the floors and walls like cheap paint, the ceilings speckled with gold, and everywhere plants blooming as though the Palace weren't really a hotel at all but a tropical garden. I felt a bit out of sorts and tried not to gawk as we waited to speak to the restaurant host.

As it turned out, we didn't have to worry about whether we could afford the Palace's overpriced ginger ale. The restaurant's host informed us curtly that all seating was reserved that evening for a reception. He directed us to the bar across the way, adding that the bartender would be happy to seat and serve anyone of legal age. We knew we couldn't sit at the Palace bar. The city's mayor had passed a recent drinking age reform. Most bartenders ignored the law, but the Palace was unlikely to be lenient.

"Well?" Frank looked at me, waiting for my decision.

I stared at the host. Now, usually I would turn right around and ignore this rebuff, but I was feeling obstinate. "You see, it's my birthday," I began, "and I was hoping to purchase a ginger ale to celebrate. I've heard the Palace serves the best ginger ale in town."

The host shrugged. "I'm sorry your birthday will be a disappointment. Good evening." He turned to pick up the phone and Frank pulled on my arm.

"Bette, we can still make it to the vaudeville show if we leave now. I'll treat us both to a drink at one of the pubs along the way." Frank was trying to cover up for the host's affront. When he grinned, two dimples appeared on his cheeks, and I couldn't do anything but agree with him then.

We turned to leave, and Miss Douglas nearly collided with Frank. She sidestepped quickly, and instead of hitting him, nearly toppled over her own feet. I caught her elbow and held her steady. Frank rushed to apologize, stumbling over his words, "Oh Miss Douglas, I'm sorry. I didn't look where I was—are you all right?"

Once she had found her balance, Miss Douglas pulled her arm back, and I stepped away, conscious now that I had held her arm for a moment too long. I felt my face flush, suddenly struck by Miss Douglas's piercing gaze. She was quite stunning in a long blue gown that matched her eyes. Her dark hair was pulled back from her pale face to give a beautiful contrast. Miss Douglas didn't answer Frank. She straightened her dress and huffed.

In the next moment, Mrs. Douglas, was at her daughter's side. She had stepped out of the parlor just next to the restaurant entrance, and I guessed that was where Miss Douglas had popped out of only moments earlier. "Darling, are you all right?" Mrs. Douglas had a high-pitched voice that was as grating as nails on a chalkboard. "Those dreadful shoes. Sarah, I told you they would never do."

Miss Douglas shot an accusatory look at Frank, and I felt him melt at my side. I wanted to punch her in the belly for it and wondered what a laugh the restaurant host would get when he threw Frank and me out of the hotel for assaulting his guests.

Three other young women had followed Mrs. Douglas out of the parlor and rushed over to Miss Douglas. I guessed they were in the hotel's plushest room to avoid the bar where the men would gather. The dance music had just begun in the ballroom, and the women were probably on their way there after the reception dinner. In overly excited voices, Miss Douglas's friends divulged the information from Mrs. Douglas that Miss Douglas had nearly collided with Frank, whose identity as Mr. Douglas's stablehand was disdainfully mentioned. Furthermore, Mrs. Douglas explained, "Sarah would have fallen, due to the atrocious shoes she had purchased, if not for her excellent balance."

Thankfully, no one mentioned my role in catching Miss Douglas. The last thing I wanted was any further attention. Miss Douglas's friends acted like the usual young spoiled nabobs that you'd expect to find at a ball. I thought they were mostly between the ages of sixteen and nineteen, but the make-up and gowns they wore made the estimation difficult. After the excitement of Miss Douglas's near accident had worn thin, the young women decided they were definitely in need of refreshment and elected to head to the reception hall for drinks before the dance. Miss Douglas looked at me just as they were leaving. I didn't expect her to say thank you.

Before I could turn to ask Frank how he had survived the awful exchange, Mr. Douglas stepped up behind us. I wasn't certain how long he had been standing behind me but guessed by his countenance that it had been long enough. He took one quick glance at Frank and a longer look at me. I felt my cheeks blush for the second time and looked away quickly.

"What the devil are you doing here, Frank?" Mr. Douglas asked.

I answered quickly, "Sir, he's my escort for the evening. It's my birthday and we came to the Palace Hotel for some ginger ale." When I'm in a bind

I have a tendency to talk when I know I should just shut my mouth. "We were just leaving. Our request for ginger ale has been refused due to the reception party. We're very sorry about the accident with Miss Douglas."

"Don't waste your apology on me." He smiled. "Frank, I see you have an apt ventriloquist. Nothing to say for yourself then?"

Frank, still avoiding any eye contact with Mr. Douglas, was staring at the ground and silent. I couldn't tell if he was mad at me, fearful of Mr. Douglas or just struck dumb by the whole affair. So I continued for him, "We're on our way out. We weren't watching our step, sir."

"Yes, and it appears Sarah wasn't either. Well, maybe we should thank you, Miss Lawrence, for catching Sarah's arm. She would have had a painful slip on this marble if you hadn't been there." He cleared his throat. "How about two ginger ales to settle the affair?" Mr. Douglas turned to the host and ordered two ginger ales to be added to his bill. He then bowed ever so slightly at us and disappeared into the bar.

The host smiled dryly at Frank and me. "You both can wait in the parlor. The rest of the party has cleared that room. I'll send the waiter in with your drinks."

Frank followed me without a word. I knew his head was hanging low even though I didn't look at him. We entered the abandoned parlor and found two plush seats in the back of the room. Frank pulled them close to the fire and sank down on one of them like a dog ready to lick his wounds. Suddenly I felt sorry for dragging him to the Palace and wished he'd speak again to ease the tension.

"Well, that was an unfortunate meeting," I began. He wouldn't look at me. A game of checkers had been left on the table by the fire in the midst of play. I picked up a red tile and tossed it at Frank to get his attention. The tile hit his nose, and he looked up at me with a grin about to break.

"What was that for?" he asked.

"Stop moping."

"Who said I'm moping? Don't I look perfectly happy?" He forced a smile.

"Perfectly." I knew Frank too well to pry further into his feelings now. We'd been snubbed, no question about it. "Well, I'm sorry we bumped into the Douglas family. What are the chances that we'd meet them here?"

"We knew they were here," Frank said, reminding me of the carriage that he had seen outside. "I feel like we're the Palace prisoners being treated to our last drink. Maybe we should make a run for it while we can still escape."

"Prisoners?" I shook my head. "We have our own private parlor. We're the Palace's own visiting royalty. The Count and Duchess of—" I paused trying to think of an exotic land. "The Count and Duchess of Harrison."

"Bette, I just can't imagine you as a Duchess. And I never thought that our old Harrison Street would ever raise royalty." He grinned. "Though I do like the title of Count."

"And we're not leaving without the ginger ale."

"Certainly not." Frank leaned in close and whispered, "For now, it's our quest." A knock came at the door and Frank quickly straightened in his chair. "Yes, my lady of Harrison, how could we think of going without refreshment?" He tossed the red tile back at me and smiled. In a louder voice and feigning a royal accent he said, "Please do come in."

The waiter entered the parlor, eyeing Frank and me with suspicion furrowing his brow. Frank reached into his pocket to find his wallet, but the waiter waved off the offered tip. He didn't say a word as he set the drinks on our table, and the door closed quickly behind him. Frank picked up the two drinks. He handed one glass to me and held his up in the air. "To my friend, the noble Duchess of Harrison, on this, her seventeenth birthday, we toast. To another happy year, whether it leads to more free drinks or a job transfer for me!"

I laughed at him and then took a sip. The tangy sweet soda water bit at my tongue and the cherry bobbed against my lips. The ice was a good contrast from the warmth of the fire, and the bubbly sensation made me feel giddy. I closed my eyes and could see Miss Douglas staring at me. I could still feel her arm in my hand as I steadied her balance. How my head had changed in that brief moment! I didn't care if Frank, or anyone else for that matter, thought me strange, but I wanted to befriend her. I didn't know how, but if I could make her acquaintance again, I was certain she wouldn't turn down my friendship.

Chapter 2
April 16, 1906

A couple of weeks passed before Mother and I had another conversation. She wouldn't speak to me the morning after my birthday, and I didn't bother to ask what the matter was. Obviously she was upset about something, and asking would only stir her up. I'd given up on wanting her to be interested in my life. Knowing that she rarely approved of my decisions or plans, it was best not to discuss anything with her.

Since I had started working with Papa, Mother acted as though simply talking to me was too heavy a burden. Papa's independent business meant no steady income for the family, and Mother had taken to sewing every morning to add a few extra dollars to the crock with mending projects. With the extra sewing work, there was too much to do, she insisted, for chatter. Sometimes I knew she was simply too tired at the end of the day for conversation. But other times I was convinced she truly believed God was going to strike me down for wearing trousers, and maybe she didn't want to stand in His way.

Unfortunately, when mother decided to speak to me again, the topic was marriage. I had come home from work early to pick up lunch for Papa and me. Mother didn't expect me, and I was quietly trying to make sandwiches without her realizing I was at home. Caroline and Mary were napping and the two boys were still at school. I heard muffled voices in the front room and guessed it was Mother and Mrs. McCain sharing the weekly tea. When Mrs. McCain came round, mother forgot about her sewing work and set aside her dishrags. They would sit down for a proper tea in the front room and my mother's jaws loosened. The walls of the front room were papered with our family secrets. We never used the front room except on holidays and Mother's tea with Mrs. McCain.

Papa and I'd had a busy morning moving trunks for a Chinese family. Unable to resist almond cookies that Mother had made for her tea, I snacked while preparing the sandwiches. My thoughts were crowded with the images of the Chinese family and their trunks. The family had just immigrated to the United States, and San Francisco was their first step on American soil. Unfortunately, it wasn't a very good step. The family had made several attempts at securing a delivery wagon for moving their trunks to Chinatown, but no one would accept their job. The other wagon drivers thought that they shouldn't have to work for the Chinese. When the family reached our wagon, they started out with an apology: "Sorry we ask. You go to Chinatown?"

Papa knew that he could ask more for moving their trunks than his ordinary rate. The other drivers often took advantage of any new immigrants, and the Chinese were especially targets for unequal rates, if the driver would take the job at all. We were the last wagon waiting at the Ferry Building, but Papa wouldn't overcharge anyone. He accepted the job immediately and offered our lunch to the three children in the family, who all seemed too thin. I guessed that the oldest boy was close to my age, but so much quieter than the boys I was used to and so thin that he could be much younger. As we moved their trunks, Papa lectured me on why it was important to welcome all immigrants and how this Chinese family should be treated as any other family. Papa told me all of this, but I don't know if he would have openly declared it to the other men at the shipyards.

When I had finished making the sandwiches, I knocked on the door to the front room. Mother called, "Yes?"

I opened the door gingerly and poked my head half in the room. "Good afternoon," I said, smiling to Mrs. McCain. "Mother, I'm sorry to interrupt, but Papa wanted to let you know we'll be home late. We took a moving job that will keep us late. I just stopped in to pick up our lunch."

She tilted her head at the angle that I knew meant, "Please explain." She had already made lunch for us and knew we shouldn't need more to eat. Our family budget was tight, and no one needed to eat more than his share of lunch. I didn't want to explain the Chinese family. I was proud that Papa had taken the job when no one else would, but I knew Mother wouldn't want Mrs. McCain to know this. She would be embarrassed and think that her husband needed money so badly that he would take any work. It wasn't about money at all, as Papa had explained, but Mother wouldn't understand. Instead of mentioning the Chinese family, I replied, "We left our lunch sack on the docks when we were loading the wagon and someone stole the sack."

Mrs. McCain nodded knowingly. "Rats. The men that work down at the docks used to be good folk, but now they're no better than rats, most of them."

Mother scowled at me. She could always spot a lie. I didn't say anything to defend myself and wondered what she might say to Mrs. McCain when I closed the door. I couldn't understand how she entertained Mrs. McCain for hours on end when she was so quiet with the rest of us. I had heard her laughing and carrying on with Mrs. McCain as though they both were schoolgirls. She rarely laughed with the family around her. I wondered if she had ever wanted five kids. It was obvious that we wore on her spirits. She only became alive when she was alone with Mrs. McCain, taking tea in the front room.

"It's so nice that you stopped in today, Mrs. McCain." I smiled at her. "Mother makes the best cookies for your teas and I had the benefit of one for a snack, so I must thank you for coming. Have a good day, ma'am." I then turned to Mother, "I'll be home in time to help with dinner."

She nodded once and waited for me to close the door. We would have words later, or at least sharp looks. I bounded out of the house and down to the Ferry Building. Papa had stayed with the wagon and the trunks, waiting for me. We'd made two runs into Chinatown with the trunks and still had at least two more to go. I arrived with our lunch and Papa smiled broadly when I handed him an almond cookie.

"Did Emma McCain make a house call?"

I nodded.

"Ah, it does your mother good when she comes." He took a bite of the cookie and caught the crumbs in his whiskers. "Does me good too." He smiled, finishing the cookie. Papa had a full red beard, but the hair on his head was dark brown and graying at the sides. He claimed he was half-Irish and half-English and that the red beard was the Irish half trying to fight its way free from the English half.

"Yes, sir. Mrs. McCain and Mother were taking their tea in the front room when I stopped in at the house," I explained.

"And I trust you didn't spy on their conversation?"

I looked at Papa with wonder. "Why would I spy on their conversation?" Thinking over his comment, I handed him one of the sandwiches and continued, "What would Mrs. McCain and Mother talk about that I would want to know? Yarn prices and mutton recipes?"

"Well, it's what the women talk about. And you have no interest?" Papa laughed and sent a spray of cookie particles into the air as the whiskers on his face shook. "Bette, I never can guess what you will say next. You're a woman, and womenfolk are supposed to have an intuition about things of this sort, but lightning will strike me dumb if I swear you don't have an inkling of what this visit was about, now do you?"

Papa made up for my mother's silence. He was always talking and joking. I shrugged and took a bite of the sandwich. Between mouthfuls of apple butter and honey, I answered, "No, I guess I don't have the right intuition. But if you know what Mrs. McCain's visit was about, tell me. You've got a smile that says I should be concerned. Will I want to know?" As soon as I asked, I felt a full-mouth of that intuition clog my throat. "Oh, Papa, wait now. Was she coming to talk about Frank and me?" I didn't want to think about the marriage, but I had a bad feeling that it was nearing time someone would want the issue settled.

Papa grinned. He was missing three teeth in the upper row and two of them were filled with silver, so when he grinned I always grinned back. But I didn't want to grin now. I could feel my sandwich edging its way up my throat, and I almost choked on the words before I could get them out, "You know I don't want it."

"Who knows what you want if you don't say?" he asked. "I know you're not like your quiet mother, and I know you'll speak your mind. Speak up now, Bette."

I pulled myself together and solemnly answered, "I don't want to marry Frank."

"Since when?" Papa didn't look at me. He chewed on his sandwich as though I had just told him the weather had turned foggy. "You've always been close. Closer than some married folks I've known."

"Close friends only. I've never wanted to marry Frank." I was swallowing fast now and squinting to stop the tears. It was hard working with men all the time and especially hard with Papa. I could lift the trunks same as a boy my age and rein in the horses better than most, but I was not a man. Again and again I was reminded of this. I struggled to stop the tears. If I were a boy I would not have this problem. I could choose to marry or not and no one would harass me. Papa was treating me like a girl again, though I did a man's job. He used my help, begrudging the fact that I wasn't his son, who ought to have the job. And now he wasn't listening to me because I was a girl. He thought I'd marry Frank if he pushed it. I always did what I was told, eventually. That's what girls do.

"We'll talk later." Papa patted his lips with his handkerchief, then folded it like an expensive linen napkin and tucked it in his pocket. He pointed at the trunks in the wagon. "We've got our work for the afternoon. Harness Trader and Midge so we can get a move on." His sentence ended in a spasm of coughing. He'd been coughing all morning, but I was in no mood to ask about it.

I sprang out of the wagon, leaving half of my sandwich uneaten on the front seat. Tears were streaming down my cheeks, and I could barely see the knots as I struggled to untie the horses from the hitching post. Trader nudged my hand, smelling the remnants of apple butter, and I pushed his muzzle away as I raced to latch his harness. I wanted to finish the moving job and see the Chinese family settled in their apartment above the red-tiled theater by dinner time. I didn't want any delays. Delays would only mean time for me to think of a reason for why I should marry Frank after all. Everyone expected it. Now I knew that Frank had asked my parents. Mrs. McCain and Mother would love to discuss the wedding details. A marriage between their children was exactly what they had planned on for years. Papa shouldn't have had to tell me about women and intuition.

Although I had thought something was strange when Frank had spoken so seriously with Papa on my birthday, I didn't really believe he could ask my parents about marriage without asking me first. Maybe he thought that I wanted the marriage as much as everyone else wanted it. I was angry at everyone. Livid. My parents and Mrs. McCain probably deserved most of the blame, though I didn't find Frank innocent. I blamed Papa for the bet placed on a gypsy's whim. I blamed my silent mother and Mrs. McCain for organizing the marriage before I could speak against it.

By the time the Lees had their trunks stowed safely in their small flat it was dusk. I knew Papa was tired from the day's work. His lungs bothered him more and more lately with any exertion, and he'd been coughing a lot. He didn't argue when I mentioned that I was planning on dropping him off at home and taking the horses to the stables alone. He simply nodded and said that was always the plan. I hated him more then, but I wasn't going to tell him how I felt. He wouldn't care. And anyway, I wasn't going to marry Frank. No matter what anyone said.

Trader and Midge took their time heading to our house on Harrison, but once they felt the reins direct them to the stables, they both picked up their pace. Horses have a way of knowing when they're headed home, and I told them that an extra ration of grain would be waiting for them at the stables. The trunks were heavy, and we'd all had a hard day. The stableboys never offered to help me with our team because I didn't have money to tip them. After I unhitched the horses and scrubbed their backs with warm water and burlap sacks, I bedded them in their stalls for the night with two fat slices of oat hay and a full scoop each of corn grain. They ate greedily, and I sat down in Trader's stall to listen to his teeth grinding.

The sounds of horses eating always made me happy. I told Trader the story of Frank and our intended marriage while he slurped water from the trough and chewed on the oats. He nudged me every so often with his velvet nose and then would go back to his meal. Trader was my favorite. Despite his name, he could be counted on through thick and thin, unlike Midge. Midge was never eager to work and would take advantage of any inch you gave her. She was my father's favorite because she was a pretty bay with racing bloodlines and a fast pace if you whipped her. I didn't like to whip the team and always let Trader set a slow, steady pace for our trips when Papa wasn't at hand.

From Trader's stall I could hear bits of the stableboys' stories from the day, and I knew I was the only woman around to hear their cussing. Reining horses wasn't work for women, as I'd been told more than once. But I loved the job and secretly was happy that I had been born first, instead of Charlie. Charlie was still young, but he was growing as fast as a weed. In a few years Papa would have him hitching the horses. Until then, Papa was stuck with me, whether he liked it or not.

After much thought on the subject of Frank, I finally decided to tell my parents I couldn't marry Frank at least for another few years. The family needed my help, especially with Papa's weak condition. For the moment, I was the only one who could handle the horses. Without my work, we'd lose what little income our family made to keep all the little mouths fed and the bank mortgage paid. An hour passed before I was ready to head home and face Mother. I rubbed Trader's head and whispered softly that I'd meet him in the morning with a bit of a roll and a treat of apple butter. The stableboys nodded at me as I slipped out of the barn quietly. I'd been working with Papa for a year now, and they'd finally come to accept my presence even if they didn't like it. Mostly everyone had learned to ignore me.

When I turned down our block of Harrison, I had a scare. The doctor's wagon was out front of our house. I ran inside and found Charlie first. "What happened?"

"Papa was having chest pains again. Doc's seeing him now."

I badgered Charlie and the other kids for more of a story, but that was all the little ones knew. Papa's lungs were bad, and we all knew that his cough was becoming more severe. Every night after the Douglas warehouse fire, the house would shake with his cough and we'd washed enough spit-lathered hankies to have our own Chinese laundry. So why was the doctor called in this time? I pushed the other kids away from the door and put my ear against the wood, straining to hear the voices on the other side. Papa was explaining his pain, and the doctor said something about his heart. I was sure I had heard Doc wrong, though, because we all knew it was Papa's lungs that were the problem, not his heart. Footsteps came up to the door and Mother walked out of the room just as I pulled the kids away. We quickly pretended as though we were all just passing in the hallway and not really spying at their room.

Mother caught my arm and pointed into the kitchen. I scurried to make dinner, knowing that it was late and the kids were half-starved. Little Caroline was scared of the doctor and was anxiously awaiting his departure. She kept her eyes fixed on Papa's door and wouldn't touch her food.

"Caroline, eat your dinner."

"I'm not hungry," she replied. "My belly hurts."

"You'll make me feel bad for not eating," I said. "I'm not much of a cook, I know. But can't you eat a little?"

"My belly hurts too," Mary added, "and the sauce tastes strange."

"Poisoned," Charlie whispered, then giggled, and added, "Bette's poisoned the food!"

Wes came right to my defense with, "It's not that awful. But I'll eat anything you cook, Bette."

"Not peas," Charlie corrected. "You'd take a beating from Papa's belt before you'd eat a pea."

To this, Mary started crying. My patience with all of them had worn thin, and I wanted to shout that no one was going to be belted by father. He was in no shape to belt anyone. I, however, could find his belt. In between her pitiful sobs, Mary kept repeating how she didn't want anyone belted.

"Quiet, Mary," I said finally. "You'll disturb Papa and he needs his rest. Just eat, everyone, please. God knows we don't need more trouble tonight."

Mary kept right on crying, worse now that I had mentioned God. She squeezed her fork in her hands and dripped tears on her plate. I tried to comfort her, but she pushed me away and threatened to cry louder, so I gave up.

"Mary's always a crybaby. Where's your doll, Mary?" Charlie pestered. He kicked her under the table, which only made the sobs louder. "Go get your doll so you can have someone to cry with."

"Charlie, enough!" I said, slapping the back of his head.

He spun around and made a face at me. "Your food always tastes horrible. That's why Mary is crying. You should learn to cook."

"I'll learn to belt you first," I said, cuffing the side of his ear. Mary saw this and her jaw dropped open in shock. Before she could wail, I hissed, "Silence, everyone! And eat the terrible food or I'll get Papa's belt." After that, the only sound was the kitchenware clattering against their plates.

When the doctor finally stepped out of Papa's room, he eyed our group at the table and mumbled something. I stood up quickly and offered him a plate. With a shake of his head, he said he had to be going home to his own family. I guessed this meant he knew we didn't have much to spare. Or maybe he had heard the children's talk. I didn't really care if he spread the rumor that Bette Lawrence couldn't cook. I really was only good at making spätzle.

Mother called me in to Papa's room as soon as the doctor left. I shut the door behind me and walked over to Papa's bedside. Lying in bed with only a faint candle glowing over his skin, Papa looked much older than I imagined him. He was in his forties and not a young man, but I didn't think him old until that moment.

"Doc's gone?" he asked.

I nodded.

"You fed him?" he prodded.

"He wouldn't have any dinner."

Papa scoffed about my cooking and the poor produce we bought as if the doctor had known and made his decision based on this knowledge. My cooking alone would make someone lose his appetite, Papa continued. I tried to ignore his comments, though it was true I was not a good cook, and our grocer did sell poor quality vegetables. Unfortunately, we could only afford the quality he sold.

Papa was silent for a few minutes, and I guessed this meant our conversation, or rather his, was over. I started to leave and he cleared his throat to stop me. "There's a delivery to be made for Mr. Douglas."

Mother was quietly staring out the dark window. I could tell by her crossed arms that she was upset. I looked back at Papa. "You'll be able to work?"

He sighed. "Doc said no. That's why I'm telling you about the job. Mr. Douglas asked me to keep an eye out for any personal packages that he might receive at the docks. He's away on business for the next few weeks. One of the ship clerks dropped by earlier to say there's a harp with Miss Douglas's name waiting for a delivery wagon to take it up to California Street. They've had it on hold at the warehouse." Papa started coughing and gripped the bed as though he might slip off with the retching. When he finally had subdued the cough, he continued quietly, "I told him I'd be picking up all deliveries for the Douglases myself, but he'll understand why I've sent you. You can manage the team well enough without me. Don't take any other jobs. Just deliver the harp."

I nodded and left the room quickly. Papa's coughing spells were hard enough to listen to when you were trying to sleep at night, but watching his body writhing on the bed was too pitiful. Once I'd left Papa's side, the full weight of my task for tomorrow pressed down on me. I was to deliver a package to the Douglas mansion, and a harp for Miss Douglas at that.

Mother followed me out of the room a few minutes later. She ate a roll and a few bites of chicken and then cleared her throat and looked at me solidly. She and Papa had the same throat clearing technique to announce they were about to speak. I waited but she refused to speak and only stared at me. I hated this worse than if she had taken to yelling at me. What had I done wrong now? After a while I said, "Papa will want me to take the deliveries alone now, I guess. Did the doctor say how long he will be bedridden?"

"No. He's only caught a cold and needing rest. He'll not be bedridden for long."

"But I thought I heard the doctor say something was wrong with his heart."

Mother waved her hand to silence me. "A cold—that's all." She took a bite of boiled carrots and made a sour face. "You always overcook the vegetables."

After Papa's comment about my cooking, this particularly stung, and I couldn't deny the charge. The carrots were near mush. I'd left Charlie in charge of the boiling water, and he'd left the carrots in the pot for a half hour at least. Charlie shot a pleading look at me, knowing I could tell Mother that he was the one to blame. After all the trouble I'd had with him earlier, I was tempted to tell on him, but I had no reason to side with Mother. I'd take Charlie as my ally over her any day. "The carrots were too old. We should have bought the better carrots at the grocer instead of the old vegetables."

"Too much money," Mother scoffed.

I'd had no further complaints about the food from the children after I threatened them with the belt. I'd bet that they had heard Papa yelling at me for the cooking because everyone had eaten the tough bits of chicken without a whisper of trouble. I left the table and heated some broth for Papa. Mother watched me, not speaking. Something more than Papa's health was on her mind, and I wondered if Papa had told her of the conversation we had about marriage that afternoon. She would hate me if I turned down Frank's engagement offer, both for Mrs. McCain and for herself. I knew Mother was eager to have me married and one less mouth to feed, but she must also have realized that with Papa ill, I was the only one the family couldn't do without now.

When I brought the broth into Papa's room he asked me to close the door. He took the mug of chicken broth and sipped it slowly, and then asked for another quilt, which I laid on his feet. His feet were always cold. I waited, half expecting him to start a lecture, but he was tired and silent. After a few minutes, he looked over at me and seemed startled that I was still at his bedside. "Why are you waiting on me, Bette? Your mother will need you in the kitchen."

I was glad he let me leave. The air was stuffy and smelled still of the doctor's medicine bag. But I didn't want to go back to the tight kitchen to clean dishes and be jailed in with Mother Silence again. The girls were playing dolls in our bedroom and would have to be tucked in soon, and the living room had been taken over by the boys with their soldiers. I decided to escape to the front room and Mother let me slip away without remark. As I passed the living room, Wes called out for me to join in the army game. He was leading the American force and clearly losing to Charlie's Spanish troops in a battle at the Rio Grande. The Americans, he insisted, were pleading for reinforcements. I doubted their battle's historical accuracy and told him that his hero, Admiral Dewey, would have made do with the men at hand. Little Wes sighed and nodded solemnly. Charlie was heartless when it came to toy soldiers. The Americans' mass grave—Mother's flowerpot—was overflowing.

The front parlor was cold, as I knew it would be, and my skin prickled immediately. We kept the doors closed to save the heat for the other rooms. I lit a candle and found Grandmother's afghan to pull over my shoulders. The afghan was used primarily to cover the one white piece of furniture in our house—a great plump fainting chair. Despite the plain pattern and lack of color, I adored the chair and stretched out on it as though I were Queen Victoria herself.

A book was lying open on the front table. I flipped the pages absently. My thoughts were too busy for reading. The trip to the Douglas mansion loomed tomorrow, and I knew there was a chance I'd see Miss Douglas. I was hoping for it, though I couldn't say why. After our last meeting at the Palace Hotel I had thought of her often. There were no girls my age in our neighborhood, and I missed the female companionship of the school friends I had made at St. Anthony. More than a year had passed since I had last been to school, and I had few occasions to see my school friends. The memory of school times and laughing with my friends, Myra and Florence, as we played in the park seemed a distant life. When I did have a chance meeting with one of the girls from school now, I was struck with the feeling that we had nothing in common. They had their studies in literature, while I had a team of horses to tend. Somehow childhood had slipped away. If I married Frank, girlhood would be gone forever.

My thoughts came back to Miss Douglas. When I had touched her arm in the hotel lobby I had felt something strange. It was almost as if we'd held hands before. Or maybe, the sense of familiarity was because we were meant to again. I couldn't decide. When I thought of Miss Douglas, I was not thinking of my school friends then or wishing for an acquaintance so I could have a tea party like Mother and Mrs. McCain. The rush of emotion was of desperation for a kindred spirit. Unfortunately, I knew Miss Douglas was unlikely to enter my life in more than a passing glimpse. And though I knew this, I yearned for even a passing glimpse.

Chapter 3

April 17, 1906

The next morning I awoke early and made a quick breakfast of coffee and stale bread. Mother was hemming a skirt and her needle didn't pause when I set a cup of coffee on her sewing table. "It's cold in here. I thought you might want something warm to drink."

Her eyes shifted briefly to the coffee. She took a sip and then moved the cup off to the side of her sewing. Her foot pressed the sewing pedal again sending the needle into another flurry of action.

"Is Papa feeling any better?" His coughing had kept me up for half the night, and I wondered how Mother could have slept at all. Mary and Caroline had managed to sleep despite the intermittent hacking. They were both still soundly snoring when I got up to dress.

Mother ignored my question. Her eyes were focused on the seam she was fashioning. I left her at the sewing machine and went to wake Charlie and Wes for school. The boys moved slowly, and I guessed they had a rough night's sleep as well. I saw them both dressed before leaving the house.

It seemed strange to walk alone on the same route to the stables that I always took with Papa each morning. As I opened the front gates, a few neighs of welcome came from Trader's stall. He always watched for me, and I paid him off for the compliments with a snack of apple butter smeared over a stale sweet roll. This was his favorite treat. Midge was full of piss and vinegar, as Papa would have said if he'd come to the stables that morning, and she nearly bit my hand when I tried to place her bridle. It took more than ten minutes to get her brushed and harnessed. Trader was, as always, diligently waiting to start the day, and took his harness without any trouble.

I guided the team out of the stableyard and headed to the Ferry Building, feeling somewhat apprehensive about the responsibility I would take on once I reached it. As if eager to find where their day's work would lead, or maybe recognizing that Papa wasn't aboard, the horses pulled hard against the reins, and I had a fight to keep them at a jog. One of the longshoremen spotted me as I turned the horses in at the wharf's hitching post. He waved and approached our wagon.

"Hello, Ed."

He tipped his hat to me. "Where's your father, Bette? He's taking the day off and letting his women work twice as hard?"

"Papa's caught a cold. I won't have too much work today anyway. Just a package to deliver to the Douglas mansion."

"Aye," Ed responded, "And there's something else for your father. A hatbox waiting with Mr. Lawrence's name—the porter told me to let your father know when I saw your wagon come in this morning." Although he always meant well, Ed had a brusque tone and ill-conceived manners. He was chewing tobacco and spit black juice at the horses' feet.

"Thank you, sir." I jumped out of the wagon and tied Midge and Trader to the hitching post. Ed followed me inside the Ferry Building and pointed the way to the porter. I found the two items waiting with Papa's name. The harp for Miss Douglas was packed in a crate with the Douglases' address and post stamps from Lisbon. After loading this crate in our wagon with the porter's help, I went back for the hatbox. It had no address. On the top of the box a neatly printed note read: "Thank you Mr. Thomas Lawrence."

The hatbox fit under my seat in the wagon. I suppressed my curiosity about it by thinking of the route I'd take up to the Douglas mansion. The crate was carefully balanced on the wagon's floorboards and tied securely so I wouldn't have to worry about the bumps in the roadway or the steepness of Nob Hill's California Street. I turned up Embarcadero and headed through the city. Past the waterfront, the rest of San Francisco was just waking. The shopkeepers swept their storefronts, the newsboys hawked their papers and the businessmen in matching black suits filtered through the financial district in a loud bustle of activity.

I tried to avoid the busy streets and instead took a side pass that went by the Opera House. Midge threw a fit when a banner at the Opera House's entryway rustled in the breeze. She was looking for any excuse to act up since Papa wasn't on the reins that morning. I yanked on her line and yelled *whoa* to slow her down, then made her stand still so I could read the banner. In bold print the advertisement listed the evening's opera: "April 17—Enrico Caruso—Carmen."

The breeze caught the banner again, and Midge bucked against her harness and tried to lunge forward. This time I reined her in with a hard backward pull that nearly upset the hatbox. She rested finally, and I caught the white glint of her eyes as she turned her head to look back at me. "Midge, I can't say that I blame you, I'm not an opera fan myself," I said, not caring if anyone heard me talking to the horse, "But God help you if this wagon overturns with our load this morning."

Trader tossed his head and the hitch jingled. I knew he wanted to be moving on past the opera house. Several wagons and carriages had already passed us up, which annoyed him to no end. We continued on our route at a steady jog, and before long the Douglas mansion came into view. Everyone who grew up in the city could recognize the houses on Nob Hill, point to each mansion and tell you which rich newsman or speculator had built it. We were fed the tales of the men who worked hard and found their riches through the sweat of their own brow—not like the kings in the European castles or the New England aristocrats. We were told that the mansions on Nob Hill were built by men who had prospered by their own will. But I had seen plenty of shoremen who sweated more than the Nob Hill folks and got nothing more than a sour-dough roll for their work. Seemed mostly it was luck that decided if you lived high on the hill or low in the gutter.

Frank came out from the backyard to grab my horses as soon as I pulled the wagon onto the Douglases' gravel drive. He tipped his hat at me. "Good morning, fair lady."

"Nice act, Frank. I know your real manners though." I jumped off the wagon and grinned at him. "And I like those manners better than your highbrow act."

Frank scoffed at this and then pointed at my pants. "What happened to you?"

"It's just a little dirt." My trousers were filthy from the knees down, splattered with mud from Midge's little uprising down at the opera house, and I was glad that Frank was the only one greeting me. "Will you help me get this crate?"

He nodded. "All deliveries are made at the back entrance. We'll lead the horses behind the main house so we won't have to lug the crate quite so far."

I followed behind Frank, listening to his description of the grounds and the mansion with an undeniable curiosity. I didn't mind that Frank knew more about the place than I did and accepted his patronizing tone for once. He pointed out the rose garden, where Mrs. Douglas and her daughter regularly took their afternoon tea, and then the three guest cottages and the maid's quarters. After he mentioned Miss Douglas, I was listening with only half an ear. "Is she about today?"

"Who?" Frank asked.

"Miss Douglas."

Frank shrugged. "If you're worried about bumping into her after what happened at the Palace Hotel, don't. She's already forgotten about the whole affair."

"How do you know?" I wasn't worried. But I was hoping to see her. For some reason my thoughts kept returning to Miss Douglas. I stared at every window of the grand house hoping that I might catch a glimpse of her.

"She couldn't give a damn about us, that's all."

I smacked my lips in feigned surprise. "Frank McCain, what happened to your manners? Just think what the sisters at St. Anthony will say. You missed church last week and now you swear like a waterfront rat."

"Ah, Bette, I thought you liked my waterfront accent." He winked. "And you know I don't give a damn about what the St Anthony sisters say. But cross me and you might find a damn rat in your wagon for your contemplation."

I tried to cuff his ear for the half-hearted threat, but Frank stepped to the side quickly. Fortunately, we'd grown too old to play out our threatened pranks.

On our way to the servants' back entrance, Frank pulled me aside to point out Mr. Douglas's automobile. Parked next to his stately carriage with plush velvet seats and gold speckled paint, the black metal automobile seemed like a hideous contraption—certainly an ugly duckling that no one would be proud to drive to church.

Frank whistled softly. "You should see Mr. Douglas in this hell-wagon. He speeds down California Street and could take out an entire family without noticing anything more than a bump under his wheels."

I laughed with the image of a family fleeing from the automobile's wrath and imagined Mr. Douglas speeding by with a gleeful expression plastered on his face. "Their automobile isn't as grand as their carriage. I'd rather have a seat on the plush velvet behind Mr. Douglas's pair of dappled grays than in this metal box."

"But a ride in this box would cost you nearly ten times the price," Frank replied. "Mr. Douglas won't let anyone but Mr. Peterson, the carriage driver, touch the hell-wagon."

"Where is everyone this morning?"

"Mr. Douglas is gone on business. He's visiting a shipping import center in Vallejo and then he's going to stay with his son in Berkeley. They have a second home there."

I knew the younger Mr. Douglas, Henry, was studying at a university but hadn't realized he was at Berkeley. And I couldn't understand why Mr. Douglas would need another house when they already had a mansion here. "Why have two houses?"

"Who knows? Rich people . . ." Frank brushed his hand along the side of the automobile and continued, "And Mr. Peterson has a week-long holiday to visit his family in Sacramento."

"So, no one would notice if we took the hell-wagon for a drive?" I challenged him half-jokingly, knowing that he'd never dream of doing that. Touching the leather interior was enough of a sin to warrant a reconciliation visit with the priest.

"Bette, you shouldn't even say that out loud!" he whispered, glancing over his shoulder at the house. "There are ears everywhere around here."

Just then the back door opened and one of the maids emerged with a basket of laundry. Frank turned away from the car quickly and stepped toward the wagon. He hollered out to the maid, "Miss Gillian, mind telling Mr. Klein that we've got a delivery here?"

The maid nodded at Frank. She set the laundry basket down by the clothesline and headed back inside the house. Frank breathed a sigh of relief. "You're trouble, Bette! Miss Gillian would sooner put me out of a job than keep any secrets."

"We didn't do anything wrong. What secrets would she have to keep?" I asked, grinning.

Frank waved me off. "Come on, help me get this crate up to the house."

We carried the crate in through the servants' back entrance. Mr. Klein met us in the hall and directed the delivery into the main house. "Miss Douglas is expecting this package and will want it opened immediately," Mr. Klein explained.

By his prim features and uppity manners, I guessed that Mr. Klein was the butler. He seemed not to care that the delivery boy was in fact a girl and treated me with the same tone of disdain that he used with Frank. After setting the crate in the front of the house, Mr. Klein had a crowbar brought in to crack the nailed wood that sealed the crate tight. I waited with baited breath to see the thing opened, expecting that they would hold me responsible if the harp was at all damaged.

The maid called Frank out of the room as another delivery wagon arrived with groceries. Frank gave me a look that I knew meant I shouldn't still be there, but he didn't tell me outright to stay or leave, so I made up my own mind and stayed. Mr. Klein and I lifted the harp out of the crate and I heard a sharp clap behind us.

Miss Douglas's voice called out, "Mother, look what's just arrived. It's beautiful! Doesn't Father have exquisite taste? Come see."

Miss Douglas walked past me as though I didn't exist at all and strummed her fingers on the strings. The rich sound filled the room, and Miss Douglas smiled as if she had a secret to share. She pulled a stool over to the harp and started to play a beautiful melody from the strings, while Mr. Klein and I listened, myself with open-mouthed amazement. Her fingers knew their place as though she had long possessed the instrument.

When Mrs. Douglas arrived in the front room she took only a second to appraise the harp and then fell into a fit about the dusty mess that the shipping crate had left. Mr. Klein and I quietly bore the brunt of her ranting about the mess until it was clear that we could begin the clean-up.

"Mr. Klein, please! Do something about all of this. Find Gillian or start cleaning this room yourself. Don't simply stand there uselessly! And show that delivery boy . . ." she paused, eyeing my trousers and then my tousled hair, " . . . delivery girl, her way out, immediately," Mrs. Douglas finished with a huff of irritation.

I helped Mr. Klein carry the remains of the crate out to the servants' back quarters, listening to the conversation in the front hall. Mrs. Douglas was congratulating her daughter's skill with the instrument. I thought the woman's shrill voice ruined the beautiful tones of her daughter's harp.

"Oh Sarah, the years of music classes have certainly paid off well," she said. "And I know your suitors will soon agree."

Miss Douglas returned, "Oh Mother, please don't tell anyone about my harp. My skills are pitiful, and I'd rather not have any suitors at all than to have you going on about how well I shall play for them."

"Sarah, don't be so childish. You will learn that men appreciate fine talents as well as fine looks." Mrs. Douglas sniffed loudly. "And one's attributes must often be pointed out to suitors."

"Mother, please. Do you really need to carry on about suitors? Don't mention anything about music when Darren is here tonight!" Sarah exclaimed.

"Sarah! Don't suppose what I shall or shall not tell *your* Darren. And," Mrs. Douglas's voice rose in a painful shrill, "don't raise your voice at me!"

I eyed Mr. Klein nervously, but he only shrugged. He didn't seem to think that a domestic fight was about to ensue, or else he didn't care, and his calmness suggested that yelling was a common occurrence at the Douglas's.

After a moment Miss Douglas spoke up, "I'm sorry, Mother, forgive my hasty remarks." She sounded anything but contrite.

Regardless, Mrs. Douglas accepted her apology and continued, "When you attend the opera tonight, I hope you will mention to Stephen Crestwell that you would be obliged if he heard your harp this coming weekend. Your father has invited him to dinner on Sunday, and I know he will accept the invitation if he has a reason to visit."

"How much for the delivery?" Mr. Klein asked, fishing a money clip out of his breast pocket.

"My father bills Mr. Douglas," I replied. I wished Mr. Klein would let me stay a few minutes longer, but I could sense that he knew I was spying.

Mr. Klein handed me a five-dollar bill. "I know your father well and I've heard he is ill these days. I expect that's why you're here in his place. Please give him my regards and tell him this isn't payment for the delivery."

How Mr. Klein would know Papa well enough to hand me a five-dollar bill for our family's charity was surprising. I tried to return the money, but he refused. Mr. Klein showed me out the back door, and the rest of Miss Douglas's conversation with her mother was lost to my ears.

Frank was busy helping the grocer and only tipped his hat as I turned the wagon round and headed out. The harp's music drifted out the open windows of the mansion, and I made Trader and Midge pass by slowly so I could hear every last note before we'd have to head down California Street.

By the time we reached Golden Gate Park, the morning fog had burned off and sunshine was streaming on the spring bulb flowers. I could have taken the horses back to the stables and run straight home to check on Papa or see if Mother needed my help, but I wasn't expected yet. After finding my favorite meadow, I unhitched Trader and Midge from the wagon. They fell to grazing on the tender grass sprouts with delight before I even had a lead line tied to their halters. The hatbox was still waiting to be opened, and I was tempted to look inside now. Only one strand of twine prevented me from knowing the contents of the package, and Papa would never know if I took a peak inside the box. I wasn't even sure if he was expecting the package.

After much deliberation on the matter, I took the hatbox out from its hiding place and sat down on the grass with this treasure. The horses were too busy enjoying the fresh grass to pay me any mind, so I slipped their leads around my waist and knotted the two ropes together as a belt. With my hands free to explore the hatbox, I slipped a knife under the twine and cut the knot. Newsprint with Chinese characters half filled the box. Under the strange paper sat a bamboo box with abalone shells fitted into the lid in the pattern of a mermaid. I opened the box and heard a faint bell tinkle. A music box! The crank was at the base of the box next to a Chinese inscription. I wound the crank tight, set the box on the grass and then gently reopened the lid. The most wonderful sound erupted with a simple turn of the gears. Trader lifted his muzzle from the grass delicacies and eyed me, obviously wondering how I was making the strange noise. I held up the box, but he had already lost interest in the sound. I couldn't place the melody, but it was familiar.

I left the music box to continue its song as I fished through the rest of the hatbox. The only other object in the box was a small red silk pouch. Opening the pouch, I explored the lining and quickly discovered one last treasure—a jade medallion hung from a silver chain. The jade had been etched with a fine tool and inlaid with silver to produce a shimmering dragon. Every flick of fiery breath was shown in exact detail. I latched the thin chain on my neck and smiled at the foreign appeal of jewelry. I would have to show Papa and could not dream of keeping it, though the weight and coolness of the jade felt wonderful on my skin. The price of a piece like this might bring a month's worth of food to our table. For the day, the treasure was all mine. The Chinese family was too kind to have sent this hatbox of treasures to Papa. He would not want to accept their gifts without giving something in return, and I couldn't think of anything we had so fine as the jade and the music box to give them.

I felt a tug on one of the ropes on my waist and eyed the horses. Trader had his muzzle pointed toward the bend in the path. I followed his gaze but saw nothing. My thoughts were still on the jade. Would someone try to steal this? Trader sniffed the air and then snorted, his head pointed north still. Horse hooves sounded ahead of us, and a carriage soon appeared on the path. I quickly tucked the jade under my blouse to hide it. The carriage was fine, and I guessed the occupants were wealthy, though I couldn't see them. Only wealthy folks, beggars and undisciplined strikers would lounge in the park on a Tuesday morning. The carriage passed through the meadow without stopping.

Just as the carriage disappeared around the bend of the path, the music box reached the last note in the melody and fell silent. I leaned back on the grass and wound the crank again to let the music flow. The image of Miss Douglas's harp came to my mind, and it occurred to me that she had played the same melody on her harp as this little box played. Suddenly a loud bark broke the tranquil sounds of the park. Trader was staring in the direction that the carriage had taken and looked uneasy. Midge whinnied softly and tossed her head. "Easy now," I started.

A bullet cracked the air in the brush behind the meadow and a loud squawking of birds protested the shot. Midge and Trader bolted from the sound of the gunshot just as a flock of birds overcast the sky. I stood up quick and yelled to stop the horses, but they were deaf to my commands. Midge reared once and took off at a gallop. Trader flicked his tail and lunged in the same direction, also at a full gallop.

For an instant I relaxed, thinking that I'd just let the horses run out their fright and knowing that Trader would come trotting back to me as soon as he realized he'd left me behind, but then I felt the long lead lines tug at my waist. I worked the knot free just as my feet were yanked off the ground. The lines whipped through the grass and I dropped my head on the ground, thankful that I was no longer attached.

Trader slid to a halt first, just a few feet from the gravel path. Midge jumped the path, then realizing that Trader had stopped, spun on her haunches and faced him. I was stretched out on the ground now over twenty feet from the horses and began screaming all the swear words I could think of at Trader and Midge. Neither horse seemed to care which only angered me more. I finally stood up, gingerly checking each limb for injuries, and then swore again at Trader.

Trader came over to me when he heard my voice, not understanding the horrible adjectives I had attached to his name. He had settled down some, but his nostrils still flared. Trader nudged my hand, which was raw from rope burn and stinging painfully. "Go away," I said, still furious.

Trader followed docilely as I went to retrieve Midge's line and called her over. I couldn't believe my own stupidity. Who would tie a grazing line on their waist? Fortunately I had untied the knot. I didn't want to think about being dragged behind two horses. I was lucky to have survived with only burns on my hands, a rip in my blouse and a tender spot on my hip. The jade piece was unscratched and I found the little music box had suffered no harm.

After a few minutes, the carriage came round the path to pass by our meadow again. This time a dog was out of the carriage and running at the horses' feet. The hound yipped a few times when he spotted me. I was hitching the horses up to the wagon and gave the driver my best scowl as he passed. Though I doubted that the carriage driver had anything to do with the gunshot being fired so near to my resting spot, he was the only person to whom I could immediately show my anger. At the rear of the carriage, the carcass of a Canada goose hung, blood dripping in a trail behind the carriage, as a trophy of the day's exploits. Shooting was illegal in the park, but the wealthy didn't often pay mind to the rules and were rarely prosecuted for any crimes.

By the time I got the horses back to the stables it was well past two. I groomed the horses and bedded their stalls. One of the stablehands asked after Papa and wondered why our team was home early. I didn't mention that Papa was sick and instead told the boy that we were having a family holiday that afternoon. It would be bad for business if the news of Papa's illness became public knowledge, and stablehands were notorious for spreading rumors.

"Hello, Papa," I said, entering his bedroom. "I've got a package for you."

"Hmm?" Papa was propped up on pillows and reading the afternoon paper. A cup of half-drunk tea and an uneaten breakfast roll waited on his bedside table. Obviously he was not feeling well enough to eat. I had a moment of satisfaction thinking that it wasn't just my cooking he refused. His face looked pale, and I could hear the fluid in his lungs as he tried to clear his throat to speak.

"Papa, don't try to speak," I said. "I'll bring you some hot tea while you explore the present. It was left at the Ferry Building—from the Lee family."

I took his cold teacup and went to the kitchen to brew a fresh cup. Mother was sleeping on the sofa in the family room and Caroline and Mary were also napping. The boys would be home from school soon, but for the moment the house was oppressively quiet. I wished I didn't have to stay.

"Look at this," Papa said as I entered the room. He coughed a few times and then pushed the music box forward. He traced the abalone shell mermaid and then turned the crank to start the music. He listened with eyes closed and smiled. "Do you know the tune?"

"No."

"Mozart. You should know Mozart, Bette," Papa replied. His smile was the first time I had seen him act lively since he teased me yesterday afternoon. "Isn't it strange that a Chinese family would give us a music box that plays Mozart?"

I tried to imagine Mozart giving a concert to a crowd of Chinese and shook my head. "Maybe the music box was made in Europe."

"I think this was made in China. The Chinese have good taste, that's all." Mozart was Papa's favorite composer.

"They also gave us this," I paused to unlatch the silver chain and pulled the jade out from under my blouse. The dragon fell into Papa's hand, and his eyebrows arched. "Isn't it beautiful? I'm sure we could sell it for quite a price."

Papa gave me a sharp look. "You don't sell gifts like this." His fingers traced the line of silver inlaid in the jade. "Do you know why they gave us these things? Was there a note asking for anything?"

"No." I paused, wondering again what we could give to the Lees in return. "I almost wish they hadn't given us these gifts. We don't have anything this fine to repay them."

"We don't owe any gifts in return. They were settling their debt to our family. Nothing is due on either side now." Papa seemed confident in this. He handed me the jade piece. "You will keep the necklace and I'll keep the music box. If I hear you've sold it, I won't speak to you again."

"Papa, I can't keep something this nice," I said, trying to hand it back to him. "If you won't let me sell it, then keep it for yourself."

"No, Bette, it's a gift," a cough interrupted his sentence and he paused for a sip of tea before continuing, "You can't return or sell it without repercussions."

Papa spoke with enough authority that I wasn't about to press the issue. Although I liked the jade, I questioned his judgment. We would be hard up for money in the next month with Papa off work, and Mother couldn't sew enough garments to keep food on the table. One look at Papa though, and I knew I wouldn't sell the jade. Somehow I'd work the wagon team and keep the business going until Papa was on his feet again. I latched the chain around my neck again and felt the jade slip cool against my chest. "Well, if I must keep it, then it will remind me of you. When I saw the dragon I thought you would like the piece."

Papa smiled. "I was born in the year of the dragon, according to the Chinese calendar."

How did Papa know about the Chinese calendar? I didn't think he had contact with the Chinese other than the few that we met at the Ferry Building or those working in the laundries. I wanted to ask him more about his connections to the Chinese, but just then I remembered the five-dollar bill in my pocket. "Oh, Papa, when I delivered the harp to the Douglas house I met a Mr. Klein, the butler. He sent his regards to you and asked that I give you this. I told him that you bill Mr. Douglas directly for the delivery charges, but he said this wasn't for the delivery." I handed him the bill. "He wouldn't take it back when I told him we were not so in need of charity."

Papa shook his head. "Mr. Klein is a good man." He coughed a few times and then finished in a suddenly tired voice, "I'll miss working with him."

I nodded and handed him the cup of tea he was reaching for. I didn't know what his last comment meant. Was he saying that he had missed Mr. Klein's company because it had been a long time since they had worked together? Or did he mean that he would miss the opportunity to work with him in the future? A knock came on the bedroom door, and I didn't have a chance to ask for an explanation.

Papa set down the tea and quickly replaced the lid of the hatbox. He slipped the five-dollar bill in the pocket of his nightshirt and gave me a conspiratory nod. "Hide the music box under the bed so your Mother won't see. I want it to be a present for her later."

I did as he asked and then went to open the door. Mother entered with a plate of toast and another cup of tea. Papa didn't mention that I had just brought in a cup. Mother was always strangely jealous of any time Papa and I spent together, and he was careful not to allow any compliment to me while she was there. I gave an excuse of wanting to start dinner and left the room.

Frank called at our house just after dinner. Mother invited him inside and asked the same question she always asked when Frank walked in our front door, "How are your mother and father?"

Frank replied, "They're both well tonight, but send their sympathies for your husband. How is Mr. Lawrence?"

I replied, "He's not well. Doc has him bedridden."

Mother shook her head. "Just a cold."

Frank nodded politely, knowing that Papa wouldn't stay in bed for a cold, as we all well knew. "My mother said she would like your company tomorrow for tea at our home. She wanted you to call at the usual time if Mr. Lawrence was not too ill to have you leave his side for a short visit."

Mother nodded but didn't answer.

Frank looked at me and shrugged. He was used to my Mother's silence. "Mrs. Lawrence, may I take Bette for a short outing this evening? I'll have her back safely before eleven."

Mother gave another quick nod. Frank always acted formal around my parents, and I tried not to laugh when he asked them for permission to take me out—as if this were a date! I didn't care where we were headed so long as I could get out of the house. Mother was refusing to talk to me because Papa told her that I didn't want to marry Frank. At least, this was my best guess. Silent people are difficult to figure out, and I had lost patience for Mother.

As soon as we slipped out of the house, Frank turned to me and said, "We have an evening for ourselves."

"Oh? And what are our plans?"

"Ice skating first, then a show."

"Where? There's no ice in the city. The last time I checked, the ocean doesn't freeze." I wondered what show he had in mind, hoping it wasn't the vaudeville show he had mentioned on my birthday.

"The fair at the Mechanics' Pavilion. They've set up the rink there for a masquerade skating party tonight."

I remembered seeing a banner for the fair. The masquerade party was held every year near the Opera House, and Frank and I used to stand outside the gates of the rink and watch the men and women skating in their costumes. Neither Frank nor I could afford the cost of one ticket, let alone two. "You know we don't have money to get in." I stood on tiptoe and spun in a circle. "Unless you intend a game of pretend like old times. Shall we stand outside the gates and skate on the street?" I winked at him. "In that case, I'll be wearing a long flowing blue gauze and doing spins on the toes of my boots and flips above your head."

Frank grinned. "Well, I don't see anything wrong with a game of pretend, although I think we're too old to wait outside the gates." He reached in his pocket and held out an envelope. "And it would be a shame to waste these two tickets."

"Where did you get those tickets?"

"My secret."

I couldn't get him to tell me, no matter how much I pestered. We made our way to the Mechanics' Pavilion and waited in the line outside the gates of the ice rink. Most of the guests were wearing costumes, and I convinced Frank that we should buy five-cent paper masks.

"The red one with the yellow fringe," he suggested as we scanned over the masks.

I nodded at the man peddling the cheap wares. "We'll take this red one and the silver one over there." The silver mask reminded me of the dragon on my jade, the weight of it was lovely on my skin, and I debated showing my treasure to Frank.

We slipped on the masks and made our way over to the rink. So long as you had a ticket, the gatekeeper would let you rent a pair of skates and enter the rink. Lights sparkled everywhere and the ice glistened. Frank pointed out several extravagant costumes, and we made a game of choosing which we liked the best. I felt quite transformed by the silver mask. The music from the bandstand, the other costumes and Frank's red mask with the yellow beak helped me forget even the headache of marriage proposals.

As we edged out onto the ice, I realized it had been a long time since I had last stood on ice. Papa had taken me once on a trip in the winter to a frozen lake, way across the bay. We had spent the day skating, and eventually I had learned where to place my feet so I might glide over the slippery ice, but my memory of that time was too distant. For the first few minutes on the rink, I clung to the rails and feared any small crevice in the ice where my blades might catch.

Frank took to the sport as though he had grown up in the arctic. He swished between two couples, made a circle, and then skated backward to meet me. Eyeing my cautious movements, he slowed his pace. "Come on, Bette. You won't get far hugging the rail. Where's your sense of adventure?"

"My feet are just getting used to the skates." I'd gotten a few bruises from my fall in the meadow that morning and the last thing I wanted was another painful adventure. "Go ahead without me. I'll catch you on the next lap."

He nodded and skated ahead with a mischievous grin. "Watch your back. There are monsters, jokers and masqueraders everywhere. You never know what or who might grab you on that next lap!"

"Frank! Don't even try!" I cussed him under my breath and hoped he wouldn't surprise me. Frank reminded me of Charlie—full of trouble and always the cause of my younger sisters' agonies. I watched Frank disappear into the crowd of skaters and finally got up the nerve to venture farther from the safety of the railing. I took a few easy strides and felt my feet glide easily over the ice, though my ankles wobbled.

Suddenly, the woman in front of me slipped. Her hands shot up in the air as her feet splayed and she toppled onto her backside. I managed to stop, inches from her skates, without falling over her. She wore a red velvet cape over her clothing and her face was concealed by a yellow-feathered mask complete with a wooden beak. As I reached my hand down to help her stand, still unsteady on my own skates, I said, "You've unfortunately fallen in front of the worst skater on the ice. I'm sorry if I'm not much help here."

She smiled weakly. "You're not the worst. I'm the one who fell. And thank you for not toppling over me."

"I nearly did," I admitted. As soon as she was standing on her skates again, she took a step toward the rail, and her feet shot apart. I latched onto her arm, catching her just before she hit the ice.

She regained her balance, then thanked me again. My breath caught in my throat when I recognized Miss Douglas's voice. Her gloved hand settled on my arm, and we cut a slow path back to the railing. The silver mask hid my face and I didn't have to explain the blush coloring my cheeks. I was nervous just to have Miss Douglas leaning on my arm, though I tried to tell myself that she was the same as any other young woman I might have befriended. Yet, I knew that wasn't true. She was the daughter of one of the richest men in the city, and well-known for being both a great beauty and a highly cultured young woman. And who was I?

Once we had a hold on the railing, she pulled her mask away from her face and wiped her eyes. Tears striped her cheeks. I handed her my handkerchief—thankfully clean—and she blew her nose.

"Thank you, again. I'm afraid I am not much of an ice dancer." Miss Douglas laughed softly. "I'm glad my friend skated ahead and didn't see me fall."

I was too afraid to speak or remove my mask, lest she might recognize me, so I only smiled and nodded.

"Are you skating alone?"

I shook my head and pointed into the crowd, then pretended as if I couldn't find my partner and shrugged. Frank was on the opposite side of the rink, spinning on his skates. It seemed that another skater had challenged him to a race as Frank and another man were pointing at each other and shouting wagers.

"Well, would you mind keeping me company for a while? I don't want to step off the rink yet, but I'm scared to go alone." Miss Douglas smiled and squeezed my hand.

"Of course." The words slipped out and I thought I saw Miss Douglas's eyebrows raise in recognition, but she said nothing. I gripped her hand

and we made an unsteady pass to the skating lane. Miss Douglas kept her fingers locked on my hand. Neither of us made it a full lap around the rink without falling, but we laughed at our follies and ignored the crowd that skated around us. She wouldn't let go of my hand. We skated together as though we had been long-time pals, and I remembered the feeling I'd had at the Palace Hotel. Maybe we could be friends after all. But her hands felt so soft that I was ashamed at the roughness of my own. Gripping reins and hefting crates had rubbed sturdy calluses on my palms. Our worlds were so different.

After another lap, Miss Douglas turned to me and said, "Before long we'll both be ice dancers! I think we may be getting the hang of this!"

I shook my head. "I think I'd have more luck singing opera than dancing on ice skates."

Miss Douglas laughed. "Do you like opera?" She leaned close and added in a conspiring tone, "You know, my mother thinks I'm at the opera now."

"Really?" I was surprised that Miss Douglas would admit her deceit to a stranger. I added, "No, I'm not a fan of opera. But why are you here at the ice rink if you're supposed to be at the opera?"

"I detest opera." She winked at me. "Don't tell anyone, promise?"

I nodded solemnly. "You mentioned you had a friend here. Was he your date for the opera?"

Miss Douglas smiled. "You're quick. Yes, my friend Darren was set to take me to the opera, but I convinced him not to." She pointed at the man who was now skating with Frank. The two young men were well matched in skill and had taken to a game of out-doing each other. I had kept my eye on Frank and the other man while skating with Miss Douglas, but I hadn't noticed that she was watching the scene as well.

"The other man with him is my escort."

"Really?" Miss Douglas smiled. "He seems quite handsome, though it's hard to see anyone's features with the masks. Are you engaged?"

"He would like that. As would both our parents." I shook my head. I was surprised that Miss Douglas would think Frank was handsome and wondered that she didn't recognize him as one of the hired help at her house. Or maybe she did, but was unwilling to admit this to me, yet. "No, we're not engaged—and won't be, if I can help it."

Miss Douglas laughed. "My feelings exactly! I don't want an engage-ment either, but Darren," she nodded at the young man circling Frank, "is courting me. I won't have to decide until I turn eighteen, but I've already had too many suitors. They want my father's money." Miss Douglas realized she had said too much and blushed. Quickly she added, "I think we were both remiss in our introductions!" She touched her hand to her chest and said, "Sarah Douglas."

"Nice to meet you, Miss Douglas."

"Oh, please call me Sarah."

I nodded, feeling tongue-tied. Sarah was waiting for me to intro-duce myself, and I knew I couldn't avoid it. I thought of using a ficti-tious name, but knew Frank might appear at any moment and ruin the scheme. Finally I mumbled, "Oh, I'm Bette Lawrence." For the first time, I was ashamed of my name. I hoped she wouldn't recognize the name.

"Lawrence?" Sarah asked, as if running the name through San Francisco's list of important people. "Has your family lived in San Francisco long?"

"Not long," I lied.

"Hmm. Your name sounds familiar. But I suppose Douglas and Lawrence are both common names." She smiled and replaced her mask. "And if we knew each other, I guess we would have remembered meeting, even without our masks."

It was unlikely that a young elite would remember the daughter of one of her father's workers even if we had been properly introduced, which we never were.

Sarah and I hadn't made it far around the rink before Frank skated up to me and exclaimed, "Bette! Look at you! I see your skates have finally settled on the ice. And you've met a very fine feathered friend."

I was glad he didn't recognize Sarah with her bird mask concealing half her face. "Yes, we're helping each other keep from breaking any bones."

"Excellent. And I've met a friend myself," Frank paused and shouted, "Darren, over here!"

Darren came around the rink with a flurry of ice. He swooped up to Sarah, linked her arm in his and bowed.

Frank noted their interaction. All four of us made hasty introductions and Frank didn't falter when he learned that it was Miss Sarah Douglas at my side. After a last circle around the rink, the four of us agreed we were ready to leave. Darren and Sarah mentioned that they should be back at the opera in time for the last act. I made an excuse that Frank and I were expected at a friend's house, and our group parted company at the rink. I didn't remove my mask the entire time, and I noted that neither had Frank. When Sarah and Darren finally disappeared into a waiting carriage, Frank turned to me and grinned.

"Well blimey, we're regular nabob socialites now," Frank said in a cockney accent. He was always trying to fake a British accent and never quite succeeded.

"I did like that, I've got to say." I was barely able to contain my amusement at the evening's unlikely meeting.

Frank's smile broadened. "My lady, I believe we acted quite the part of two vagabonds. Darren told me he admired the 'vagabond' costume. Our fine rich friends must have suspected this was unusual attire. Good thing you picked out the cheap masks and neither of us dressed fancy!"

I laughed. "Do you really think that Miss Douglas didn't recognize either of us?"

"She showed no sign of it."

"Well I'd guess she'd never forgive herself for spending an evening with a pair of wharf rats."

"Darren, too. His father is a lawyer on the exchange and his mother was a concert violinist. Regular socialites." Frank clasped my hand. "At least we know we can hobnob with their kind! Not that I'd want to make an everyday occurrence of it, mind you."

"Of course not. The rich are plagued with dull lives, and we'd be wearied of their idle troubles were they to be our close friends." I didn't really believe this and Frank knew I was joking. We had both talked of our dreams of living in mansions on Nob Hill, and I knew Frank was infatuated with the Douglas family as well as the rest of Nob Hill's elite.

He nodded. "Well, the rich, God love them, are regular bores, my dear."

We traded our skates in for our boots and tossed the masks. Frank and

I were both exhausted from the skating, but we still had time before I had to be home. Frank directed us to a streetcar heading toward the north side of the city, and I arched my eyebrows. "Just where is this show?"

Frank shrugged. "The North Beach area."

"We can't go there, Frank. You know our mothers would kill us." He was setting us up for an adventure to the Barbary Coast, and I knew right off that it was a bad idea.

"Bette, don't worry so much. I wouldn't take you to an act that wasn't fitting for a lady to see."

"Would you take your mother to this show?"

Frank turned away without answering. I would have argued more, but I was flushed from the skating and knew I didn't want the evening to end yet. The cable car lumbered up the hill, and I turned to watch the passing houses. The night was strangely warm and the air felt charged. The fog layer had set in, blotting out the night stars, and the moon, barely visible, cast an ornery yellow glow from the south.

We left the cable car at the end of the line and walked the rest of the way to the Barbary Coast. The vaudeville show that Frank had picked for us to see was in an outdoor plaza between two bars. We crossed an intersection where women stretched out of a whorehouse, half-naked, challenging every pedestrian to admire their bosoms and legs. I pointed to one of the women. "She's too attractive to be dangling herself out for men to purchase."

Frank blushed and pulled my hand. "Don't point, Bette."

I sighed. "Well, it's true. Have a look at her face. I wonder how a woman that pretty would end up in a window for men to buy."

We passed by another woman, and she overheard my remark. "Don't worry, honey," she said with a tired smile, "that one's paid well for her work. She'll earn more in her life than you'll dream of with honest sewing work."

Frank pulled my arm and we passed by the women quickly. He scowled at me when we had cleared of her earshot and said, "Bette, why would you say such things around here, of all places?"

I shrugged, surprised to hear the fear in his voice. "Well, I would say such things anywhere, I suppose. It just never occurred to me before. I don't venture to the Barbary Coast for a good look at the women of the night often enough, I guess."

"I'd rather you not talk about it anymore," Frank said, his tone curt. "We'll be in a fight with one of the women's managers if you keep it up."

"Managers? You make it sound as though they are honestly employed." With one look at his set face, I decided to drop the subject. "Are we near the plaza?"

Frank pointed to the next intersection. "So long as you don't get us in any fights, we'll be there shortly."

"Are you afraid?"

Just then a door flew open from the hotel saloon ten paces ahead of us, and two men tumbled out onto the street. Frank held up his hand to stop me, but I was already frozen. The men rolled on the ground, each fighting for a handhold on the other's throat. Three other men soon burst out of the same door, one carrying a bucket of water, which he tossed on the two men entangled on the ground. The water didn't faze the wrestlers, so one of the other men tried to pull them apart. The third man fired a gun in the air, and suddenly everyone was still. The wrestlers rolled apart and stared at each other, heads swaying.

Frank grabbed my arm, "It's Henry Douglas," he whispered, "There, the man on the ground on the left. He's the young Mr. Douglas, I'd swear it."

I wondered why Henry Douglas was here, in a bar fight on the Barbary Coast, when he was supposed to be at the university across the bay. And what was the coincidence of meeting Sarah and Henry Douglas on the same night? Henry was trying to stand, and it was soon obvious that he didn't have all of his wits about him. "I think he's drunk."

Frank nodded. "And soon in a heap of trouble. The police will be here before long."

Five or six more men came out of the hotel's saloon, surrounding the men, and angry words were bantered from the two factions that had formed on each side of the wrestlers. A police whistle screeched, and the men scattered down the street. I yanked on Frank's arm. "Let's go. I don't want to meet the police."

He started to follow me and then turned back to the hotel. The young Mr. Douglas was still lying in the gutter. "Go on ahead. I'll be right behind you." He raced toward the body.

I stared at him, unsure if I was angry at Henry Douglas or at Frank. The police would arrive any minute, and the last thing I wanted to do was explain to my mother how the three of us were arrested. Frank tried to pull Henry to his feet, but the limp man was heavy in his arms. Ignoring better judgment, I ran over to help. We hefted Henry up between us and headed down the sidewalk, half dragging his feet. The police whistle blared again, and Frank shot a bewildered look at me. "We'll be caught, no doubt."

I pointed at the hotel where we'd passed the scantily clad women, and Frank nodded. We pulled Henry up to the door and Frank gave it a good kick. The door swung open and Frank hollered, "Where's the back way out?"

A startled bartender gawked at us. Fortunately, most of the guests of this bar were upstairs, with the ladies no doubt. The bartender took a quick look out at the street and then turned to us. "We don't want any trouble here."

"The back door, please?" I asked, feeling an ache at my side that was either from Henry's weight or from the fear of being caught.

The bartender clenched a dishrag in one hand and a bottle of whiskey in the other. We eyed each other tensely.

"Please, sir. You don't want the police in here."

He pointed down a hallway. "The back door's on your left as soon as you pass through the hallway."

We dragged Henry past the tables and chairs, down the narrow hallway and out the back door, hearing the sound of the police just gathering on the street outside the hotel. As soon as we had made it to the back alley, Henry seemed to awaken from his drunken spell. He tried to push away from Frank and then squinted at me. "Who the hell are you two? Where'd that other bastard go? He stole my money."

His speech was slurred, and he spit out every word with bits of blood. It was obvious that he'd been knocked in the mouth and his upper lip was already starting to swell. Frank tried to quiet him, explaining that the police were looking for him and that he had better concentrate on an escape plan.

We left the alley, with Henry still limping between Frank and me and leaning heavily on our arms, and made our way to the cable car station. Frank kept to the side streets and alleyways that we hoped the police wouldn't check. Once we were past the line of hotels that lined the notorious Barbary Coast, we slowed a bit and Henry tried to walk on his own.

"I need to get down to the wharf," he said, still slurring his words. "The boys will leave without me. We have a boat there, waiting to take us back."

"Back to where?" Frank asked.

"Berkeley." Henry paused, glancing at the street behind us. "Where are we now? I'm turned around."

Frank nodded at the street ahead of us. "We're almost at the cable car station. We'll take that back to Sacramento Street and get you a hotel for the night in a better part of town."

Henry was adamant that he get back to Berkeley that night. Frank tried to argue, but before long gave up, and we headed down to the Ferry Building. We deposited Henry in a scull just preparing to make its last run across the bay for the night and gave the captain Mr. Douglas's information. Fortunately, one of the men on board recognized Henry. Mr. Douglas was well-known at the waterfront and Henry would be taken care of, simply because of his father's name and money.

We left the Ferry Building and I breathed a sigh of relief. Frank clapped my shoulder and laughed. "Well, that was an interesting turn, wasn't it?"

I nodded. "A bit unexpected. And frankly, I don't care if we never go back to the Barbary Coast to see that show." Frank looked shamed by this comment, and I quickly tried to restate it. "I mean, I've had enough adventure for the evening. Truly, I've had a wonderful time."

He smiled and slipped his arm in mine. "So have I. And thank you for helping me with Henry. We probably put ourselves in more danger than he was worth, but . . ."

"Mr. Douglas will thank you."

"For Henry's sake, I hope his father never finds out about this."

We took the long route home to avoid the crowd at the waterfront bars, and I was happy to have time to think. Frank was curiously silent, and I wondered if he too was replaying the evening's events in his mind. After a while, he grabbed my hand and squeezed it warmly. I felt my skin tingle and thought how different Frank's hand felt from Sarah's.

"You know, Bette, I need to ask you something. I've been waiting all night." He gazed upward as if he was searching for stars in the night's fog. When he looked back at me. His lips were tight and I could feel the tension in his grip.

His seriousness took me by surprise. I knew what he was thinking and couldn't help but pull away. Although I had thought of an answer if he'd ever crossed our lines of friendship, I wasn't ready to speak now. I tried to keep my voice light, "What is it then?"

"I've almost asked you a thousand times. But I've been too worried about your answer. We've known each other for so long."

"We're nearly brother and sister. You can ask anything." I couldn't refuse him, not when he looked at me, expecting so much. But I wasn't ready to answer.

He got quiet with this. After a minute, he continued, "No, we're more than brother and sister."

I shook my head and laughed. "Well, I do like you better than Charlie or Wes, but you still vex me as much as either of my brothers."

Frank caught my arm and made me stop. "Bette, I'm being serious." He looked down at my hands. "I've talked to your father, and, I'd like to ask—"

"Frank," I interrupted, "don't." I felt nauseous and my legs were weak. Long ago I should have stopped this.

Frank stepped back as though I had just spit in his face.

"I want you as my friend, my brother." I squeezed his hand, but he pulled it loose from my hold. "I don't want anything more."

"Since when?"

I thought of my father and remembered that he had asked me a similar question. My family expected Frank and me to marry. We had always been close friends. Why did we need to be anything more? "Since forever." The words slipped out before I thought how much this might injure him.

"You mean that?" Frank listened to my silent answer only long enough for the moisture to well in his eyes. He turned away from me and headed back down the street we'd just come up. He didn't look back at me, and I knew well enough not to give chase. He'd never forgive me if I saw his tears. Maybe he'd walk long enough to forget about any talk of marriage.

I continued along the street alone, suddenly lighter and free from a burden I hadn't known I'd been carrying. The pavement was wet from the fog and smelled wonderful. I passed a billboard with a picture of Yosemite and an advertisement for a vacation. The cliffs of Half Dome rose up from the valley floor and Yosemite Falls flowed in the backdrop of the billboard. "Visit the heart of California . . ." I read the ad with a sudden realization that I could travel there one day. In fact, I could go anywhere. I was not bound to marry Frank.

An automobile roared past me and I jumped up on the curb. It was unusual for a woman to walk alone, especially at night, and I could sense the passengers' eyes on me. A carriage followed the automobile and the driver whistled as he came upon me. Ignoring him, I turned down a side street and quickened my pace toward home. I wanted to be left alone and knew only sleep could let me escape from this city tonight.

Chapter 4
April 18, 1906

I awoke with a start. A sound loud as a firecracker had yanked me awake. I waited to hear it again, but there was only silence. Maybe I had been dreaming of fireworks. At some point in the night Caroline must have had another nightmare and crawled into my bed. She was sleeping on my left side with most of the blankets wrapped around her little frame. Just as I closed my eyes, I heard another sound—a low rumble as if the earth was stretching to crack her back. I bolted upright and grabbed Caroline. The mattress bucked on the frame and I could barely keep hold of Carol. The whole floor rose up at me as the bed lunged away from the wall. The cross that Mary had hung above the dollhouse smashed to the floor, and I heard her rustling on the other bed. She was bawling into the purple quilt.

"Don't worry, Mary. We're here with you. It's only an earthquake," I said, trying to reassure her despite the shaking in my own voice. Carol, miraculously, was silent as a mouse. Suddenly the rolling motion gave way to a violent shake and loud thunder crashed everywhere around us.

This second shake made my little sister cling to my neck so tightly I thought I might choke. Mary had managed to cross the room and climb into my bed. I loosened Carol's hold and the three of us huddled together with the blanket wrapped over our heads.

"It'll be over soon." I'd been through a few earthquakes before and knew that it was best if we stayed put, but I had a horrible feeling that this quake wouldn't stop. The rolling continued, and our bed was pitched as easily as a scull in a storm. Mary whimpered about her dolls, and Carol only trembled, still quiet as if she'd been waiting for this and knew just what to expect. When the rolling finally slowed, I pulled them both close to my body and carried them to the doorway. The floor and the walls started heaving around us again, and I wondered how long the walls would stand.

We got to the doorway and, just as I reached for the handle, the door swung at me. Mary cried out and tried to make a break for the bed. My hands held her so tight I knew there'd be bruises on her shoulders. Carol held the wood frame tightly and pointed toward the stairwell that was lashing about. "Look! It's a snake!"

Mary was petrified of snakes and shrieked at this. I finally convinced Mary it was only the stairwell and Caroline was imagining things, and she promised to stay in the doorway with Caroline. No sound came from the boys' room, and I had to check on them. Glass shattered at my side as I crossed the hallway. The window facing the street shattered just inches from my face, and the sound wracked my body like bullets. The door to the boys' room opened with a nudge of my foot and I spotted Charlie first. He was frozen on his bed with eyes as big as a doe's. Wes was missing, and I checked the first place I could think of. There he was, hiding under his bed, naked and wild with fright. He slipped out of my grip the first time I caught his wrist and stubbornly refused to come out of the hiding place.

"Go away. Leave me alone!"

The next thrust of the earth sent his body tumbling forward. I latched onto his arm and he didn't resist this time. Once he was out from under the bed, I wrapped a blanket around him and then called to Charlie. Despite his fear, Charlie diligently followed me to the doorway. As soon as we reached it, the shaking stopped.

Glass littered the hallway. "Don't move, Caroline." She had taken a few steps toward me and I could imagine tiny shards of glass impaling her bare feet.

"Bette, I'm scared. I want to cry, but I'm too scared." She said this in her soft, strangely logical voice, and did not cry.

"Go get your shoes. Mary, help Caroline with her shoes." Maybe I knew that the earth wasn't finished. All I could think of was getting everyone outside. We had to hurry. Our home no longer felt like a safe den. I had never wanted to run from it so much as I did now.

"Wes, you need to get dressed," I said, pointing to his dresser, now knocked on its side.

"I won't move." He crossed his arms. "I won't touch the floor."

"Come, now, Wes. We have to get out of the house and you won't leave naked." I helped him pull on a pair of trousers and found his shoes, then crossed the hall and grabbed my own clothes. Mary and Caroline managed to get their feet in their shoes just as the ground started to shake again.

We were all in the hallway, haphazardly dressed. "Down the stairs, quickly. And no crying!" I hushed Mary's sobbing with a mean glare. Charlie jumped into action this time, grabbing Mary's hand and bolting down the staircase. I carried Wes and Caroline, barely keeping up with Charlie. Mother and Father had their room on the first floor, under our rooms. I told Charlie to keep the others in the doorway between the kitchen and the hall. I could hear Father coughing and banged my fist on their door, "Mother, Papa, are you all right?"

No one answered. After a moment, Mother opened the door. Somehow she always managed to appear calm. I wondered if she just didn't realize what was happening. How could she look so sedate?

"Where are the children?" she asked.

Just then the ground started to move again. I pointed to the hallway. The gentle rolling of the floorboards under our feet had pushed the children against the wall and they each had a piece of wall to cling to near the staircase. The aftershocks were getting shorter. I prayed it would be over soon. "Is Papa all right?"

She shook her head, but aloud, said, "Yes."

A great crack erupted and both of us clutched the doorway as the rolling intensified. I stepped out of the doorway just in time to watch the brick fireplace pull away from the wall. The chimney toppled with a cloud of dust rising like an explosion, and the sound of falling bricks and mortar was deafening. The children began crying immediately and, hoping that none of them were injured, I yelled for them to be quiet. For the first time, I desperately wanted the peace of silence.

Mother was watching Papa. Her face was ashen. I could see him, half crouched, half lying in bed. His body was seized with his coughing. The latest tremor had stopped now and the ground was again solid under foot, though I thought I might never trust it again. I couldn't wait for another aftershock. "I'm taking the children out of the house. Can you manage Papa?"

She nodded.

I gathered up the whimpering, but unharmed, flock in the hallway and made for the front door. As soon as I opened it, the first wails from the neighbors filled the air. All around us, houses had tumbled off their foundations, chimneys had toppled, like ours, and glass and bricks littered the streets. Charlie was as good as gold when I gave him orders to lead the others out to the front yard. "Keep everyone together, and don't move past the front post."

I went back inside and found Mother trying to move Papa. She couldn't lift him and tears were streaming down her face, though she was silent as always. "Mother, let me help," I said softly.

She turned to me. "We can't move him."

"Go outside to be with the children."

"You can't lift him alone." She tried to lift him and then staggered back as his body slipped out of her arms onto the mattress. Papa was oddly quiet, and I had a brief horrible thought that he might have died, yet his rasping breathing belied this. He seemed only unconscious. "God, we'll die here," Mother whispered.

"No. Go outside to watch the children. I'll follow behind you with Papa. He'll walk for me."

Mother's eyes were wide, just like Charlie's had been, and I was worried I'd have to argue more. She turned from me and started out of the room. Gripped with fear and frozen in place, I watched her back disappear. I doubted that I was strong enough to move a full-grown man on my own and wondered if Mother had left because she believed that I could, or if she was ready to let Papa and me die there when the walls crumbled.

Suddenly Mother was back in the room and shouting my name. I blinked and felt a rush of relief. Mother continued, "We'll both carry him. Or we'll drag his feet if we have to."

"We can't drag him. There's broken glass in the hall." I searched for something we could use to support Papa. "He needs a cane. Maybe we could find the broom."

"He couldn't use a cane. He's too weak. And we won't find the broom in this mess." She spread her hands out, gesturing to the chaos that had claimed their once pristine bedroom. Plaster from the walls littered the room along with a smashed statue of Jesus on the cross and a painting of a Parisian garden. Mother's gaze focused on the crucifix. She sighed heavily. "We need to move him, Bette."

I nodded and went to help heft Papa up to a sitting position. He would not respond to me when I told him to stand, and his eyes were glassy. Mother was right. It was painfully obvious that Papa was barely strong enough to rise, let alone limp out of the room with a cane. I pressed my hand against his chest and felt his heartbeat. His cough that followed further confirmed that he was still alive. I had never considered Papa's size before. He was always bigger than me, average for a man, and nothing more. But as soon as Mother and I had our arms around his waist and tried lifting him, I realized how slight his frame was. The bumps on his spine were sharp and his ribs had no cushion. Maybe he'd been losing weight and I hadn't noticed. With little struggling, we managed to get his body balanced between us. He didn't try to fight as we stumbled through the kitchen and down the hallway to the front door. When we reached the last step on the walkway, my muscles were shaking under the weight. He thrashed a bit, suddenly coming to, and Mother lost her hold. I nearly collapsed on the sidewalk as I shrugged his body off. Charlie helped me get Papa into a sitting position, and we leaned his back against the lamppost so he wouldn't fall over.

People were streaming out into the street everywhere. Instinctively, I looked across the road at Frank's house. The damage to their property was severe. The second floor appeared to have sunk halfway through the first floor, and the chimney had toppled as well. I watched the front door of his house closely, expecting someone to emerge at any moment.

Mother must have been thinking of the McCains as well. She was stealing looks at their house while tending to a cut Mary had gotten on her palm. "Should I go check on them, Mother?" I guessed she was concerned about her friend Mrs. McCain, and maybe Mr. McCain, as well as Frank.

She shook her head. "We should stay here together."

The fire wagon's bells sounded in the distance, and Charlie turned his attention from Papa to search for the smoke. He was always hoping to spot the smoke spire when a fire team rang the bells. He pointed toward the south and reported, "Look, Bette, there's the fire."

"Don't worry," I quieted him, "the firemen are on their way." I was worried his excitement would frighten the other children.

"I'm not worried. I want to go have a look." Charlie wanted to be a firefighter, and Mother had a hard time of it keeping him from running off whenever he heard the bells ring. He'd been caught gawking at the scene of a fire several times before.

By the glint in his eyes, I knew his temptation to run toward the smoke was strong. Charlie and I shared the same desire for excitement, but I couldn't understand his fascination with fire. Almost immediately after spotting the first smoke cloud, Charlie spotted a second fire a few blocks away from the first. "Look at that! There's a bigger blaze over there! I bet the firemen won't have enough water for both!" His voice was high-pitched with excitement.

"Charlie," I said, shaking his shoulder sternly, "enough of that." I leaned close and threatened, "I'll have your backside with the horse whip if you scare Caroline and Mary."

Charlie squinted his eyes meanly. "You're not going to touch me. Only Mother or Father could whip me. I'd beat you first."

I cuffed him on the ear and he started whining. Father awoke as if from a trance. "Charlie, stop that whining. You listen to Bette, you hear!"

Charlie quieted promptly, but he shot a scowl at me. Mother was at Papa's side now. She clutched his hand and whispered something in his ear.

Papa seemed to disagree with whatever Mother had said. He waved her off and then fell into another round of coughing. His voice was barely audible when he spoke again. "Bette, go check on Jack and his family. No one's come out of there."

Mother crossed herself and bent her head as if she were praying but didn't argue with Papa. I knew she didn't want to lose me. She couldn't manage the children and Papa alone. Papa noticed my reservation and added. "Go on, Bette. The McCains may need our help."

It was strange how Papa had suddenly come back to life. I wasn't about to challenge him but wondered what help we could give to the McCains. Papa coughed again. He hadn't moved from his position by the lamppost, and he sat perfectly upright like a chief calmly surveying the disaster around him.

"Don't stay long," Mother whispered to me. From the look in her eye, I knew she was angry that Papa had asked me to go, but she wouldn't say that.

I turned to Charlie and said, "Until I get back, you're in charge of the younger ones. Don't let anyone out of your sight, understand?"

Charlie nodded. He was still upset that I'd hit him, and he wouldn't meet my eyes. I started across the street, feeling the ash and mortar dust fill my nose and coat my throat. Smoke clouds had replaced the usual morning fog in an ominous gray haze that seemed to thicken with each minute. Soon the sunlight might be choked completely, covering the shambled city sidewalks in shadows. I reached the front porch and hollered, "Hello! Anyone home?" The sight of their ruined house was painful. A feeble cry sounded from somewhere inside. I called again, "Hello? Who's there? Are you hurt?"

This time there was no answer. I tried the door but the lock was set. A window on the first floor was smashed, and I considered crawling inside, but the leaning support beams under the front balcony made me reconsider this plan. The last thing I wanted was a pile of bricks to bury me alive should the beam give way. I circled around to the back of the house yelling, "Hello! Mr. McCain? Mrs. McCain? Where are you? Frank? Anyone here?"

Disoriented by the rubble of fallen bricks, I searched for the back door and when I couldn't find it, realized that the first floor entrance was simply gone. The top floor had sunk straight to the ground. I prayed that no one had been on the first floor when the quake hit. Fortunately, I knew Frank and his parents both had their rooms on the second floor. Most likely, everyone was asleep upstairs when the second floor crushed the first. I broke away the remaining shards of glass on a second-floor window and crawled inside. The bedroom was empty and the sheets were in disorder as though the occupant had left suddenly. My mind was spinning with what-ifs. This was Frank's room. His smell was in the room. His books had toppled off the shelf above the bed. His picture of Athena was on the floor. His lamp had been broken to pieces. I called his name, my voice barely above a whisper.

As I moved through his room, I heard a child's laughter and shivered. I knew I had imagined the sound. Frank and I had played in this room more times than I could count. The walls breathed with our voices. It was our laughter that I heard. Somehow, the earthquake had released the sounds that the walls had absorbed when the plaster cracked and the seams split.

Someone's sobbing interrupted my thoughts. My body moved as if in a dream, past Frank's bed where he hid money between the mattress and the bed frame, past the desk where we had drawn treasure-hunting maps, through the doorway where our height measurements had been etched on nearly every birthday, and then down the hallway. A half a dozen shadows could have hidden Frank, and I checked behind the doorways almost unconsciously, remembering where I had found him when we used to play hide-and-go-seek.

The hallway was too quiet. Damn the silence. Who said that silence was peaceful? I longed for any sound now. I went to Frank's parents' room and knocked on their door. No response came and I finally tried the handle. When I first gazed around their room I couldn't place what was wrong, and then once I saw it, my vision so clouded that I could barely see at all. The green wallpaper and the brown carpet were a fuzzy blur. My focus point was the bed. A crossbeam from the ceiling had smashed through the center of the mattress. Frank's father had caught the beam in his chest. His blood drenched the bed sheets, and the stench of it made any step closer to the body impossible. I didn't bother to check his pulse. No doubt he had died instantly. Mrs. McCain was not in the room. I called her name softly.

Suddenly the floor started to shake. It's only an aftershock, I told myself, grabbing ahold of the wood-lined doorway. The shaking continued, and I felt my stomach tighten. I vomited on the floor as soon as the trembling stopped. It had lasted less than a minute and yet my nerves were frayed. My hands shook worse than the floor had, and I imagined the roof crashing on me every time the rafters groaned as they settled into their new position. I couldn't stay but I hated to move past the doorway. From somewhere in the house a soft sobbing came, and I screamed for Mrs. McCain as I ran from the room. The smell of my vomit and the sight of Jack's body were too much. "Mrs. McCain, Mrs. McCain!" I screamed again.

A feeble moan answered my call. Then a louder response came as I headed toward the stairway. "God have mercy," she said. "Take me now . . . Please don't leave me here alone."

As I rushed down the stairway I realized that there were half as many steps as usual. The second half of the stairway had smashed into the kitchen. "Mrs. McCain?" I called again.

No answer.

I searched the kitchen and found her huddled on the floor under the table. She was stone cold and looked like a ghost, but she was breathing and I could feel her pulse. At my touch, she shrank back from me. "Where's Frank?"

Mrs. McCain wouldn't answer me. She brought her hands up to cover her ears and stared straight through me as though I were a ghost.

"Mrs. McCain? Are you hurt?"

Her lips trembled but there was no answer. Her eyes had the strange look of one who had just stumbled from an opium den. I doubted if she could recognize me at all.

"Where is Frank?" I repeated the question speaking very slowly and gauging her response. She was in shock and maybe struck dumb now. After a moment, she fell to speaking in some unintelligible language. I tried to shake her, to wake her from the dream state she had entered, but she only fell to shrieking when I tried this. The shrieks were intolerable, and when I tried to cover her mouth, she sank her teeth into my palm. Before I could think, my hand pulled back from her mouth and then lashed at her cheekbone in a swift strike. As my hand recoiled I felt my heart stall in my chest. What had I done? How could I have slapped Mrs. McCain? "God forgive me," I whispered, watching her eyes focus on me.

She seemed to see me for the first time and leapt back now as though she had just felt my hand on her cheek. "Get back! Get away from me! You killed my husband!"

"No! I didn't kill anyone!" I stared at her in utter surprise. "What are you saying? It was an earthquake, Mrs. McCain. The earthquake shook loose the rafter beam that killed Jack. How could I have done that?"

She wouldn't listen to me, and I was afraid of what she might try. I had never seen someone so out of her mind. She fell to shrieking again and held her hands over her ears so she might block out the sound of her own voice.

"We have to get out of here," I said, trying to keep my voice calm. "We have to leave. Let's get your coat and go. Where is your son? Where is Frank?"

At the mention of Frank's name, Mrs. McCain finally was quiet. She seemed to see me for the first time. "Gone. He's gone."

Her words hit with the same force as a slug in the belly. I could barely stand and had to catch myself against the stair railing. If I had anything left in my stomach, I would have vomited again. Mrs. McCain had started crying and I hated her tears. I wanted to cry for Frank, but I couldn't. We couldn't both cry. Frank must have died, just as his father, but I needed to see the body to be sure. Mrs. McCain was not right in her head. She could have imagined his death. Maybe he had disappeared. One thing I knew, I had to get Mrs. McCain out of the house before I lost my mind as well. Blocking any thoughts of Frank, I took her clammy hand and got her up on her feet.

She stood shaking, and I was worried she'd collapse if we didn't move quickly. I grabbed her arm and headed out of the kitchen, whispering a silent prayer as Mrs. McCain followed behind me. After climbing the staircase to the second floor, we left the house through Frank's bedroom window. It was nearly unbearable to pass through Frank's room the second time. I hated the scent of his bedclothes. I wanted to scream his name, believing that he might only be hiding under the bed, like Wes, and would come to me when I called. Yet I knew the room was empty. I tried to ignore the sharp pang of loneliness and fought to keep the images of Frank's empty room out of my mind. My family was waiting for me.

Mrs. McCain let me lead her over to the lamppost where Papa sat. Mother and the children were at his side. My hands were shaking and I hid them behind my back so Mother wouldn't see. At first no one spoke. Mother hugged Mrs. McCain, which only caused her to start crying again, this time in horribly loud sobs interrupted by her gasping Jack's name. I wished I could leave rather than hear her repeat his name over and over. The image of Mr. McCain's body was too fresh in my mind. The children were too afraid to ask any questions. Papa looked directly at me. "Where's Jack?" he asked.

"With God," I answered. "He went to be with God."

"And Frank?" Papa asked. "Where is Jack's boy?"

I wrung my hands, feeling the calluses on my palms, feeling Frank's hand in mine. I couldn't answer him. I just stared at Mrs. McCain and Mother. Emma McCain was lucky for my mother's love, but I didn't think it would be enough. The woman had just lost everything—her home, her son, her husband, her life.

"Bette," he said harshly, "Answer me." Papa started coughing then. He clutched his chest and coughed again.

Caroline reached up and grabbed my hand. I picked her up. "Don't be scared," I said. "We are all here. Our family is safe."

She gazed at me with a strange expression and in my ear whispered, "Will Papa go away soon, like Mr. McCain?"

Shaken by the question, it took a moment for me to answer. "No, Papa just has a cold. He just needs a doctor." Tears squeezed into my eyes, and it took all my strength to keep from crying.

"Don't cry, Bette." Her thin arms hugged me, and she rested her head on my shoulder.

Although Mother argued against it, I headed back inside our house to bring out food for breakfast. I knew the children were hungry. The house was as quiet as a tomb. I entered the kitchen and found a sack to fill with a loaf of bread, honey, butter and a canteen of water. I found Charlie's box of soldiers in the kitchen and added this to the bag, then headed upstairs to find Caroline's pink blanket and Mary's doll. For little Wes, I grabbed the first things I could find—a book from his school and a rubber ball. His box of soldiers was nowhere in sight and I knew he would be crushed to hear that his clean little troops were lost. For myself, I grabbed my wool coat and my journal. I wondered if there would be enough pages left blank for me to write all that I had seen and felt between yesterday and today.

We made breakfast in the street, and no one had to tell the children to behave. Even Charlie was scared into good conduct by the news of Mr. McCain's death. Papa asked me again about Frank. I answered him the only way I knew how, "Mrs. McCain says he's gone, Papa."

"Like Mr. McCain?" Caroline asked.

"No questions now, Carol. Eat your bread." I couldn't answer her. "The honey will warm your little belly."

Before long the police came round to announce they were preparing to evacuate all of the homes on our street. The voices of men arguing with the police orders were swiftly swallowed up by whistles and dog barks as a fire wagon passed Harrison. This sight and a few ominous gunshots seemed to rally the neighbors who were on the fence about obeying the evacuation order. Soon there was a general agreement among the men of the neighborhood that it was indeed time to move, and the packing up began in earnest. It had been only an hour since the earthquake, and we had watched the fires south of Market Street spread. For some reason, the firemen were not getting a hold of the blaze. Charlie was begging to go help the firemen, and I had to scare him with threats of eternal damnation if he left his mother's side for even a moment. The wind had started and the police were afraid our block would soon be at risk for burning.

Mother looked at Papa and then at me. She was unsure how to proceed, and I thought for her this time. "Mother, go inside the house and pack the cedar chest with everything we will need for a day. They won't take longer than a day to get the fire stopped." I wasn't certain of this, but the words sounded reassuring to my audience. "I'll go to the stables and bring the wagon here. Midge and Trader are probably wild with fright over this quake."

Papa nodded. "Yes, Bette, go for the wagon. And mind the time."

I wondered what he meant by this. Did he think I would dawdle now? Our family was being evacuated and we stood to lose everything we owned. How would I not mind the time?

As I set off, Charlie was on my heels, begging to come along. I shook my head and pointed back at the lamppost. "Charlie, neither of us will forgive each other if something happens while we're both away. You have to stand guard for me. Watch the children close and don't let Wes wander off."

"But I want to go to the stables, please, Bette," he whined. "I'm just as fast as you, and I can help harness the horses."

"You're too old to whine." I shook my head. On any other day I would have let him come along. Not today. "Go on now, there isn't time to argue." Without looking back I knew he wouldn't follow me. Not even Charlie would misbehave today.

As I ran toward the stables, I passed a fireman and saw that a group of them were standing by a house whose roof had just caught fire. The firemen seemed immobilized by the sight of the blaze. Their hoses were empty and lay everywhere on the street as useless as snakeskin. A man passing by on the street kicked the fire hoses and laughed sardonically.

"The whole town will burn!" he exclaimed. "There's no water, see! There's no water for the noble firemen to spray on our churches. God shook the earth and the water mains broke."

He was a crazed man, I thought. His words couldn't be true. Our city was surrounded by water. The firemen would fight the fires.

He continued, "God wanted to burn down the city. Mark me, the whole town will burn!"

I didn't stay to listen, but the man's rant about God's judgment repeated in my ears as I raced down the road. If the firemen could not fight the inferno, our block would burn in a few hours. We had no time to lose. South of Market had already lost several buildings, and everywhere people stood about gawking at the earthquake-ruined structures or the burning embers. The smoke made my eyes sting. I reached the stables and found the place in complete disorder. No stablehands were about, and I instantly feared that someone had taken our horses. Fortunately, I heard Trader's neigh as soon as I entered the far side of the barn. Father's carriage was missing, but our wagon was still in the yard. Trader and Midge paced in their stalls and whinnied to each other nervously. I wondered what they had thought of the quake. As I prepared the wagon and harnessed the horses, I kept expecting one of the stableboys to appear. What had happened to Nathan? I prayed he was safe with his family. Everyone had fled the stables, and ghosts seemed to be watching me from every dark corner. I stowed a bag of grain under the wagon seat, knowing that the horses would have a hard day, and led the team out of the stable. As I opened the gates, I spotted smoke rising from the barn's roof like steam on hot bread. Just then I heard a muffled whinny. Throwing the reins around a tie post, I promised Trader I'd return and raced back inside the barn.

All of the stalls, save one, were empty. The one remaining horse, Terra, belonged to Mr. McCain, or rather, had belonged to Mr. McCain. Terra was a sweet old gray mare, slightly lame in the front left leg, but as dependable as Trader. Frank used to ride Terra. Mr. McCain's chestnut gelding, Guinness, was missing. Probably one of the stablehands had stolen him, I reasoned. I threw a saddle on Terra and fitted a bridle on her. Although she was an old horse, I knew Frank had thought highly of her, and there was no way I could leave her behind. Trader tossed his head, rattling the harness, when he saw me leading Terra out of the stable. The roof was really smoking now, and Midge was antsy. I tied Terra to the back of the wagon and gave her face a reassuring rub.

When I took up the reins, Midge set off at a quick trot and Trader followed suit. I could tell they were going to give me trouble when Midge reared at the first sight of fire in the warehouse across from the stableyard. It took all of my strength to pull on the reins and keep them from galloping when we passed the burning building. An officer stopped me just as I neared the street leading to our house. He was on foot and tried to commandeer my wagon, but when I told him I was evacuating my family, he let me pass.

Mother had the cedar chest packed and waiting for me. We loaded the chest and the children into the back of the wagon. I offered the dappled gray to Mrs. McCain and she looked at me as though I had slapped her face again.

"How could I ride her?" she asked. "Terra belongs to Frank. Why did you take her out of the stable? Frank will come for her. You should have left her. That was stupid to take her."

I had to answer. "The barn is burning. If Frank had come back for her, he would have found only a pile of ashes." This quieted Mrs. McCain and I continued, "We can't have everyone in the wagon and I'm the only one who can rein the horses. Someone must ride."

Papa spoke up, "I'll ride."

"No, you won't," Mother said quickly. "Charlie will ride. He's big enough to handle the old gray."

Papa pulled himself up against the lamppost, heaving and unsteady, then managed to teeter his body to the back of the wagon. We all watched him unlatch Terra and place his foot in the stirrup. Mother was shaking her head. Papa looked over at me, and I ran to help him into the seat, filled with misgivings for this plan. For once, I sided with Mother. At this point, Charlie could handle Terra better than Papa could. But I knew better than to waste time arguing. Mrs. McCain and Mother sat on the front bench with me and Charlie jumped into the back of the wagon silently. I shot him a conciliatory look, but he wouldn't meet my eyes.

I'd say it was a bad dream, except it was real and so much worse than I could have imagined. Eventually you wake from a nightmare and the world is just as it was when you last closed your eyes. The world could never be just as it was again.

We were all afraid the house would burn soon. The police had told Mother this much, but they couldn't say when. They said, "We have no water. The pipes must be broken. We're very sorry." No one could stop the fire, and it was only two streets away now.

We'd heard that the gas lines had broken with the quake. And it was rumored that someone had started a fire with an ill-placed match. The firemen couldn't put out the blaze because the quake had taken out the water lines as well as the gas. There were already six fires on the horizon. The city was surrounded with water, and yet there was no water to fight the fire.

I desperately wanted to wake from the nightmare. It feels very strange to stare at your house knowing it will burn and powerless to stop it. I thought of all the things I'd lose when the fire reached my room, but I had no more thoughts of crying. I saw Charlie and Wes playing army in the kitchen, and Mother kneading dough. I heard Father's voice waking me, softly so Caroline and Mary would still sleep, that first morning that

I went to work with him. All of these memories would burn. But my eyes were dry. Numb from the sight of Mr. McCain's body and numb from the smell of Frank's empty room, there were no tears to shed over a house.

Everyone in the wagon was quiet as I snapped the lines and headed the team down the street. Papa wanted us to go to the waterfront and take a ferry across the bay, but Mother and Mrs. McCain were both deathly afraid of boats, and there'd been enough fright in their world that day. The army had set up two evacuation camps—one at the Presidio and one at Golden Gate Park. We settled on the park in part because Mary and Caroline thought we could have a picnic there. No one had the heart to make them understand we were not going to the park for a picnic.

The trek to the park was easy, ordinarily. But the streets were now filled with brick rubble and a stream of people, some of whom were walking down to see the blaze, most of whom were walking up with us to the park, and everywhere was traffic. One street I bypassed altogether when I saw the sight at the end of the block. A carriage had overturned and four horses lay dead on the ground, their bodies half covered by brick and plaster. The scenes in the streets were like the pictures I had seen of wars in Papa's newspaper. Soldiers directed the queues of men and women while the wagons trails seeped deeper into the heart of the city. The smoke was bothering Papa. I could hear his cough worsen and knew he was using up the last of his strength riding Terra. I wished he had decided to rest in the wagon. Half a dozen times I tried to argue him off the horse, but he wouldn't listen. Charlie kept his eyes on Papa like a young hawk and, less than a block from the park, I heard him yell, "Bette, stop! Papa fell!"

Mother's cry followed Charlie's shrill voice, and I pulled up the team and leapt off the wagon. Papa lay on the cobblestone gutter. My stomach turned when I saw his face covered in blood. I grabbed a handkerchief and blotted the red ooze, finding the wound on his forehead. It was a clean cut just as if his skin had been a cracked eggshell. With the cloth pressed against his head, I searched for other wounds and found none. He seemed too weak to sit upright, and I guessed that he might have just slipped off the saddle. Mrs. McCain and Mother were immediately at my side, pushing me away to have a look at him. Mother was the first to make the announcement, "Bette, you'll drop off the children and our crate at the camp. Jack's old gray will stay with Emma. Then you'll take your father to the hospital."

We left Mrs. McCain and Mother with Papa and drove the wagon to the park. Charlie happily took my orders to stand guard over the children and the crate until Mother and Mrs. McCain arrived. I didn't say good-bye for fear it might mean that I wouldn't see them again. But Caroline looked me directly in the eye and said, "You come back quick, Bette, or you'll be in trouble."

I nodded and turned the horses around. Papa was unconscious by the time I got back to Mrs. McCain and Mother. We laid him in the wagon and wrapped a wool horse blanket around his heaving frame. Before I left, Mother gave me only one order, "Don't leave his side. Emma and I will be with the children." When I started to leave, she grabbed my arm and whispered hoarsely, "Don't think of coming back without him."

Probably she was worried Papa would leave her just like Mr. McCain had left his wife. I couldn't think of anything to say. I touched my hat, like the men always do, and turned down the street, heading back to Mission Street. The hospital was down by City Hall, and I'd have to go against the flood of people and wagons. Most of the streets were torn apart from the quake and filled with rubble, and there were few roads that were passable by foot, let alone wagon.

Before I had gotten more than a few blocks, an armed guard stopped me and said he had commissions to take my wagon and the horse team. When I showed him my father, wrapped in blankets and with the pall of death on his skin, the guard gave me a pass to go to the hospital. I worried that it wouldn't be long before another less lenient guard approached me. How would I get on if someone took the horses and wagon from me? I'd known both of the horses for as long as I could remember, and the thought of a soldier taking the team and running them to death plagued me every time I passed anyone in uniform.

By the time I reached the hospital, I had designed a plan. Two more soldiers and one police officer tried to take my wagon. I told them that the ambulance wagons were overloaded and I was running the sick to the hospital. Then, I repeated this story at the gates to the hospital and was given a Red Cross armband.

Unfortunately, the hospital was not accepting any new patients, and I was directed to the temporary hospital at the building across the street. I felt my world spin as I realized this was the same building where Frank and I had gone ice skating only last night. A nurse took Papa's information from me, and she set him up in a bed on the floor of the main temporary ward. Papa awoke with the movement. He seemed quite disoriented, but well enough to speak.

"Where am I?"

"Papa? You're at the Mechanics' Pavilion." I didn't want to say the word hospital. His face was ashen and his lips close to blue. I could hardly bear to look at him, and yet I couldn't keep my eyes off his.

"Where's Mother?"

"She's with the children. I've taken them to the park." My words were catching in my throat and I knew I would cry soon.

"How badly damaged is the city?"

"Bad." I had no reason to be dishonest now. He might as well know the truth, and I never could lie to Papa anyway.

"Have they gotten the fires controlled?"

"No, Papa. There's no water."

"Then the fires will have to burn themselves out."

He was quiet for a moment, and I worried he might have lost consciousness. "Papa?" He made no response to my voice but soon opened his eyes and coughed again. I hated his cough.

"Bette, you must do something for me."

"Yes, Papa, anything."

"Go to the Douglas house and check on the women there. Mr. Douglas is out of town and he may have left no one responsible. Have you heard if the houses on Nob Hill are in danger of burning?"

"I haven't heard. But without water . . ."

"You'll take the wagon up to Nob Hill and check on them. Mrs. Douglas and her daughter may have been left alone."

The thought of leaving Papa hit me with a wave of nausea. I couldn't leave him. "No, Papa. I'm to stay with you, here. I promised Mother. Mrs. Douglas and her daughter can fend for themselves. They've got a carriage and plenty of horses."

"No. They won't know how to drive the carriage." Father pointed at the nurse who was handing him a cup of coffee just then. "I'll be in safe hands here. This is a hospital after all, no?" He thanked the nurse and feebly reached for the coffee cup. When he had the cup in his shaking hands, I helped him lift it to his lips. All around Papa I spotted men and women in the makeshift sick beds sipping coffee. Coffee seemed to be the only medicine the nurses were dispensing.

Papa touched my wrist. "Bette, don't waste time here. Go to the Douglases' now. You always listen to me, not your mother. Since when does she have anything useful to say anyway?" He smiled wryly and briefly seemed like his old self.

I hated to leave him, but Papa was stubborn, and the longer I stayed at his side, the more agitated he became and the worse he coughed. Kissing his hands, I promised to return quickly. I'd take him to the park so our family would be together again. He vowed he wouldn't be in the hospital longer than a day. I left him with a heavy heart. Mother would never forgive me, but it was Papa's order I had to obey.

The Red Cross armband got me through several police barricades, but before I reached Nob Hill, I was asked to carry two injured firefighters back to the hospital. The firemen were quiet passengers and I worried that they might not hold on until I reached the hospital. Fortunately, they both survived the transfer to a medic's ready arms, and I turned the wagon around again and headed back up to Nob Hill.

Trader and Midge were wearing down with the hard climbing through the street rubble, and neither liked the blanket of smoke. We were all relieved when we finally made it to the crest of California Street and found the Douglas mansion. No one ran out to greet me when I entered the yard, and I instantly thought of Frank. Was he really gone? I rushed this thought out of my mind quickly.

I knocked on the great front door after hitching Trader and Midge next to the water trough. The smoke from the fires burning on Market Street had risen up to the hills, and the air choked my lungs. No butler answered the door. I knocked again, then called, "Hello? Anyone? Hello?"

The door opened finally. "Hello," Sarah said. She appeared quiet but obviously quite shaken. "Can I help you?"

"Actually I've come to ask if you need help. My father sent me. He worked for your father. We have the wagon, and I delivered the harp the other day . . ." My voice trailed off as I realized Sarah didn't seem to be listening. From somewhere in the house came a low wailing. Sarah looked at the door handle as though she were about to close the door. I felt awkward coming here alone, and Sarah didn't seem to want me. "You're probably busy with your preparations to evacuate . . . if you don't need any help, maybe I'll just leave."

"Yes, I think that would be best." The wailing grew louder, and Sarah glanced over her shoulder nervously.

"Is someone hurt?" I asked tentatively.

"Oh, no." She paused and eyed the Red Cross armband. Another wail came from behind the door. "Well, it's my mother. She's not well. I think the earthquake shock affected her mind. And all of the servants have run off."

"You shouldn't stay here," I ventured, feeling suddenly bold. "The fire can't be stopped and it will reach Nob Hill before the day is out."

"The fire chief knows Father. He won't let the fire reach Nob Hill." Sarah sighed. "But Mother is worried."

I wanted to explain that her mother's fear was warranted. Regardless of who her father knew in the fire department, there was no water to stop the blaze. Today, connections were meaningless. Sarah's gaze was on the horizon and I wondered if she really thought she was safe from the coming blaze simply because of her father's connections. I couldn't say anything to comfort her, and I knew I should tell her the truth.

"How close is the fire?" she asked.

"Close. They won't stop it before it reaches the hills." I didn't know this for sure, and I don't want to frighten her. Yet, I knew she had to evacuate. "Miss Douglas, you can't stay here. They're making everyone leave their homes."

"But I can't leave. The servants have all gone to be with their families. It's just Mother and me here now. Father isn't due home for another three days." She rubbed her eyes as if it was only the smoke that had brought on the tears. "We'll wait this out here."

"Please, can I see to your mother at least?"

Another long wail echoed from the back of the house. Sarah nodded finally. She didn't try to hide her tears now. "Maybe you could come in. Seeing someone new might help distract her."

With the Red Cross armband, I felt as though I had some right to nurse the sick, though my training had only been in ambulance driving thus far. Sarah showed me through their grand house to her mother's room. I wish I could say how their house appeared, but I don't think I looked away from Sarah at all. I was scared, really quite scared, and had no desire to stay long in the mansion directly in the fire's path. My hope was to convince Mrs. Douglas that we must leave immediately. I would then take Sarah and Mrs. Douglas directly to Golden Gate Park so I could get back to Papa.

Mrs. Douglas took one look at me and started moaning. She caught sight of the Red Cross armband and reached out to touch me, then began reciting a Hail Mary. Sarah tried to quiet her, to no avail. I took one look at the woman and decided Sarah's assessment was correct, Mrs. Douglas was not well. She seemed to have a sickness in her head, but I guessed her body was without ailment.

"Can you find some warm water and a washcloth?" I asked Sarah. Ordinarily I wouldn't have dreamed of ordering her around, and she seemed a little surprised at the request. But I had no idea where to look for supplies. She nodded quickly and ran to find the items.

While Sarah was gone, I struck up a conversation with Mrs. Douglas. Or rather, she ranted while I intervened with attempts at logic. She was intent on staying in the house, even at the cost of dying there. After a short wait, Sarah returned with a starched white linen of finer cotton than I had ever seen. The initials JLD were inscribed on the center. I wetted the cloth and wiped Mrs. Douglas's face, softly repeating three Hail Mary prayers. When I was finished, I stared directly at the woman and, in my best authoritative voice, said, "Now you will get up, Ma'am, and dress promptly."

She had seemed almost in a trance while I wiped her face and prayed over her, and now she heard my order and, much to my surprise, obeyed. With easy agility, she rose out of bed and took the clothing that Sarah handed her. Sarah had chosen too fine a dress for our trip, but I didn't argue. I found a coat for her to cover the fine clothing. Someone that we passed on our way to the park might recognize a nabob and try to take advantage. Her gaudy wedding ring might attract attention as well as the gold necklace on her throat. But I was in no mood to create a problem.

Sarah led her mother out of the bedroom, and met me in the hallway. "We will have lunch now," Sarah announced.

I wanted to argue, fearing that the more we prolonged the evacuation, the worse the trip to the park would be. And I was afraid of leaving Papa alone for long at the temporary hospital. The nurses were too busy to take proper care of all of the sick, and I knew I should be at his side. Finally, I conceded that taking lunch was a good decision since I'd settled the horses in the Douglas barn and they needed time to eat. My own stomach was growling as well. We might all be better off after a lunch break.

The servants had left the Douglas women alone, but they had ensured that no one would go hungry. A feast of fine cold cuts and cheese with thick, fresh sourdough was waiting for us in the kitchen. At first Mrs. Douglas wouldn't eat the sandwich Sarah prepared for her, but after some coaxing and a stern nod from my corner, she began to nibble. I've found that certain occasions can make even fine looking food tasteless, and I could barely eat the Roquefort cheese and roast beef after the first bite. I stared at Sarah and then at her mother, wondering if either heard the distant rumble that had just started. The grandfather clock in the kitchen chimed half-past two. I listened intently to the distant rumbling and knew that the dynamiting had begun.

Papa had told me stories of when they used to dynamite buildings in the city to create firebreaks when an inferno was raging out of control. Those fires that Papa remembered occurred before I was born and before our city fire department had constructed the best water system in the nation. But the best water system could not withstand the earthquake that ripped open streets and yanked brick and mortar off rock solid foundations. Sarah noticed that I had stopped eating and offered me a plate of chocolates. I took one, just to be polite, and slipped it in my mouth. The chocolate dissolved to reveal a bath of rum liquor.

"Have another," Sarah said with a faint smile. "You look like you could use a half dozen."

"Forty probably wouldn't be enough after today." I laughed, although I didn't know why. Sarah had a chocolate in her mouth, and Mrs. Douglas took one as well, and then they both smiled at me. We continued popping the fat squares of dark chocolate and grinning as we waited for the rum centers to burst open.

After five of the delicacies, I began to feel sick. I wasn't certain if it was the chocolate alone or the strange circumstance that I was in and decided I needed a break. "I must check on the horses." Sarah and Mrs. Douglas seemed surprised by my rude manners but let me leave unchallenged.

I ran to the barn, trying to avoid any view of the smoke-filled valley. Trader and Midge had finished their alfalfa flakes and I gave each one a handful of grain. Trader caught the scent of chocolate on my fingers and pushed his muzzle through the grain to find it. Every few minutes the thunder of dynamite rang out. The sky was a sickly red-gray color and the air was foul. From the garden on the south side, I could see Market Street and the desolation beyond the line of fire. I couldn't make out our house and guessed it had already burned. As I followed the line of destruction, I realized the Mechanics' Pavilion was completely ringed by the fire. Had they moved the patients, or was father still there, awaiting death? I stared at the pavilion, immobilized by the fire and the deafening dynamite. Suddenly I felt a hand on my arm, and I wheeled quickly to the side.

Sarah stepped back, apologetic. "I'm sorry to startle you. I was calling your name, but I guess you didn't hear me."

"I was watching the fire." I pointed to the flames surrounding the pavilion. "I left my father there. The hospital next to the pavilion was destroyed by the quake so they set up a temporary hospital at the pavilion."

"And now it appears the pavilion will burn," Sarah said. "But there's no need to fear for your father. They will have already moved the patients."

"Where?" I wondered. "Where can they move everyone? The fire will burn everything the earthquake hasn't yet destroyed. And where can they move so many sick and injured people?"

"They'll find a way." She paused, then continued, "And the fire will be stopped before nightfall. Don't worry, Bette. The firemen will put out the blaze soon, I know it."

I was startled to hear Sarah use my name. She was staring at the pavilion, and I wondered if she was thinking about our ice skating adventure there last night. How light my heart was last night while we skated together. Now the world we knew was being destroyed before our eyes.

Another burst of dynamite brought a startled cry from Sarah. "What's that for?"

"They're dynamiting the buildings," I replied.

"I know, but why?"

"To stop the fire." A cloud of smoke rose up from Fifth Street. The cloud obscured the damage that the dynamite had enacted.

"I don't understand why they don't use the water to put out the fire. Why are they destroying everything with dynamite?"

"The water mains broke in the earthquake. Dynamite is the only defense." I pointed past the pavilion at the charred streets near the waterfront. "That's my neighborhood, over there. And everything is going to keep burning unless the dynamite stops the blaze."

"Not here," Sarah replied indignantly. "The fire won't climb the hills."

"Can you see Rincon Hill?" I found her hand and squeezed it. She didn't pull her hand away but stared at me with a mix of surprise and confusion. She tried to find the landmarks of Rincon Hill, but I knew she wouldn't see anything. Smoke obscured the view. I continued, "You won't see the buildings. They've already burned. Sarah, the fire won't stop because of a little hill."

Sarah didn't answer. We stood quietly watching the smoke and dust clouds as though it was all a dream—a nightmare. When Sarah finally spoke, she had tears in her eyes. "How could Father have left me alone with Mother? He's over there with Henry, over there, somewhere . . ." She pointed eastward, across the bay.

Henry . . . I'd almost forgotten about Sarah's brother. Henry had been lucky to get on that scull last night. If Frank and I hadn't run into him, he might not have escaped the city alive. But if Henry or Mr. Douglas were here, Sarah and her mother would have evacuated hours ago. Sarah would probably be on a ferry sailing across the bay to Oakland or Vallejo. Now they would have no way to leave except on foot or my wagon, and I knew the fire would eventually reach their doorstep. Mr. Douglas might try to cross the bay to rescue them, but I doubted he would find a way to reach the house from the east port. Smoke and rubble now obscured all of the streets. After watching the scene below us, my eyes had begun to burn with the stench. I squeezed Sarah's hand and then let it go. "We need to evacuate," I began. "If we wait any longer, I'm afraid the roads will be impossible for the horses to manage. Can you pack a trunk with necessities for you and your mother?"

Sarah nodded. "Where will we go?"

"The evacuation camp. The army set up space at the Presidio and at Golden Gate Park." I thought of Mother and Mrs. McCain and hoped they had found the children and were setting up camp. It seemed so strange to be on Nob Hill with Sarah when my family needed me. "I'll make a trip down the hill to find out how impassable the roads are from here. We should leave when I get back. Can you have your mother ready within the hour?"

Sarah nodded. She suddenly stepped forward and hugged me. "Thank you."

Instantly stiffening, I pushed away from her. "Please, don't thank me. I haven't done anything." My voice was too sharp, and I wished I hadn't reacted to her touch. I doubted Sarah ever thanked Frank or her other servants. "I'm only here to obey my father's last wishes."

"Don't think of his last wishes. You don't know that he won't live. Our minister says that you never know what God will do for our loved ones if we pray."

I shook my head. "Who is God?"

Sarah's mouth dropped open, but she didn't answer. I turned to leave then. Maybe I was an awful Catholic, I thought, realizing I would have plenty to tell the priest at the confessional, assuming I survived. Sarah and her family were staunch Protestants of English descent. She would probably concede my godlessness to a mixed Irish and German background and discredit the Catholic Church for my wayward soul. I didn't much care. Today, God had turned his back on us.

After sending Sarah inside to tend to her mother and the preparations of a trunk, I headed down California Street on foot. I wanted to give the horses as much rest as possible, knowing that this next trek to the park would be anything but easy for the tired beasts. The smoke had gotten thicker and the fire was progressing despite the dynamite. The horses would have a tough time simply breathing the dust and ash, let alone navigating the demolished streets.

I passed lines of men and women evacuating the downtown area, but it was some time before I found a police officer. As I approached him, he gave me a sharp look of reproach.

"We can't have any lookers down here, Miss. Get along with your family, now." The officer pointed to a group passing us on the street. "The whole area is being evacuated."

"I know, sir," I started. "But I left my father at the Mechanics' Pavilion—the temporary hospital. Do you know how the patients are there? Will the fire burn there?"

"They've moved all the patients to the camps. Your father is either at the Presidio or at Golden Gate Park."

"Everyone was moved?" I asked, surprised that the hospital would have managed this.

"Everyone who wasn't already dead." The policeman sighed at this last statement and then turned to help a woman who had just fallen.

I turned and walked with the crowd for a few paces, unsure of which direction I should head. Suddenly, I saw a friendly face. It was Mr. O'Connor, our family's butcher. He recognized me right off and gave me a hug.

"Lass, you're not alone, are you now?" he asked.

I shook my head. Mr. O'Connor called all girls *lass* or *lassie* and insisted this was a term only meant for recognizing beauty. Hearing him say lass now nearly made me want to cry. Nothing would ever be the same as it was for the waterfront. The neighborhood I had known was gone—or would be if the fire hoses never filled with water. The fire would destroy every neighborhood it met. Mr. O'Connor had been more than our butcher. He was a close friend of my father's, and he was Charlie's godfather. "My family is already at the evacuation camp—Golden Gate Park."

He nodded. "And why aren't you with them?"

"Papa was ill. I took him . . ." I couldn't continue. Something told me that Papa had already joined Mr. McCain. You have no proof of this, I told myself. Just as there was no proof that Frank was alive, or dead. Both of them were lost. What could I tell Mr. O'Connor about Papa?

"Come, lass, what's the matter?"

"My father was sick, so I brought him to the hospital, but I don't know where he is now." I shook my head, thinking that my mother would blame me, and not caring about her judgment now. "They've moved the patients."

Mr. O'Connor put his hand on my shoulder. "Lass, God will look after him."

I pulled away from him then. Why was everyone placing so much trust in God? "I promised my mother I would stay with him."

Mr. O'Connor tried to console me with an embrace, but I fought my way loose and turned to scramble over the rubble. Maybe he sensed the wildness that had slipped inside me. Papa was with Mr. McCain in heaven, I thought again. I had no proof, but I didn't need to see his body to confirm my intuition. What good was this intuition, I wondered grimly. Papa had joked about this sense and now it was too late to tell him that indeed I had it.

"Lass, you need to get back to your family," Mr. O'Connor insisted. "You have brothers and sisters to take care of." He patted my shoulder. "Ye can't leave that all to your mother. Go on, now. Back to them. Don't wander the streets being a waste. Go on, God will look after your father."

Mr. O'Connor's voice followed me as I made my way through the crowd. Once I had escaped the group and Mr. O'Connor's voice had drifted out of my head, the anger dissipated. I turned onto Sacramento Street and saw the Chinese evacuating along this road. It was a strange sight to see the women in bright robes and the men in dark rice hats with children holding on to ropes behind them. Everywhere people were trying to pull their trunks, and I thought how lucky we were to have the wagon and the horses. I wondered where the Lees were and if they had safely evacuated already. The jade piece was heavy on my neck as I thought of their generosity. I wished I could find them now, but everyone seemed lost in the dust and rubble. Finally, I turned back up Nob Hill and made my way back to the Douglas mansion.

Sarah had packed three trunks instead of one. She looked aghast when I told her there was no way we could carry more than one trunk. The others would have to be left behind. She fought this idea so bitterly that I was worried she might decide against leaving altogether. We finally came to an agreement. Mr. Douglas had a taste for wine and had constructed a cellar behind the house. Sarah selected one trunk to take with us on the wagon, and we stowed the other two, along with the harp, in the cellar. I didn't ask what the trunks contained, but I guessed their wealth was more than I could well imagine.

When we had the wagon ready, Sarah went inside to find her mother. I rubbed down the horses, chattering to them in the language of tongue clicks and humming my father had taught me. The sounds meant nothing to me, but it soothed both Trader and Midge. Sarah reappeared at the front of the house with a look of frustration.

"What's wrong?" I asked.

"She won't leave her room. I can't convince her about the fire." Sarah sank down on the first step of the grand entryway, between the two marble pillars with the large stained glass door behind her.

"I'll try to coax her," I volunteered.

"Don't," Sarah said, shaking her head. "Don't bother. I think you should leave with the wagon. Get back to your family and find your father. I'll stay here with Mother."

"No, Sarah," I replied adamantly. "The dynamite seems to be doing nothing more than making dust down there. The firemen can't put out the blaze without water. By nightfall your house will be consumed." I paused, but Sarah didn't make any argument against this. "If the fire continues, you'll both be dead by morning. I can't have that on my conscience."

I walked past Sarah and into the house. Her mother was back in bed, silent now, and appeared almost tranquil. I touched her shoulder to awaken her and she screeched, "Get out! Get out off my room!" With her bed sheets pulled up around her she stared through me with wild eyes. I knew then that Sarah was right. Mrs. Douglas would not move in this condition. I left her in the room and joined Sarah on the steps outside.

"You're right. There's no moving her."

"And you should leave now. If my mother comes out of this spell, we can leave on foot. The walk to the park isn't so long."

I doubted that Sarah had ever traveled anywhere in the city by foot, let alone a trek to the park with the roads in their current condition. "No. If you stay, I have to stay as well."

I thought of Caroline and her harsh warning for me to come back to the camp. I hated Mrs. Douglas, but there was no way Sarah and I alone could move her. Sarah touched my knee and I looked over at her.

"Thank you." Sarah started to say something about her mother, but the sound of an approaching carriage stopped her.

We both ran to see who was coming up the drive. Sarah recognized the driver and shouted a hello to him. She turned to me. "It's one of our neighbors, Mr. Packard."

Although I had never seen Mr. Packard in person, I knew of him. He had a reputation as a ladies' man, and his wealth was widely discussed. Mr. Packard had made his millionaire fortune as a business developer, but everyone gossiped of him now only because of the women who were said to frequent his mansion. I'd also heard that Mr. Packard had never married. No one knew what he planned to do with his money when he died, but there were plenty of rumors. Many women had an idea where he should spend it, but I was glad none had been able to catch Mr. Packard's coattails. The stories that the stableboys told of Mr. Packard's women provided hours of entertainment.

Mr. Packard jumped off the front seat as I caught the horses' reins. He was shorter than I'd expected and not that handsome. He did have a nice mustache that curled at each end, and he smelled of sweet soaps, just like Sarah. Trader and Midge were excited for the company of other horses and the four called back and forth to each other as I led Mr. Packard's team to the water trough.

Mr. Packard tipped his hat to Sarah. "How are you, Miss Douglas?"

Sarah curtsied. "I've seen better, sir."

"Haven't we all?" He nodded. "I thought I might come check on the Douglases before I left. Your father didn't leave any men about, did he?" He didn't wait for Sarah's answer. "I said to myself, Packard, you must check on the Douglas women. They might be alone. And again I see that I must listen to myself."

Already Mr. Packard annoyed me. He acted as if his duty to God had just been fulfilled by the one act of pulling his carriage around the block to check on the Douglas women. And the fact that Sarah was smiling and carrying on with him as though a horrible tragedy wasn't in progress frustrated me even more.

Mr. Packard continued, "I had heard that all of your servants left. I was hoping the rumors were false. One knows the true worth of our help in times as these. To think, not even your butler remained?" He cracked his riding whip at this unpardonable act. "And I know your father overlooks too many faults of his servants, leading to accidents of this nature. He isn't due back to town for a few days, correct?"

Sarah nodded. "Along with Henry."

"Well, they will have a tough time getting into the city at all with this chaos everywhere." Mr. Packard paused and motioned in my direction. "But perhaps my concern was for naught, as it appears that you have garnered a wagon and maiden to carry you to the evacuation camp." He angled his crop at Trader. "Though, these steeds may have been better placed on pasture. And with a girl at the helm, I can't imagine you'll get far. Really, Sarah, you could have chosen better. I see you've got your knack for picking help from your father. No doubt this is the cause for your delay in evacuating."

I wanted to spit at his damn fine boots and kick his horse. Fortunately Sarah spoke up too soon. "No, that's not it. My mother is in a state and won't be moved. We can't leave the house, she insists."

"She has no choice," Mr. Packard said, shaking his fist. "The army patrol has informed us that the entire Nob Hill will be evacuated. No exceptions. The patrollers will be here shortly, and I'm afraid they are not men that well-bred women should reckon with. They won't take kindly to anyone who disobeys orders."

"They won't reckon on my mother." Sarah sighed. "She won't listen to any reason. The soldiers would have to drag her out of the house before she'd leave. What choice do we have but to wait here?"

Mr. Packard clicked his tongue. "Perhaps you have also not heard about our mayor's declaration."

Sarah glanced at me with a concerned look, then turned back to Mr. Packard. "No, we haven't heard anything. What has the mayor decreed? A state of war?"

Shaking his head, Mr. Packard replied, "A shoot-to-kill order for any looters or anyone disobeying military order. And I wouldn't doubt it at all if they used that order to point a pistol at anyone disobeying the evacuation order. In fact, I've already heard several shots fired on our hill this afternoon."

Although Mr. Packard's *well-bred* manners annoyed me, I wasn't about to ignore his warning. "Perhaps, sir, you may have more luck in convincing Mrs. Douglas of evacuating." To the unctuous appeal, I added, "You certainly have Sarah and me convinced."

Sarah nodded. "Yes, please, Mr. Packard. You would be a great help."

Mr. Packard grudgingly agreed to try his words with Mrs. Douglas. Sarah led him inside the house while I waited with the horses. I couldn't hear their voices, but after ten minutes, Mr. Packard stepped out of the house looking grim.

"Will she come?"

"Not by my influence. She's not well. It's a shame the men of the house are all gone. Leaving the women at a time like this . . ." Mr. Packard clicked his tongue on the roof of his mouth and shook his head. "Well, I've done what I could."

I wasn't surprised when Mr. Packard took his set of reins from my hands and boarded his carriage. Men of his well-bred nature often cared only for their own hide. He turned his horses down the road and disappeared beyond the bend. If I had my wits about me, I would have shamed him into helping us somehow. Instead, I only stared at the rear of his beautiful carriage and thought that I wouldn't want the world to end with this as my last memory.

Sarah emerged from the house and scanned the courtyard. "Did Mr. Packard pull his carriage around to the stable?"

"No."

"Where is he then?" she asked, with a hint of irritation in her voice.

"Halfway down California Street, probably." I tried a smile. "He left in a hurry. Maybe he was late for a date."

"Bette! How can you joke now?" Sarah grunted then turned to stare in the direction Mr. Packard had taken with his hasty escape. "Maybe I can stop him. Maybe I can bring him back here," Sarah said. "There's no way we can get Mother out of the house without him. How could you let him leave?"

"Well, I couldn't wrap myself around him and hold him here," I returned defensively. "He had every right to leave and no responsibility to you or your mother—at least that I'm aware of."

"No, he has no ties to myself or Mother!" Sarah was angry at my insinuation. She knew Mr. Packard's reputation with women as well as I did.

"Ties to whom?"

Sarah and I both spun around to gape at Mrs. Douglas. She stood on the porch, watching us, dressed for an afternoon at the park complete with a sparkling yellow dress and a wide-brimmed blue sun hat with yellow silk roses.

"Mr. Packard, Mother. He has such a nice carriage for a drive to the park." Sarah did an excellent job of recovering from the shock of seeing her mother in what appeared to be her normal mental state. "But have no fear. Bette has offered her wagon, and we have our trunk already loaded. We'll be enjoying our picnic in no time and will probably see Mr. Packard again shortly."

Mrs. Douglas smiled gratuitously at me. She had a set of keys in her hands and searched until she found one that fit the front door lock. I didn't have the heart to tell her not to bother locking the door. Within a few minutes, Sarah and Mrs. Douglas were seated in the back of the wagon on several green silk cushions squeezed on each side of the trunk. Sarah had taken the cushions from one of the sofas in the parlor. Fortunately, Mrs. Douglas didn't notice. I turned the horses onto the driveway, and we set off at a quick trot. Mrs. Douglas and Sarah chatted in the back of the wagon about which delicacies one should bring for an afternoon picnic, while I concentrated on the horses. We had to slow to a walk as soon as we hit the main road, and Mrs. Douglas called up to me to ask why I had slowed the horses.

"We're taking the direct route to Golden Gate Park."

"There seems to be quite a bit of traffic. Maybe today is not a fine day for a picnic." She paused for a minute, and I wondered if she was aware of the rubble in the street, the smoke and dust choking the air, or the men, women and children that we passed. The pedestrians made slow progress, dragging their belongings in crates or hand pushcarts and many people had abandoned their heavy items on the side of the road. Now it seemed that the lucky ones were the children of God with nothing save the clothes on their backs. For the first time the poor had an easier walk, and I wondered if they considered themselves lucky.

Mrs. Douglas continued, "Well, then we should go to the Ferry Building. We can take a passage to Berkeley." She addressed Sarah in a lower voice, taking pains to exclude me. "Wouldn't it be nice to join Henry and your father in Berkeley for the afternoon?"

Despite Sarah's protests, Mrs. Douglas insisted that I turn the wagon around and head toward the Ferry Building. In a way, I thought it might be a good idea. Depositing Mrs. Douglas and Sarah on a boat headed across the bay would relinquish me of their care and might be the safest thing for them. But I doubted if we could still get through to the Embarcadero or if any of the piers were still intact. Trader and Midge were both reluctant to turn around—so much so that I had to jump out of the wagon and grab their bridles to turn the wagon. I took a detour road that skirted Nob Hill and headed straight into the streets of Chinatown.

All of the sights and smells that we passed en route to the Ferry Building were a blur and intensely clear all at the same moment. I was stopped twice by armed soldiers and informed that I must give up my wagon. Wagons and horse teams were in shortage, and the army had apparently received orders to take control of any horse team they found. Sarah came to our rescue both times by handing out gold coins. I didn't ask where she had hidden the gold and neither did the soldiers. They simply pocketed the gold and waved our wagon through countless detours. We miraculously reached the Ferry Building at what I would have guessed was sometime after sunset, had the sun braved the dark smoke clouds that afternoon.

I helped Sarah and her mother out of the wagon. Sarah set off to find a ship clerk while I stayed with the wagon. The Ferry Building was mobbed with evacuees awaiting passage out of San Francisco. Mrs. Douglas fell into a conversation with a beggar woman who was ranting about God and pigeons. For some reason, Mrs. Douglas did not seem to comprehend that the woman was an ordinary street beggar. When Nob Hill burned, both women would be homeless, and perhaps Mrs. Douglas in her estranged state understood as much. The women were debating whether pigeons might be in heaven. Mrs. Douglas argued against pigeons behind the pearly gates while the homeless woman argued for the pigeons, on account of their close relation to doves. I kept my distance from the two women, but kept a close eye on Mrs. Douglas. The last thing I needed was to lose her now.

Sarah finally returned to our wagon with a low countenance.

"Any luck?" I asked.

"All of the boats leaving tonight are full. Apparently the Ferry Building will soon be evacuated and everyone not on a boat will be sent—on foot—to one of the evacuation camps."

"Can you send a message to your father?"

"I asked about that." Sarah sighed. "Both the phone and telegraph systems are down. We can't send word to anyone." She glanced at the wagon and suddenly seemed to realize who was missing. "Where's my mother?"

"Arguing about God and pigeons." I pointed Mrs. Douglas out, and Sarah hurried over to her.

Somehow, Sarah managed to pull her mother away from her conversation. Before the two returned to the wagon, Mrs. Douglas let out a squeal of excitement and pointed down the street at an approaching figure. In the dim light I had trouble discerning the man's features. Mrs. Douglas apparently knew him, but I was cautious until he neared the Ferry Building and I finally recognized Mr. Packard's coat and hat. Where were his carriage and horses?

Mrs. Douglas and Sarah headed Mr. Packard off before he could reach the building. With pained indignation, Mr. Packard explained that his carriage and horse team had been stolen by soldiers. Apparently he hadn't brought enough gold to bribe them, as Sarah had done. Poor Mr. Packard had traipsed on foot the long route to the Embarcadero. I held no sympathy, secretly pleased that he looked much worse for the journey and none the ladies' man befitting his reputation now. Although Sarah had no luck in securing a passage on a ferryboat, Mr. Packard was determined to try his mariner connections. Sarah sent Mrs. Douglas with him, in a very smart move, by saying that her mother was frightened to be alone without a male companion in this neighborhood. She added that Mr. Packard would acknowledge the benefit of Mrs. Douglas's company, as Mr. Douglas was well-known by the shore men and touting the name might secure passage on a private boat—if any were still at port.

Sarah climbed up in the wagon and took a seat on the green cushions as soon as her mother disappeared with Mr. Packard. I took the opportunity to tend to Trader and Midge with a handful of grain and a bucket of water. They ate and drank too greedily. Both were ready for the day to be over as much as I was.

I brushed the horses down with a burlap sack and checked their hooves for rocks that might have lodged in the crevices of their feet or shoes. Midge had suffered an injury to her front leg, probably by stepping wrong on some of the street rubble. The hair just above her hoof was scraped clean off and the skin was red and tender. Blood had mixed with dust and dried in a thick cake around the wound. I noticed now that she was favoring the leg and rested her weight on the other hooves when she stood.

Father kept wound salves and soap in a small sack tied under the wagon's front seat. Remembering this, I boarded the wagon and rummaged through the sack until I found the items I needed. Sarah noticed me but didn't ask what I was up to. At this point, we were both tired of conversation. I felt her eyes watching me as I washed Midge's wound and applied a dab of salve to the skin. Trader nudged me a few times to see what I was up to, but Midge remained perfectly still while I cleaned and dressed the wound. I guessed she was in quite a bit of pain judging from the penetrating injury and wondered how much longer she'd be able to place weight on the foot.

"Bette, can I ask you something?"

"Yes?"

Sarah didn't say anything. She was perched on the green cushions with her gray cloak wrapped around her and her gaze cast toward the bay. Only a few boats remained in port and their numbers were quickly declining. The color of the water matched Sarah's cloak precisely, a somber gray that reflected the smoke-filled sky and reminded all of those awaiting passage across the bay of their luck. We were not dead yet, nor was there any reason to suspect we would live long.

Finally, she met my eyes and asked, "Why did you act like you didn't know me last night at the skating rink? I recognized you right off, but I pretended I didn't know you. You were afraid to take off your mask, weren't you?"

"Maybe." I turned away from Sarah and leaned down to pick up the rag and salve by Midge's feet. I knew Sarah was watching me and I was too nervous to look at her again. Trader whinnied and I moved to his side, placing more distance between me and the green cushions. What would Sarah think of me?

"Why were you afraid?"

I shrugged.

"Am I that scary? A monster?" She waved her hands above her head and growled menacingly.

I couldn't help but laugh and the tension between us eased. She smiled back at me, still waiting for my answer. "Well, I wasn't sure you'd speak to me if you knew who I was. My relations would prevent me from becoming friends with someone—" I paused. "Well, you're the daughter of Mr. Douglas."

"And?" Sarah interrupted. "I don't see how our fathers affect our friendship. In fact, my father often mentioned that your father was one of his best workers."

"Exactly." I didn't expect Sarah to understand. My family was poor and hers was rich. They could lose their house on Nob Hill and build another in a month. My family would be dependent on charity, again. Mr. Douglas had been Papa's employer until the accident at the docks. After Papa was injured, he had given our family more charity than Sarah knew. Sarah was quiet, finally. I knew she was watching me, and I tended the horses long past when they needed my attentions just to keep from looking up at her. For some reason, I was afraid of Sarah and simultaneously drawn to her. I knew no reason to explain it, and I only thought to keep my distance.

After a half-hour passed, Mr. Packard and Mrs. Douglas emerged from the building. They had managed to find one boat still waiting at the pier in addition to the already overfilled ferries, which were just disembarking. A friend of Mr. Packard's owned this private boat, and the owner had been convinced, at great trouble, to take extra passengers. But the owner insisted on no more than two. The boat was small and couldn't handle any additional weight.

Hearing this, Sarah quickly decided our fate. "Bette and I will take the wagon to the Presidio and Mother will go with you, Mr. Packard."

Mrs. Douglas immediately protested leaving Sarah behind, but Mr. Packard argued that it would be the best solution since only two could ride in the boat and it was his friend who owned the boat. Therefore, he must be on board. And, he added, once Mrs. Douglas reached the mainland, she could locate her husband and they would send a boat to the

Presidio tomorrow morning to retrieve Sarah. Moreover, time was of the essence. Mr. Packard's friend was intent on leaving the pier immediately and no time could be wasted on a revision of plans.

I stood by silently listening to the arguments on both sides. What luck! Sarah would stay with me, at least through nightfall. And I still had no idea why I was so happy to hear this. Mrs. Douglas made a show of a tearful goodbye as she kissed Sarah and then was dragged away by Mr. Packard's strong arm. Sarah and I watched Mrs. Douglas and Mr. Packard hurry down the pier past the Ferry Building. In short order, they would be in relative safety while we faced a night in hell.

"Well, then," I started. I didn't know what to say next so I turned back to the horses. Trader nudged his nose against my hand and I rubbed his head. He was tired, and I think he knew that our night was not yet over. He sniffed my hand again for grain. "No, boy. There's no more." I sighed and started to turn around when Sarah stopped me.

She hugged me tightly and I could feel her crying, quiet sobs that rattled her frame. I didn't say or do anything to stop her. She was more alone in this city than I was and suddenly less fortunate. How she would weather the night outside the Douglas mansion remained to be seen. After a moment, she let go of me and wiped her face with a white hand- kerchief. She cleared her throat and in a weak voice asked, "Are the horses ready?"

"Yes." I didn't tell her about Midge's injured foot or that Trader was still hungry. It was probably better that only one of us had to worry about the horses.

"Then I suppose we should be on our way before they start evacuating the rest of the Ferry Building refugees." She climbed aboard the wagon without further word.

Before boarding the wagon, I checked Midge's foot again and whis- pered, "This is the last run of the day, Midge. I know you can make it. And, Trader, I'll give you a whole bucket of grain when we're done with this trip. With a couple of carrot tops and apples for good measure—just as soon as I can steal some."

For the first time since I had driven the team, Midge dragged. We kept a slow pace as we snaked our way through the bloody gray mist that discolored the night. I think the horses made their way more by scent than sight, and I had to pull them up short several times when I realized we had turned down the wrong street.

We passed several buildings that had already burned to their foundations, and the smoking remains were an unsettling sight. I had decided to take Broadway Street, hoping that if I kept to a main thoroughfare I'd have a better chance at finding a clear path. Much of the street had been abandoned to the fire. Knowing that the destruction was everywhere and my city was ruined filled me with a strange hopelessness mixed with unfiltered anger. I thought of praying, but who was my God to let this happen?

Trader tossed his head and tried to balk away at the sight of dead horses lying at the side of a broken wagon axle. It looked as though someone had driven the horses, and the wagon, to death. As we passed the slain team, my stomach tightened. Trader tossed his head and tried to turn down another street. I couldn't blame him for hating the sight, but we had to pass the street where the horse bodies lay. "There's no other way around." I slapped the reins on his neck and yelled at the horses to encourage them both to move on. Trader turned the white corner of his eye at me, and I could have sworn he was cussing. "Trader, I know this must be hell. But we've got no choice."

With more cursing, they finally skirted past their dead comrades and pulled the wagon down the street. We passed the still smoking Telegraph Hill and slipped along the northern edge of Chinatown. Trunks littered the street, and I couldn't help but wonder what treasures might be wrapped inside. More than once I considered pausing to let the horses rest while I tried a trunk. But I didn't stop. Maybe the thoughts of Sarah sleeping soundly on the green pillows preyed on my mind more than I knew. I wanted desperately to join her. Sleep would be a welcome relief from the nightmare that surrounded me on all sides.

Suddenly a light flashed ahead of us and I caught my breath, waiting. The light flickered out almost immediately. I pulled the reins, and the horses slowed to a stop. Sarah was silent in the back, still sleeping. Midge was grateful for the break and immediately rested her sore hoof. I listened carefully, trying to slow my uneasy heartbeats, and then heard the footsteps. Through the red fog, I could see less than ten feet in front of me, and I had no idea from which direction the footsteps were approaching. The light sparked once more, still ahead of us.

"Are you alone?" a voice asked.

"No." My skin prickled with uneasiness. The Chinese voice sounded young and somehow familiar. "Show yourself," I said in a hoarse voice. "Don't be a coward on this night." I was gripped with fear that this man whom I could not see might be a ghost of a dead Chinaman. What wrongs had he suffered in life and what now lay in store for me as his retribution? "Show yourself!"

A match flickered and soon a candle was glowing. I recognized Lee's oldest son immediately. He bowed his head as he stepped closer to the wagon. His hands gripped a lantern, but the candle was close to the wick's end. "I can't keep the light." The flame burned brilliantly through the cut glass panes. "They'll see me."

"Who will?" Lee's son didn't answer me. His eyes seemed crazed, and I thought he might have lost his mind. "Where's your family? Are you lost?" So much of the city had crumbled and what was not shaken from the earth had burned. Everything was so much worse than Caroline had dreamed. She had known two weeks ago and I had ignored her. But there was nothing I could have done to prevent this.

"The soldiers . . ." He tried to explain something but seemed to not know the right words and his shoulders slouched in frustration. Finally he said, "My family's gone." Lee touched the side of the wagon and then collapsed on the ground. The glass panes of the lantern shattered on the cobblestones and the candle's wick flickered and died.

I jumped to the ground and pulled his body out from under the wagon. He was breathing but unconscious. Although Lee's son was close to my age, he weighed almost nothing, and I managed to heft his body into the back of the wagon as easily as a sack of flour. He fell between the green silk pillows and the trunk opposite Sarah. Sarah snored on, unbelievably. I stared at the two bodies in the wagon. My charge had been doubled. Two lives were dependent on me, and I had no idea if any of us would survive the night.

Losing the lantern was unfortunate. I picked the candle stub out of the pile of glass and climbed back in the wagon. The horses didn't want to move when I slapped the reins. Neither Midge nor Trader noticed the flap of the crop and I didn't want to whip them. We waited in the middle of the street for at least ten minutes with the horses ignoring my coaxing until I finally relented and climbed back off the wagon. I grabbed hold of Trader's bridle and started walking at his side. He followed me, and Midge finally gave in. She was lame in her right foot and I was sorry I had to make her walk another step, let alone a thousand. The next hour passed in a blur. I remember falling several times, and each time Trader's nose pushed my back, forcing me to stand up again though I only wanted to lie on the pavement and sleep forever. He was my only lifeline. If not for Trader, I would never have had to wake from the nightmare.

Chapter 5

April 19, 1906

At dawn, I saw the green grass lining the boundary of the Presidio. A military guard was pacing the sidewalk near the entrance gate. He saw me approach and jogged over to catch the reins.

He said something unintelligible and repeated it twice. The only part I understood was: "Well, you've had a rough night, no doubt. Barely alive."

"Barely."

He pointed toward the hillside facing the bay. "Follow the path and you'll run into another guard. He'll give you an assigned tent and direct you to the medical tent."

I didn't need a medical tent. I needed a cot and a warm blanket. Trader and Midge stumbled behind me as we made our way through the army's training ground. As explained, another guard was waiting for me near the first hill. He asked me my name and whether I was traveling with any relations. I guessed they were starting a census to determine how many lives had been lost, but I didn't want to know the number.

"I have no relations with me," I answered.

"You're alone in the wagon?" he asked.

What he meant to ask was, how could a girl be driving a wagon team in the dark? All of the streetlights were out and, if not for Lee's candle, which I lit several times over the past few hours to check the route down Broadway Street, there would have been no way I would have reached the Presidio by dawn. "No. I have two passengers. Sarah Douglas and," I paused, realizing that I didn't know Lee's son's name. I tried to think of a name quickly so that the officer wouldn't be suspicious. "And a Son of Lee."

"Chinese?" He spit out the question with his face twisted in a grimace.

I nodded, feeling my jade pendant swing on my neck. What had the Chinese done to this ugly soldier to make him hate even the word? He could easily see in the wagon, so I didn't bother lying. "My father worked with the Lee family and they are upright citizens." I had to defend the family to this guard even if he wouldn't listen to me. "The rest of the Lee family perished in the disaster yesterday."

"We are placing the Chinese in a separate area from the other evacuees. He'll have to get out of your wagon now and walk to the Chinese camp." The officer scribbled my name and the names of my two passengers in his notebook. "How many were in the Lee family? I have to record all casualties."

"Four casualties in the Lee family. I don't know their first names."

"Surname is adequate for the Chinese list." The gatekeeper pointed down the road and groaned. "I don't believe it. Another load."

I turned to look in the direction he pointed and spotted two soldiers in a wagon that looked familiar. After a moment I realized that it was Jack McCain's. Someone had taken the wagon from the stableyard, and apparently the army had later assumed control of it. But I didn't recognize either of the two horses pulling it, and the wagon had never held any contents comparable to its present load. The soldiers had covered the wagon in a white sheet, but the sheet left the load partially exposed— shoes, sleeves, pants, arms and legs jutted out at irreverent angles. The mound of bodies was nothing I could have imagined before the night that had just passed.

The gatekeeper sighed. "Ah, here's the second load for the mass grave. Today will be a long day."

My worst fear was that I might recognize someone heading for the mass grave. With the gatekeeper distracted by the approaching death wagon, I slapped the reins and urged Trader and Midge down the path toward the campground. Poor Midge could barely place any weight on her right front leg, and I felt horrible for forcing her. She moved so slowly that I was worried the gatekeeper might remember my Chinese passenger, but he let me pass without further comment. My wagon was the least of his worries. The gatekeeper's notebook would soon be full of names, and I wondered with a swell of nausea if Frank McCain was among the bodies now in his father's wagon. We had ridden so often in the backboard of that wagon. But the image of the McCain wagon that would haunt my sleep now was of the bodies piled too high on the splintered, sagging planks.

I decided to get Sarah and Lee's son set up in a tent and then tend to the horses. Midge was barely able to walk now, and I feared the worst for her foot. Trader was hungry and tired, but he carried on without complaint. Sarah awoke when the wagon moved off the paved road to the dirt path.

"Bette?" Sarah's voice gave away the obvious dismay she must have felt to be waking up in a wagon in the middle of an army campground.

I smiled. "You're awake then? I was surprised when you fell asleep. I had guessed that the wood planks and the bumpy ride wouldn't much compare to the beds you're used to."

"How long have I slept? I don't remember anything . . . after leaving Mother with Mr. Packard at the Ferry Building the night is a blur. Where are we?"

"The Presidio." I pulled the horses up at the tent number that the gatekeeper had assigned to me. Our white canvas tent was already set up at the edge of a field of tents. I couldn't count all of the tents that were waiting for evacuees to fill them, nor the number of tents that were already filled with families who had arrived yesterday. I wondered how my own family was faring at the Golden Gate camp. "After we set up here, I'll find out where we can send a message to your father. I've already notified the gatekeeper that you're here, so if your father checks, he'll know you're here waiting for him."

Sarah nodded. She stretched her arms and started to climb out of the wagon. As soon as she spotted the other passenger, she gave a startled yelp. "Who's this?" Sarah shot an accusatory look at me. "Do you know there is a Chinese boy in the wagon?"

I hated the tone she used to refer to Lee's son, but now wasn't the time to start an argument. "Yes, I had some idea. I threw him in there with you." I smiled at her expression of dismay and then added, "He was unconscious at the time." I held up my hand to help Sarah climb out of the wagon so she wouldn't have to pass by Lee's son. Sarah paused as though she were unwilling to take my hand. I continued, "I know his family. He's harmless. Barely our age I think, and definitely no risk to you. Everyone in his family has died and he's alone now. I found him when we were passing Stockton Street. He collapsed and I had no choice but to take him."

Sarah was clearly upset but she didn't say anything more about Lee's son, and I was glad he was still asleep. We left him in the wagon, and Sarah set off to investigate the tent and set up a bed roll while I found an officer who showed me where I could get water and hay for the horses. While Trader and Midge ate, I tried to have a better look at Midge's foot. The cut, which had seemed small last night, was now a deep and festering wound with the leg swollen to nearly twice the size of the other. She pulled her foot away at the slightest touch and tried to bite me as I lifted her hoof to check the underside. Among the packed in mud and mortar dust, my fingers scraped against a firm, sharp object. Midge could barely stand the pain as I picked out the dirt and finally isolated the shard of metal that had lodged in her sole. Somehow she had stepped on this metal, and it had penetrated the surface of her sole and drilled through her hoof to emerge at the fetlock. I felt nauseous as I stared at the metal, wondering how I could remove it. How had I missed this last night?

The officer who had helped me find the hay came over to see Midge's foot. He took one look at the fetlock and said, "Well, now, that's a bad scrape."

"It's only the half of it." I lifted Midge's hoof and pointed to the metal. Suddenly I couldn't think about it more. I stood up and shrugged. "Maybe she just needs some time off the foot and some hot mineral soaks after I pull out the shard."

The officer's breath whistled through his teeth. "No, miss." He took his revolver out of a hip holster and held the handle out for me to take. "I'm afraid she needs more than mineral soaks."

"No, sir." I shook my head and stepped away from the gun. "No, sir," I repeated, envisioning Midge's head with blood oozing down her white blaze. I had watched a horse die at his master's hands after a broken leg, and I refused to do this to Midge.

"I'm sorry, but it's the only humane thing to be done. I'll do it for you, if you can't stomach it." The officer grabbed ahold of Midge's reins and started to pull her away from the alfalfa hay.

I shrieked and grabbed his arm, pulling the reins out of his hands, "No!"

He looked at me as if I were hysterical, and well I might have been. In a softer voice, he continued, "I'm afraid it's got to be done, miss. That's more than a cut. Her foot is infected, and she's in too much pain. Would you rather she die slowly, unable to stand from the pain?"

I couldn't speak. I saw my father cradling Midge's head while she ate grain after a long day of work. I heard her call to Trader and his returning neigh. "She just needs some time and some soaking."

"No, miss. I've seen this before. Even if you can get that metal out of the hoof, the foot will still fester, turn green then black, and she won't walk again. It's only humane to finish this now."

"Humane? How can killing her be humane?" I was out of my mind with horror. No. I could never kill Midge. It was just a bad wound. I needed more salve and some mineral water to soak her foot. I needed a pair of pliers to yank out the metal. Midge's head dropped low and she brushed her lips over my hands, then sniffed at her right foot. Her agony was so plain that I couldn't stop the tears now. "Salve will help, won't it Midge?" Midge sniffed my hands but had no answer for me.

"She's got you here to safety," the officer continued, "this is the only favor you can return to her now." He set the gun in my hand and pointed at the far side of a band of trees. "Lead her over there and let her take a bite of some tender sprouts. Then put her out of the misery she's in."

I don't know how I moved, but I know I didn't lead Midge. She followed me at her own pace. Trader watched us walk away but didn't try to follow. Somehow he seemed to know better. The gun was too heavy and I hated the cold metal. In a slow procession that didn't last long enough, we reached the far side of a band of trees, separating the temporary camp from the bay side of the army training grounds. I let Midge forage in the moist grass that the officer had told me we would find. She seemed half starved and I don't think she was listening, but I started to tell her everything I could remember that my father had said about her—how she was the fastest mare in the barn, the most spirited he had ever met and his most well-loved horse. I added that she had saved my family and my friends and that Trader would miss her dearly. Then I pointed the gun between her eyes.

The bullet came out too fast. I had only aimed the barrel and found the trigger when the world turned red. Midge crumpled to the ground slow and without any grace. First her knees buckled, and she looked at me with fear in her eyes and cried out, then her belly hit the wet green grass, followed by her chest and her neck. After the gunshot's echo there was only silence. I watched Midge's head, colored red now with her blood, slowly fall to the earth. I wished I were blind, tears everywhere, my eyes swelling shut to block out the horrible thing I had done. But I could still see, and Midge's body would not go away. I felt a hand on my shoulder, shuddered, and collapsed next to Midge. My hand brushed over her wet muzzle and turned red with blood. The soldier took the gun or I threw it at him, I don't remember which, and then I stood up and started to run.

On the other side of the hill, the ocean met me. The angry torrent that crashed on the rocky beach below was deafening and I stared at the waves, numb and knowing there was nowhere to run. When I finally closed my eyes, I could hear my father calling my name. His breath mingled with the water slamming into the cliffs. Somehow I convinced myself to walk back to camp, but I avoided the far side of the trees where Midge's body lay. Trader was still tethered by the alfalfa, but he was too restless to eat. He would take a bite of the hay, start to chew, and then pause to lift his nose to the wind and flick his ears sideways to listen. I knew he was waiting for Midge. They had pulled father's wagon together for the past ten years.

When I returned to the tent, I found that Lee's son had left. Sarah mentioned that he had set off an hour earlier hoping to find the Chinese camp. Although Sarah didn't admit that she had told him to leave, I thought that this might be the case. Our tent had been transformed with two bedrolls, a wool army blanket, several pillows and Sarah's trunk. The place felt strangely homey. Sarah had also gotten an extra breakfast ration for me—two pieces of toast and a slice of cheese. I didn't feel hungry, but I ate to satisfy Sarah.

After eating, I decided I couldn't stare at the wagon anymore. It reminded me too much of Midge. I found the soldier who had loaned me the gun and asked if the army would need another wagon. Indeed, there was both a shortage of wagons and horses. He offered me a great sum for Trader and the wagon together, but I couldn't part with my horse and took a stamped certificate from the U.S. Army for the sale of the wagon alone. The soldier claimed the certificate was redeemable for one hundred dollars, but I wasn't sure if I believed him. He helped me clear out the wagon and then brought a new team of horses over. In a few minutes, two sorrels were hitched to my father's wagon and the soldier waved as he set off down the path.

Sarah talked to our neighbors in the tent village, trying to find out if anyone knew where messages could be sent. Apparently a mail center had already been set up, and she went off in search of this. Although the horses were supposed to be kept away from the camp, I hitched Trader next to the tent. I couldn't afford to lose him and knew he was uneasy with Midge gone. I tried to explain to Trader what had happened to Midge, as if he could understand my words. He kept his eyes on the path where he'd last seen her disappear as if he expected her to trot over the hill any minute.

After a while, I brought one of the army blankets out to the grassy spot where Trader was tied. I didn't want to leave him alone, but I was exhausted from the long night and had to lie down. Trader nuzzled my head, sniffing at my hair and then left me alone to sleep. One look in his big amber eyes and I knew that somehow we'd get through this mess. He was the only one who could steady my thoughts.

I awoke to a tap on my shoulder. Sarah sat down on my blanket. "I don't know what to do," she started. "There's no message from father for me and no one has heard of any boats coming from Berkeley."

The sun was high overhead, and I knew I'd slept several hours, but it felt like only minutes. I stared at Sarah, trying to concentrate on what she had just told me. She had every right to be consumed with her problems, but I wanted to scream at her to be quiet. I didn't care about how long she would have to wait at this camp until her family found her. The point was that someone would come for her. My father's name was not listed among the sick at the Presidio. I had been told that everyone in the temporary hospital at the Mechanics' Pavilion had been taken to the Presidio, yet my father was not here. I held hope that Papa had been sent to Golden Gate Park instead of the Presidio. But it was a slim hope.

I'd have to make the trip across town to the park to locate the rest of my family, and maybe Papa would be waiting for me there. But something told me that he was gone already. Caroline's dream had come to mind several times since I left Papa. She had told me about the earth shaking and a fire that followed. It seemed impossible that Caroline had known the whole nightmare before it played itself out for the rest of us . . . She had wanted to warn everyone, but I had silenced her. Now Papa was missing, as was Frank. I hadn't thought much of Frank in the confusion. Was he alive or only ashes now in his old house just like Mr. McCain? Maybe he was wandering the city streets lost. I hoped that he had found his mother and the rest of my family at the Golden Gate camp and that everyone was only waiting for me to return.

"Sarah, I'll be leaving after Trader has a few more hours rest."

Sarah looked startled. "Where will you go? I have to wait for my father to come here. Mr. Packard and Mother will tell him to find me here."

"Yes, and you should wait here. But I have to find my family. I've left them at the Golden Gate camp, and they don't know if I'm alive or dead now. And I have to tell them about my father . . ."

"He's not among the hospital patients here, is he?"

"No." I rubbed my eyes so Sarah wouldn't see the tears.

She placed a hand on my shoulder and kissed my forehead. "Certainly you must go to find your family. You know, I haven't thanked you for last night."

"Please don't." I wanted no reminder of the nightmare that had occurred last night. "I only hope that Mr. Packard and your mother had a safe trip across the bay last night. By now, they've probably met your father in Berkeley and are arranging for a boat to be sent here."

"I haven't wanted to think about my house, but do you know if Nob Hill burned last night?"

"We could find out." I stood up and tugged on Sarah's hand. She followed me up to the front gates of the Presidio. A soldier let us climb one of the Army's lookout towers. At the top of the tower, a thin spacer between the bricks provided a view of the charred city. Nob Hill was indeed gone. Sarah pointed to California Street and followed it to the cross street where the Douglas mansion once stood. The mansion's foundation was still smoking, but the walls and the roof lay in heaps of ash. The huge marble pillars that had lined the front entryway now stood with nothing to support but an airy ceiling. Sarah didn't cry. I expected that she might, but instead she only asked where my house had once stood. Unfortunately, there were no good landmarks south of Market, and the Embarcadero had a thick layer of fog creeping up the bay and obscuring the houses that had once stood near the waterfront. But I knew my house had burned to the ground. I pointed toward the east bank neighborhood. "I live there, somewhere in the rubble down by the waterfront."

"We've both lost everything," Sarah said with a note of hopelessness.

"No. Just the houses where we once lived." I turned away from the view of the charred city. Sarah squeezed my hand. The tower was dark, and for the first time all morning, I felt a moment of peace. Some things were clearly beyond my control and here that was the most evident. I don't know exactly why, but I kissed Sarah then. Her lips were soft and warm against mine. Instead of pulling away, she wrapped her arms tightly around me. I buried my face against her collar and started to cry, silently.

After a while, Sarah brushed her fingers through my hair, smoothing the tangled locks. "You should go find your family, Bette."

"I don't want to leave you," I said, surprised at my brash words.

Sarah smiled. "Oh, I'll be fine. But if my father doesn't send a boat for me . . . will you come back to check on me before nightfall?"

"Yes." I felt so close to Sarah then and hated the thought of leaving her alone in the camp. There were strange men all around, and it was no place for a young woman to spend the night alone. Yet, my family was waiting.

Trader was reluctant to make another trip, and I had to convince him with a carrot that I had stolen from one of the soldiers' horse rations. Unfortunately, there was no saddle, and I wasn't happy to make the long ride bareback. My trousers were already filthy though, and I doubted I could look much worse covered in horse dirt.

Sarah had decided to spend the rest of the day near the main water dock of the Presidio, hoping to catch any news of a boat sent for her. We promised to meet that night at the tent. Lee's son had not appeared since early that morning, and I was concerned that he might be lost. Sarah was confident that he had found his 'kin' and had reasonably decided to stay on his side of the camp. Feeling the jade bounce against my chest as Trader trotted down the path, I made a vow to check in on Lee's son as soon as I had found my own family.

Although fires still burned in several parts of the city, the route from the Presidio to Golden Gate Park avoided the areas consumed by the infernos. I didn't push Trader to keep a fast pace. The rubble in the streets made us both cautious. Around noon the dynamite blasts started again at irregular rhythms, reminding me of a drummer that couldn't find his beat. And with each blast, Trader tossed his head and whinnied. I knew he was asking for Midge, who no longer heard or returned his call, and every note of his voice felt like a knife jabbing a fresh wound.

I climbed off Trader as soon as we reached the grass of the park. The number of tents had nearly doubled since yesterday, and I wondered how I'd find my family in the sea of canvas. The first person I recognized was the nurse who I had left my father with at the Mechanics' Pavilion. She was in a large crowd gathered around a wagon serving lunch and didn't look up when I shouted to her. I couldn't lead Trader through the crowd to reach her, but was reluctant to leave him tied up alone here. Seeing the nurse filled me with the hope that Papa had been brought to this camp after all. I made my way to the tent with the large Red Cross flag and inquired after a list of the sick. My father's name wasn't on their lists, but no one had any record that he had died. Finally, I tied Trader up to the water trough and set out to find the nurse.

The woman was still by the lunch wagon and now employed at serving food. I got in line with no intention of eating and caught her attention as she tried to spoon mashed potatoes in my bowl. "Ma'am, excuse me. But I don't want any potatoes."

"That's what we have." She dished the potatoes into my bowl.

"No, I mean, I want to talk with you. You were the nurse that was with my father at the Mechanics' Pavilion."

A man in line behind me pushed his bowl in front of my chest and tried to nudge me forward. Instead of moving away, I handed him my full bowl of potatoes. He acted confused but took the bowl anyway. The nurse squinted at me. "I don't know, miss. You don't look familiar. And there were too many fathers that I saw to yesterday. Today, I feed the living. I had my fill of sick and dying, so they gave me a break today." She coughed into her coat sleeve. "Try the Red Cross tent. Or try the Presidio. Most of the patients at the temporary hospital were sent there. They have a list of everyone. You can find all of the patients in the Red Cross tents."

"But, ma'am, my father isn't on their list. He's not on the list at the Presidio camp either," I insisted. "Thomas Lawrence, my father. I told my mother I wouldn't leave his side, but I had to . . ."

"Then he's missing now." She filled the next bowl with potatoes and shrugged. "What did you saw his name was?"

"Lawrence. Thomas Lawrence." I could hear my voice shake and tried to steady my breathing. That was his name. And I knew before she looked at me that he had no use for the name now.

The woman shook her head and filled the next bowl with potatoes. "Aye, Lawrence. He has a family here, I think. You're his relations?"

I nodded. Had she been listening to me at all? "Yes, I'm his daughter. I left him with you yesterday at the Mechanics' Pavilion. He only had a cold."

"Aye, I remember. Pneumonia." She grunted. "Thomas Lawrence died of pneumonia yesterday morning at eleven."

I fell back from the line and turned away from the nurse's eyes. I had left Papa at the pavilion at half past ten. If I had stayed another thirty minutes I could have been there when he passed. Maybe he would have held on a little longer if I were there to hold his hand. I had to tell my family that he was gone. We were left with no home, few possessions, and too many mouths to feed. I was now responsible for everyone and would have to find a way to take care of them with at least the clothes on my back, Trader, a jade necklace and a certificate from the army for the wagon.

After leaving the food line, I went to the water trough to untie Trader and then searched out the soldier who was in charge of the Golden Gate camp's roll. The soldier with the list of names quickly informed me of the tent number where I would find Thomas Lawrence's family. My eyes watered as he repeated Papa's name. It was all I could do to turn and walk down the numbered rows until I reached my family's assigned campsite.

Caroline was the first who saw me. She was sitting on my mother's trunk, which they had left outside the tent to be used as a table, and swinging her blanket over her head.

"Bette!" she shouted. Caroline jumped off the trunk and ran toward me. I lifted her up and hugged her tightly. She jabbered away about all of the things that she had done that morning and then paused as she saw Trader slowly marching behind me. "Where's the girl horse?"

"Midge hurt her foot."

Caroline's eyes were wet almost immediately. "She went to heaven also?"

"Yes, I'm sorry." My sister understood too much, I thought sadly. Children were not supposed to know so much of death. Mother had come out of the tent now and Mary was at her side. Charlie and Wes were playing with some of the other boys at the camp, and Mother called to them in a stern voice.

"Where's the wagon?" Charlie asked as soon as he saw me and gave me a quick hug.

"The army took our wagon," I answered. "They needed it to help clear the streets and carry people to safety."

Wes tugged on my sleeve and reached his hands up to me. I set Caroline on the ground and lifted him up on my hip. He was too heavy to hold for long, but I appreciated his warm hug. "We missed you, Bette," he said, much too serious for his years.

When I set him on the ground, I turned to Mother. She didn't hug me like the children had, and she didn't ask me any questions. She knew that if I was alone it was because her husband was dead. I opened my mouth to speak, but there were tears in her eyes already. Mary held on to Mother's apron tightly and looked at me with a pained expression. Finally, Mother asked after Papa, and I had to tell them all the horrible truth.

"He's gone, Mother. Passed of pneumonia at the hospital."

Mother stood stone still. Her hand covered her mouth as the tears streamed down her face. A moment later she had ducked inside the tent and closed the flap. Her sobs filled the air. For once, Mother was noisy. The children stood about struck dumb. Charlie gave Mary's hand a squeeze and she promptly hugged him. Wes leaned against his big brother, crying softly. I was proud of Charlie, standing so tall and showing no fear, but I knew he too would need to cry over this.

Caroline was holding my hand, and when I glanced down at her, she whispered, "He's with God, Midge and Mr. McCain, isn't he, Bette? At least Papa has his horse and his best friend."

"Yes, Caroline." My voice was weak and I didn't want to speak anymore. Caroline didn't seem surprised. She just sat down on the dirt and started to hum the Mozart song that Papa always loved to dance to. I wondered how she could remember that. Mary sat down near her and asked why she was humming. She didn't seem to understand what had happened.

I didn't expect Mrs. McCain's reaction. I hadn't seen her on the other side of the tent, but she had watched my arrival apparently and listened to the story of how our wagon had been taken by the army and father had died at the temporary hospital yesterday morning. After Mother's sobbing had slowed, Mrs. McCain stepped forward and hugged me.

In a low voice she said, "My husband is gone, Bette, just like your father. But I know my son is alive. He's still alive for you."

I pushed away from her and shuddered. The image of Jack McCain's wagon full of dead bodies flashed in my mind.

Mrs. McCain grabbed my arm and continued, "You must find him, Bette. Caroline had a dream last night that you came back to the camp leading only one horse. In her dream you left again to find Frank—"

"No," Caroline interrupted. "It was different. In my dream your horse had red on his face."

Blood red, I thought. Caroline's dreams made me nervous. She saw something that the rest of us didn't understand. Maybe Frank was alive. If he was, where could I find him? I rubbed my eyes, trying to clear my thoughts. I wanted to find Frank desperately. To Mrs. McCain I said, "You've checked the records for his name here?"

Mrs. McCain nodded. "And one of our neighbors went to the Presidio camp this morning to check for the missing relatives. He said Frank's name wasn't listed among the living or the dead there."

It would be impossible to confirm the identities of half the bodies in the mass graves this soon, but I didn't tell Mrs. McCain this. "Yes, I'll go search for him. But Trader is exhausted and needs to rest."

Mrs. McCain nodded. "So are you."

"Mostly I'm hungry."

While Mrs. McCain opened the crate to find a snack for me, I looked around the tent, sensing something was missing. Finally, I realized that Terra, Mr. McCain's old gray mare, was gone. I asked about her, knowing it was probably not a good sign if she was missing.

Charlie gave me the story. A soldier had taken Terra on the first night at the camp. He had told them that the army was commissioning all horses and wagons, but he hadn't offered anything in return for taking the horse. Probably Terra was already dead. An old lame horse wouldn't last long under the army's care.

Mrs. McCain fed me a few dried apricots and a slice of bread with Mother's apple butter that had miraculously made it into our trunk. Mother had left Mary outside the tent, and I could hear her inside crying still. I was glad that I didn't have to tell her Papa had died alone. Finally I had found a benefit to my mother's silence. She didn't ask the question I was afraid to answer. How could you leave your father alone to die? I would take this secret with me to my own grave.

After a few hours of rest and a burlap sack rubdown for Trader, courtesy of Charlie and Wes, I left my family again. I entrusted the army certificate for the wagon to Charlie, telling him that if he so much as dropped a grain of dirt on the paper, I'd skin his hide. No one asked when

I would return. It was understood that I would be back with Frank, but only Caroline knew this would be true. The rest of us were doubtful.

Wes begged to ride with me, but I convinced him to stay as Charlie's aide. Charlie now understood that he was the eldest male, and he didn't even suggest leaving the family. At eleven years old, he was ready to take on more responsibility than his scrawny shoulders could carry. Caroline trotted along with me as I left our tent and only stopped when we reached the park gates.

"Good-bye."

"Where will I find Frank?" I asked her, only half-serious.

"I don't know. My dream ended too soon."

I nodded. "Be a good girl, Caroline."

She turned and skipped down the park lane toward the tents. I watched her form disappear behind a tree and then climbed up on Trader's back. "Time to go, boy. There's no long rest for us until tonight."

We took a different path this time back to the Presidio, keeping along the western edge of the city where the ocean pounded the shoreline. Trader liked the beach, and we moved faster on the hard-packed sand at the water's edge than when we navigated the rubble-filled city streets. Unfortunately, the beach ended and we had to take the last quarter mile through the city. In this part of town the earthquake had done little more than topple a few fireplaces, crack plaster and break glass windows. The fire was miles away, and the occupants of the houses on the west shore seemed secure in their homes. I envied them but tried not to dwell on this. Losing everything makes you envy basic possessions, but I knew this wouldn't help my lot.

Suddenly I saw him. I knew it was Frank before my eyes could focus on his haggard face. He was riding Guinness, his father's favorite horse. "Frank!" I called to him and put my heels in Trader's side to urge a trot.

Frank looked up at me and his face instantly broke in a wide grin. "Bette! Now, bless the devil! How are you here?"

We both jumped off our horses and embraced as if ages had separated us rather than a scant forty-eight hours. "I've been sent by your mother to find you," I replied. "And it seems I've succeeded. How did you survive alone?"

"I don't hardly know," Frank answered. "Our house is burned to the ground, and yours too, Bette. Is your family safe?"

I nodded. "Except my father. He died yesterday. My mother is with the children and your mother as well, at Golden Gate Park. They were expecting you, but I'd given you up for dead."

"So little faith?" Frank laughed. Then a shadow came over his face and he bowed his head to rest on his horse. "Ahh, I have little faith left, as well. You heard that my father was killed in the quake?"

"I'm sorry."

Frank continued, "Just after the first quake, I heard my mother scream. I ran to their room and saw the trestle that had landed on Father's chest. I tried to lift it, but I knew there was no use. He had died instantly. You're certain my mother is well?"

I nodded. "I've just seen her. She's at the Golden Gate Park waiting for you."

"Thank God, at least for that." He bowed his head and continued softly, "I carried Mother out of their bedroom. She was hysterical and refused to leave the house. I had to get out. I couldn't stay with her—"

"It's not your fault for leaving. It was horrible." I rested my hand on his shoulder and he turned to hug me. For a minute, I waited for him to let go. When I started to pull away, I felt his silent sobbing. He leaned against me and I held him tight, absorbing the violent shaking that ripped through his body. I knew he could have lifted that trestle from his father's frame, but it would have been no use. Instead, he had carried his mother to safety, and then run. Grieving makes some lose their minds, and I didn't blame him at all. He had no idea the fire would follow his heels.

Frank's crying slowed after a while. He wiped his eyes and looked away from me, as if embarrassed. I kissed his cheek and he tried to force a smile. "Finally I get a kiss from my Bette?"

"I'd give you another, but it might go to your head," I teased softly. I wondered why he had taken Guinness, his father's horse, instead of Terra. Frank had always been closer to the gray mare, but she was old now and lame too. He couldn't have known that he had left her in the barn to die, had I not found her. Soon he would hear that the army had taken Terra. I wasn't sure which fate was worse—to be run and whipped to the ground by soldiers or left in a barn to burn. I shuddered. "We shouldn't stay here long. I have a responsibility back at the Presidio, and your mother needs you at the Golden Gate camp. Was that the direction you were headed?"

Frank shrugged. "I've been wandering lost. I'd given up on God and was about to ask the devil for advice."

"Well, I'm glad I found you before the nuns could hear that."

He laughed, sadly. "Yes, I'm glad you found me."

"And now that you're found, I have to ask a favor." I knew that my family would expect me to return with Frank, but it was getting late, and I had to go back to the other camp to check on Sarah. "Since we're both fatherless today, we both have our families to care for. Will you see to mine until I get back to them tomorrow? Mrs. McCain and Mother are sharing a tent, and the officer at the entrance to the park will give you their tent number."

Frank nodded. "What are you going to do?"

For some reason I was reluctant to tell Frank about Sarah. He knew me well enough, though, that I didn't dare risk a lie. "I have to go back to see Sarah, Miss Douglas. She's waiting for her father to send a boat to the Presidio."

"Sarah Douglas?"

I nodded. "The rest of her family is waiting for her in Berkeley. You know, their house burned just like ours."

"Ashes to ashes. Yes, things seem equal now. But when this nightmare is finished, the city will be rebuilt, and the Douglases will still be rich and we'll still be poor."

"Perhaps." I conceded that Sarah Douglas would never be at my level, even if now we both shared the pleasures of homelessness. This was only temporary. I continued, "But my father asked me to look after the Douglas women. They were alone when the earthquake hit."

"Mark my words, Bette. Miss Douglas won't remember your kindness as well as some poor bugger you lift off the street." He sighed. "But I understand your duty. I'm sure your father would have asked you to take care of her family. He was attached to Mr. Douglas and always said he was a good man. But I wouldn't bet on him repaying all that he owes your family."

"What do you mean?"

"We both have our obligations now, don't we?"

I resented Frank's haughty tone but decided not to push him further. We'd both had a rough time of it the past few days, and some things were better overlooked. Yet, I wondered what Frank meant by saying that Mr. Douglas owed something more to my family.

Frank clapped my back and jumped astride Guinness. He gave a soldier's salute and then headed down the street in the direction I had just come. My heart was much lighter now that I had seen Frank. I knew he could take care of himself, but I had worried anyway. I gave Trader a rest and walked the rest of the route to the Presidio. My thoughts were now directed to Sarah.

I desperately hoped that Sarah's father had not yet sent a boat to retrieve her. In part, I didn't want to spend the night alone, and I knew that by the time I reached our campsite, it would be too late to turn back to Golden Gate Park. However, another reason played in my mind. I wanted her company. Why had I kissed her in the tower? This question drifted in and out of my mind several times without any explanation. And why had she returned the kiss?

Sarah was not at the tent, and Lee's son was nowhere to be found on the Chinese side of the campground. I went down to the pier hoping to find Sarah there. She spotted me first and called out as she was on her way up the steps from the water's edge.

"No news from your father?" I asked.

She shook her head. Then she reached out and took my hand. "Did you find your family?"

"My mother and my brothers and sisters are safe. They're at the Golden Gate Camp." I paused. The water lapped up on the shore and again I thought I heard my father calling me. His voice was part of the shore break now. "My father died yesterday."

"Oh, Bette, you're not serious?" She knew I was and didn't wait for an answer. She embraced me quickly. "I'm so sorry. If you hadn't left him to come for my mother and me . . ."

"Then he would never have forgiven me," I finished. "I half knew he was gone, but I was still holding out for a miracle, I guess. There's one bit of good news today . . . Do you remember Frank McCain? He was my partner at the ice skating rink where we met on Tuesday?"

"Frank? Yes, he's one of our stablemen. And he's your suitor?"

"Not exactly. He's my good friend, and he'd like it if we were engaged, but I'd prefer otherwise." I sighed. "But the good news—I met him just past Seal's Cove. He was missing from his family and I had feared the worst. It was a blessing to find him alive."

"Yes, you must be quite relieved."

I thought her curt tone was strange but tried to ignore it. Perhaps she wasn't fond of Frank. We walked back to our tent in silence. When Sarah spotted Trader she cooed and rubbed his head.

"I've got a present for you, sir." Sarah reached into her pocket and produced a carrot, much to Trader's delight.

"Where'd you get that?" I asked.

She shrugged. "The army horses have more than their fair share."

I thanked her for thieving. Trader deserved it.

After a dinner of rolls and cheese, courtesy of the army, Sarah and I retired to our tent. The army had ordered that no lights be lit. They feared a new fire might start. Fortunately there was a good deal of moonlight. The fires were still burning in certain parts of the city and dynamiting continued, but the north wind cleared the smoke from the Presidio and we had enough light to see, mostly.

Sarah pulled a box out of the trunk as I sat back on the bedroll and tugged off my muddy boots. She handed me the box and said, "I found a present for us, too. Unlike the treat I found for Trader, I came across this one honestly."

I stared at the box, picking out the image of the Alps and the word "Schokalade" and remembered the box of chocolates that we had feasted on with Mrs. Douglas yesterday. Somehow the chocolates had made it into Sarah's trunk. She pulled off the lid and popped one of the rum squares in her mouth, then urged me to follow suit. I took one and grinned.

"There's no reason to eat like beggars on stale rolls and tasteless cheese, simply because we're sleeping outside." Sarah took another chocolate. "I say, let us well feast as the ladies do at the English courts or the Viennese tea parties."

Our bellies were full of chocolate before long, and the dose of alcohol warmed my blood. I could tell that Sarah was feeling the effect as well. We lay back on the blankets and talked of costumes we would wear if we were dining at a Viennese tea. After a while, we both grew quiet. Sarah placed her hand on mine. Her tone of voice changed to serious as she asked, "Why did you kiss me in the tower today?"

I shrugged, then sat up and took another chocolate so my mouth would be full and I wouldn't have to answer. Sarah guessed my ploy and snatched the chocolate from my fingers, and placed it between her lips. She leaned toward me and brushed my lips, letting half the chocolate slip into my mouth as she bit into it. I felt dizzy and closed my eyes as the chocolate melted on my tongue. Sarah winked at me as soon as I opened my eyes, and then kissed me again.

"Why did you do that?"

She shrugged. "I like kissing you. Do you think that's wrong? In Europe, women kiss all the time."

"You've been to Europe?"

"No, but I've heard the stories and eaten the chocolate." She laughed. "My mother told me about a party she went to in Paris. All the women kissed each other, and not just when they were making introductions. In fact, the men kissed each other as well."

I smiled. "Sounds like a drunken party down on the Barbary Coast. Are you sure it was Paris?"

Sarah snorted at my comment. "My parents would never go to the Barbary Coast."

"Have you been down to the Barbary Coast before?" I considered telling her about Henry, but decided against it. My eyes were on Sarah's lips and I could hardly wait to feel them again. But something made me stop. I'd never thought of kissing a girl before I met Sarah.

"No. The most reckless I've been is escaping operas to go to the Ice Skating Masquerade." She paused, and then reached out to touch my arm. "I almost kissed you then—when we were catching our breath at the side of the rink. You looked so beautiful."

"I was wearing a mask!"

"But I knew it was you. And your lips weren't covered by the mask. Neither was the rest of your body."

My skin turned impossibly hot and I hoped Sarah wouldn't see my blush. She laughed and playfully pushed my shoulder. I could feel my breathing quicken. It was all I could do to try to relax.

She continued, "You know, my mother has a friend who's an actress in New York. She's never married. In fact, she refuses to sleep with men. She only invites women to her bed." She paused. "I wouldn't mind that. But I'm no actress. Ordinary women could never get away with that, I suppose."

"I think you could be an actress. You're very pretty and people would certainly enjoy watching you." I smiled. "At least, I would."

Sarah giggled. "My father would disown me if I became an actress."

"Would he disown you if you told him you liked kissing women?"

She ignored my question. "I think I might enjoy acting but only if I could pick the best scenes and have my choice of co-stars—the best co-stars to make me look good, you know. And, I do like kissing women." She grinned. After a moment she asked, "Bette, are you in love with Frank?"

I opened my mouth to answer but couldn't think of how I should reply. Sarah shifted away from me. She was just far enough away now that our skin was no longer touching. I wanted to pull her back but didn't move. I thought of kissing Frank. He was so different from Sarah. "No. I'm not in love with him."

She nodded, obviously uncomfortable. "But you're going to marry him."

"No," I answered immediately. "Frank and I are only close friends. We're not engaged. If I had my choice, I'd never marry." As much as to myself as to Sarah, I repeated, "We're not in love."

Sarah raised an eyebrow. "Love doesn't always determine these things. Some women have no choice but to oblige their parents' wishes." She sighed. "And some situations require marriage. Can you get on without marrying someone?"

"My family expects that I'll marry Frank," I answered. Sarah's remark was more candid than I wanted. My situation in life was different from hers, but I didn't need her to point this out. "I could get on alone, unmarried. I won't be rich, but I could take care of myself."

"Well, then I hope you won't marry. As for me, I don't want any of the suitors I have met yet. Mother wants me to marry some rich idiot. Father says I'm too young. Henry might not marry either. But it's different for men." Shaking her head, she added, "No one would think badly of my brother if he decided to forego marriage for his career."

"Maybe not."

"Of course not." Sarah paused and met my eyes. "I don't like the thought of sharing you with Frank."

"I don't belong to Frank."

"No, we don't really belong to anyone, do we?" She sat back on the blanket. Her hand rested on my arm. I loved the warmth of her and the brush of her fingertips on my skin. She let go of my arm and grabbed one of the pillows, hugging it to her chest.

"What's wrong?" I asked. She shrugged and tossed the pillow aside. I took her hand and squeezed it gently.

I reached out to caress her cheek, then traced down the line of her jaw until I reached the point of her chin. She turned toward me, quietly watching. I brushed her dark hair off her shoulder and kissed her lightly.

She tilted her head as I pulled away. "You're scared of me?"

"No." I hid my trembling hands in the rough blanket. "I hardly know you."

"Do you feel it too? A strange desire . . ." her voice faded. I wondered what she was thinking, but her emotions seemed masked now. She pushed the one window in the tent open a little further, lightening the blankets and our few possessions. The window was really just a slit in the canvas, folded back and providing only a dim shaft of moonlight. She turned back to me and though I felt the desire she spoke of, I couldn't answer her.

"You're beautiful," she whispered.

I felt my cheeks warm with another blush. "No, I'm just . . . You're the beautiful one."

Sarah smiled. She pulled me close and opened her lips as she kissed me, her tongue touching mine. Sarah had been in my thoughts for so many hours. The closeness that I felt toward her now seemed to salve the wounds that the past day had carved. My thoughts were blurry, and when she touched me, I only wanted more. Overcome, I had to turn away. Sarah looked a question at me, but didn't ask what was wrong. She tossed one of the silk pillows at me. I could tell she was confused. The tent was filled only with the noise of our breathing and everything felt too tense. "We should get some sleep," I said dryly. "It's been a long day."

Sarah's lips were tight and I wondered if she was upset at me. She stretched out on the bedroll and I lay next to her, barely breathing. I wished she might speak. What had just happened? My thoughts were filled with my own excitement and uncertainty, and the sound of Sarah's breathing. I wanted Sarah to touch me again, or at least to look at me, yet her eyes were closed and I worried she might fall asleep. I turned on my side. "Sarah, I'm sorry. Is everything all right?"

She opened her eyes and stared up at me, then nodded. "I guess so." She shifted up to her forearm and kissed my cheek. Her fingertips brushed over my lips. "I don't even know what it is we're doing here."

"Neither do I." After a moment, she brought my hand to her lips and kissed my palm. Sarah moved to touch my face again, avoiding my lips. She traced my profile and then my neck. Her fingers felt softer than feathers. Slowly, her hand moved down the front of my chest, and she gazed up at me as I responded to her touch. "You're right, we should sleep. We can talk about this later."

I nodded, doubting we would speak of this again. Sarah would be gone from my world as soon as her father found her. Maybe that was for the best. I stretched out on the blankets and closed my eyes. Her arm rested on my belly, as if she'd laid claim to me. I loved the weight of her hand. Sleep came easily.

Chapter 6
April 20, 1906

I awoke what seemed only a few hours later. Sarah lay at my side, perfect even in the darkness. Piles of blankets were tucked around us and our heads rested on the green silk pillows. At first I wasn't certain why I had awoke at all. Then I heard the scratching sound and knew someone was at the door of the tent.

The sound had not wakened Sarah, and she only murmured when I moved her arm off my shoulder and rose up from the bedroll. I pulled on my trousers and blouse, and then grabbed my jacket. Before opening the tent flap, I pulled the blankets up to cover Sarah's body.

Lee's son apologized for waking me, "Your horse . . ." His voice faltered and he started to make a hand gesture and then stopped.

I slipped out of the tent quickly. "What's wrong?"

He pointed to Trader's rope. No horse was attached to the line. The muscles in my throat immediately tightened. I could barely swallow, and I struggled to speak. "Do you know where he is?" My voice was shaking and showed all my weakness. How could I have let Trader slip out of my hands?

"A soldier took him."

"A soldier? Are you certain of this?"

He nodded.

Every semblance of right and wrong disappeared. A soldier had stolen Trader. "When?" I rasped. "Did you see which way he rode?"

He pointed east. "I don't know exactly."

"Thank you for waking me." I bowed my head, hoping that he might recognize this gesture more than my impotent words. I ducked inside the tent and woke Sarah. It would be hard to leave Sarah and the warm tent.

"Trader's gone," I said quickly. "I have to go find him."

"Now?" Sarah grabbed my arm, trying to hold me still. "You can't go out tonight. They've been dynamiting." Just as she said this another load of dynamite exploded, somewhere near enough to shake us. The sound was more chilling than close thunder. "They've blasted our city. You won't find your way in the dark with all the rubble."

"Don't worry. I know this city." I stepped out of the tent and Sarah started to argue again. I held my finger up to my lips to quiet her. "I'll be back by sunrise."

Lee's son was waiting for me. "I have a debt to repay. You saved me last night."

"Is that why you were watching my horse? Why didn't you stop the soldier?" I was angry and didn't want to lose time talking.

He opened his mouth as if to explain and then said simply, "I'm Chinese."

"What difference does that make?"

"To the soldiers?" Lee's son left the question, his answer, unfinished. "I can help you find your horse."

"Look, I didn't save you. I just gave you a ride in my wagon." I started out along the path, heading toward the front gates of the Presidio. All of my thoughts were focused on Trader. I imagined his whinny, recalled the smell of his coat and every feature of his face. But there was little to guide me tonight. Our barn was east of here. Maybe I would head east and find him. Maybe Trader wanted to take himself home.

"My name is Ming," he said, following me. "Lee Ming."

I ignored him at first, then tried to make him turn back when I realized he was following me. He was more stubborn than I anticipated. When we had almost reached the gates, I pointed at the guards whose backs were to us. "Lee Ming, or Ming Lee, whoever you are . . . thank you for waking me. You repaid the debt between us. Now, please go back to your tent. You'll put us both in danger if you follow me."

"Call me Ming." He smiled. "What's your name?"

I was frustrated and the last thing I wanted to do was have polite introductions. "Bette. Bette Lawrence."

"Good. Bette, I'll meet you on the other side of the gate."

Before I could argue, he had disappeared into a thicket of brush at the side of the path. As I continued toward the guards, it occurred to me that Ming spoke nearly flawless English. He seemed to struggle to find the right word, and his voice had a heavy accent, but unlike his father, Lee senior, Ming was almost fluent. I wondered how he had learned the language so fast since his family had only been in San Francisco for a little over a week. I guessed that he had practiced with the sailors during the long boat ride from his old home to San Francisco. Or maybe he'd learned English in his school before reaching America. I really had no idea of his previous world.

The guards were sleeping on their posts and didn't wake as I slipped by them. I saw Ming hop over the fence farther down the hill and then jog over to meet me a block away from the guards. We headed down Broadway Street at a fast pace and didn't talk, both of us searching the dark side streets as well as vision would allow. Only moonlight lit the pavement, and the fog was drifting inland. Combined with the still lingering smoke, the fog limited eyesight to twenty or thirty feet in any direction.

Ahead of us, I heard horse hooves and quickly pulled Ming to the side of the road. We hid in the shadows of the entryway to a boarding house as four soldiers passed on horseback. Unfortunately, Trader was not in this group. The soldiers turned off the main road and headed south. After a few minutes, we escaped the shadows and continued down the path, but Ming kept glancing over his shoulder. Finally I asked, "Do you hear something?"

He scanned the street. "I think we are going the wrong direction."

"You saw the soldier head this way," I argued.

"Yes." Ming took another few steps and then paused. "I thought I saw him . . . But we are heading to the fire. A soldier who steals a woman's horse wouldn't be brave."

"Which way then?" I strained to keep my voice soft, though I wanted to scream. Whenever I closed my eyes the image of the bullet exploding into Midge's head came into my mind. What if the soldier rode Trader until he came up lame? In the dark with all the rubble it wouldn't take long . . . A soldier would just shoot a lame horse and steal another.

"I don't know," he admitted. "Why would the soldiers be out tonight? Why don't they sleep?"

I shrugged. We were wasting time. I wanted to continue down Broadway until we reached the fire. Suddenly, I remembered the signs I had seen in my trip between the Presidio and Golden Gate Park. Nearly every standing post had a sign that detailed the mayor's order against looters. Any looters that were found would be shot on sight. The soldiers must be searching the streets for looters, and if they found Ming and me, chances were good that they would shoot before asking for our defense. I told Ming this much and then sat down on the curb. A large fissure separated the curb from the street. Everywhere there were reminders of the horrible earthquake. I had heard that the water lines could not be restored until the rubble was cleared from the streets, and there was no telling how many more blocks the fire would consume before it burned itself out. Maybe it would burn until it reached the ocean.

Ming sat down on the curb next to me. He reached forward and touched the jade on my necklace. "My father was rich in China. All of his children wore jade for good luck. My mother wore ruby. I have nothing of my father now, except this." Ming slipped his own jade amulet out from under his shirt. His piece was similar to mine, but a snake instead of a dragon was carved on the backside.

"My father is dead as well."

Ming nodded. "I'm sorry for your family. He was a good man."

"So was your father. I never thanked him for this." I touched the jade and then hid it under my blouse. "Which direction should we head?"

Ming pointed to the south. "We should follow the soldiers. It is better to keep your enemy in sight, and one soldier may lead us to others. And to your horse."

We walked for hours, spotting soldiers occasionally, but never Trader. I lost track of the street names and the directions, but I was certain that at some point we circled our path at least twice. Just before sunrise, Ming directed us back to the Presidio. I didn't argue. In my mind, Trader had already been shot and lay dying now, just as Midge had, with his face covered in blood and the coldness of morning seeping into his body. He wouldn't be alone. Everywhere the street was littered with dead horses, overworked and injured, they were killed and left unburied. Just like I had discarded Midge, someone would discard Trader if I didn't find him soon. Maybe it was already too late.

When we reached the front gates of the Presidio, Ming said a quick goodbye, promising to meet me later that day, and then dodged around the eyes of the guards. The Chinese were not allowed to leave the camp at all. I was questioned by the soldiers and claimed that I had gone for a morning walk because I had lost my horse. I told them that I had seen a soldier take my horse and was trying to track down the thief. The soldiers shook their heads and called me a liar, then hysterical, though I never yelled or spoke above my normal tone. I left them quickly, hoping that I wouldn't be reported for any of the charges they threatened.

Sarah met me at the entrance to the tent. "Did you find him?"

"No. Trader's gone."

Sarah tried her best to console me, but it was of little use. Without Trader, I was lost. I hated the thought of facing my family again, this time empty-handed. After breakfast, I accompanied Sarah down to the pier, and we inquired after any planned launches to Berkeley or any news of vessels from that direction. One of the sailors we met said he had been on the boat that carried Mrs. Douglas and Mr. Packard to Berkeley. Sarah was happy to hear that her mother's voyage had gone smoothly, at least as smoothly as could have been expected given the events of that day. The sailor, however, knew nothing more of Mrs. Douglas after she disembarked the boat he had been hired to attend. We sent a message to the Berkeley harbor in this sailor's care as he mentioned he was setting sail later that afternoon for this destination. Unfortunately, he could take no more passengers on his boat, but promised to take Sarah on the next journey tomorrow if she were still stranded at the Presidio.

Sarah decided she would spend the day at the piers, checking each boat for news from her father. She knew I had to find Trader and didn't ask me to keep her company at the dock. For my own, I wanted to see Trader's body if he had been shot as much as to find him alive. I couldn't stop my mind from running the course of horrible punishments the soldier might enact on Trader. I imagined the soldier whipping Trader until he collapsed, or spurring his sides until blood oozed from his beautiful coat, or forcing him to gallop on the cobblestones until his shoes wore through and his hooves cracked or the bones shattered, and then finally the soldier would shoot him. The last thought was the worst. My mind had too perfect an image of this.

I hiked the entire length of the Presidio and then wandered down to the beach on the edge of Seal's Cove. Ming accompanied me for most of the journey, nearly always a silent companion. I was grateful for the second pair of eyes, and I think he kept me from diving off the edge of the cliffs when we came to Lighthouse Point.

Ming was excited to see the sea lions basking on the rocks by the lighthouse beach. He claimed they had no sea lions in the waters of his country. "How can they swim when they are so fat?" he asked, laughing as a big male tried unsuccessfully to climb a large rock.

"The fat ones are slow on land," I agreed, "but they will keep up with our fastest skimmers in the bay, and a dozen sailors can't beat a sea lion on the open water."

We watched one young sea lion jump off a high rock and nose-dive into the water with a big splash. Ming clapped his hands. I couldn't help but smile at him. Maybe this was how I would act if I saw the animals that Ming had known in China.

"I would like to swim with them," Ming said. "Do you think I could?"

"The water is too cold. You'd freeze. The sea lions wouldn't want your company anyway. They only want fish."

Ming hung his head. After a moment he brightened, "Well, I might become a fisherman then. I could spend my day watching the fat sea lions."

I laughed. "You wouldn't like the sea lions if you were a fisherman. They fight for the same dinner."

Ming nodded, but added, "There are plenty fish for our appetite as well as the sea lions. We will share dinner."

We stayed by the lighthouse for a while longer and then wandered farther down the beach. I asked Ming to tell me a story from his childhood and he obliged, describing his village in China and the school that he attended. His father had in fact hired a tutor to teach Ming English when he was only seven years old. As he was the eldest son of an important man, Ming explained that he received more privilege than the other boys did in his village, and he was ill prepared for the rude treatment his family received when they arrived in San Francisco. Some time in the early afternoon, Ming suggested we head back to camp and I followed unwillingly. I hated to think that Trader was truly gone, yet the more we searched, the less hope I held. And though I wanted to find him alive and well, I started to think that it would be better if Ming's theory were true: "Maybe he bucked the soldier and ran off. Maybe he has found a place with good grass and another horse to keep him company."

Ming and I parted ways at the entrance to the army camp. I made my way to the tent and quickly discovered that Sarah was gone. The trunk had been moved out of the tent and only one green silk pillow, a bedroll and a wool blanket remained. I wondered if she had left the green silk pillow for me. I had no way to tell how long ago she had left, but decided to check the pier for any news of her.

Mr. Douglas spotted me as I approached the docks and gave out a shout of greeting. I guessed that Sarah had already told him the story of our journey from their mansion to the Presidio, or maybe Mrs. Douglas had, if she finally regained her senses. Mr. Douglas patted me on the back and thanked me for, in his words, "Saving his beloved women."

Their boat was already loaded with Sarah's trunk and was nearly ready to push off. Sarah begged me to come with them and Mr. Douglas agreed that I should, until he heard that my family was waiting for me at Golden Gate Park. Sarah asked after Trader and I grimly replied that I thought he might be dead. Mr. Douglas had already heard the story that a soldier had stolen him, and since he knew my father and said he owed me a great deal now that I had saved 'his women,' he promised to find a new team for my wagon and even offered employment. I didn't ask what sort of work Mr. Douglas would allow me, as a woman, however able, to do, but thanked him for the generosity. I was still holding out to find Trader, but now that Sarah was leaving, I would have to abandon the search and go back to my family.

After Mr. Douglas boarded the boat, Sarah turned to me and whispered, "You'll not forget last night?"

"How could I?" The words made my eyes water and I quickly brushed off the tears. The last thing I wanted was to cry with Mr. Douglas and all the men about.

"I'll be back." She kissed my cheek. "Remember, in Europe, women kiss all the time."

I blushed just the same. I held on to her hand as she stepped on the mainstay of the boat and only let go when the boat's captain called, "Away with the ties."

Now that Trader was gone, the thought of Sarah leaving me made me inexplicably lonely. With a heavy heart, I watched their boat pull up anchor and disembark. Sarah kept her eyes on me until her father distracted her with something. Why had I let myself believe that the daughter of a rich man like Mr. Douglas would be friends with me? She was leaving the city and might never return. I was stuck here and would have to make my way out of the mess, if not for myself, then for my family. I finally turned away from the scene and headed up to the campground. The army cook was serving beans and cornbread and the smell awakened my hunger. I got in line and tried not to think about eating my dinner alone. Maybe Sarah would want to see me after this nightmare was over, but I doubted it. We were worlds apart, however strong our emotions might seem, and both of our families already had marriage plans for us.

Although I knew it was against the army's rules, I decided to take my dinner over to the Chinese camp and sit with Ming. I didn't want to think of Sarah anymore and hoped Ming wouldn't mind seeing me.

He greeted me with a smile that assured me I was welcome on his side of camp. Ming was sharing a tent with a family that his father had known. He introduced me to the family, first in Chinese and then in English. I bowed and thanked them for letting me sit on their side of the camp. They bowed back and then the father of the family said something to which all the children started giggling, but I wasn't certain why. I couldn't tell if I'd done something wrong, and Ming didn't translate.

The Chinese had only been given rice for dinner. When I realized this, I had Ming mix his meager portion with my beans and split my cornbread with him. Rice alone was certainly not a meal, but our mixed food wasn't much of a feast either. Still, Ming was happy for the supplement. I felt horrible that the soldiers were serving plain rice to so many people. Ming said that there were more important reasons to be angry with the soldiers, but he wouldn't go into any details. I had the sense that he didn't quite trust me yet. And I couldn't blame him.

At dusk I left the Chinese camp and headed back to my empty tent. Trader's lead line was still tied to the center pole inside the tent. I kicked the rope and then felt sorry I had. This rope was both a reminder of my loss and my last remaining attachment to Trader. Untying the lead line, I wrapped the rope in a circle and held it up to my nose. His scent had soaked into the cotton fibers. I wanted nothing more than to keep this smell in my mind. I lay back on the army bedroll and rested on Sarah's pillow. I knew I needed sleep, but my thoughts were troubled. I wished Sarah were still here and wondered if she would think of me again. Then I thought of father. I missed him so much, but I had to quickly push his image from my head. I couldn't get past the thought that I'd left him to die alone. I heard a horse whinny in the distance and cursed myself for losing Trader. Without him, I wasn't sure how much more I could handle.

It seemed the whole camp was fast asleep when I climbed out of my tent. For the first time I was grateful for the fog. A thick blanket of gray had rolled in from the shoreline and would provide the cover I needed. I guessed the time was somewhere close to midnight. Nearly two hours had passed since I had heard the night patrol blow his whistle for ten o'clock curfew. Why he bothered with the whistle, I don't really know. With orders against lanterns or any open flames, few people lingered awake for long after sundown. And the mayor had forbidden the sale or consumption of alcohol as well, so anyone who wanted to stay awake would find himself cold, lonely and nearly blind in the dark.

Thus I found myself happily alone, save the company of a few sleep-deprived soldiers, most of whom I trusted as well as a mean dog with a soup bone. I kept my eyes to the ground and moved quickly past any soldiers I met. They didn't question me, and I guessed that any of them who noticed me were probably bored with their duty of watching the evacuees. Apparently they didn't think I was a threat.

I found the army's stable easily, having already staked out the directions in the light, and tried the front gate. A padlock was set and I knew of no other way inside. I toured the outer paddocks until I found one stall door that had been left ajar.

A buckskin gelding greeted me with a half-hearted snort as I slipped inside his stall. He let me pass through and I climbed over his feeding trough into the main corridor of the barn. A few other horses lifted their heads and poked their noses through the slats of feeding troughs to see who had caused the commotion. The horses, however tired from the day's labor, were light sleepers and as I tiptoed through the barn, I got a long look from every horse in the place. Fortunately for me, their keepers were heavy sleepers. Two young soldiers, ostensibly the stable guards, were snoozing in the tack room and didn't wake as I padded past them.

Much to my disappointment, neither Trader nor any of his tack could be found in the stable. I wondered if I should have trusted Ming. Maybe he had lied when he said that a soldier had taken Trader. Why was Ming watching my tent in the middle of the night anyway? He claimed he wanted to repay the debt he owed to me, but did I trust him not to steal the horse himself and then sell it? Certainly he needed money as much as anyone did, and was he only leading me in a goose chase last night and this afternoon? Why would he want to help me find Trader?

Questions about Ming's objective crowded my thoughts, and I nearly missed the sound of approaching footsteps. At the last moment, I ducked behind the grain barrels as a soldier turned down the main corridor. Between two barrels I found a space wide enough to hide and still have a view of the soldier. As he came closer to the barrels, I realized this was the same man who had given me the gun to shoot Midge. That gun still rested in his hip holster. He paused in his trek through the barn to check on the stable guards and raised quite a call when he caught them snoozing. The two stablehands jumped awake and bolted out of the tack room, with the higher ranked soldier threatening to whip them for their transgressions. "Sleeping on duty is grounds for discharge," he said, with seething anger.

I kept to my post between the grain barrels, watching as the stablehands brought the soldier's horse, the same buckskin I had met earlier, and quickly tacked him. With a few more harsh words, the soldier left the barn and the stablehands both breathed audible sighs of relief.

"Officer Piedmont's got a thorn up his arse," the taller stablehand began. "Or else he was dropped on his head—regular pissant he is."

The other stablehand added, "More than a thorn in that man's arse . . . even his horse don't well like him. Did you see that buck sidestep when Piedmont tried to mount him?"

"Ha! I'd do the same!" shouted the tall stablehand.

Both young men laughed at their joke and then argued over cleaning the buckskin's stall. They couldn't agree and soon retired to the tack room. I doubted that they would fall back asleep now and needed an alternate way out of the barn. Just then, the barn doors burst open with Officer Piedmont again. He called for the stablehands to saddle five horses and the two men jumped on this order.

From what I could gather by the excited talk of the five soldiers who entered the barn ten minutes later, looters had been caught pillaging the rich homes on Van Ness Avenue. Second only to Nob Hill, the aristocrats of San Francisco called Van Ness Avenue their sanctuary. The news that circulated around the tent camp had detailed the Van Ness Avenue evacuation yesterday. And I had heard that the firemen had waited to begin dynamiting the area until today. The approaching fire was held off at Van Ness by demolishing countless numbers of town homes and flats in order to save a handful of mansions.

The poor had lost their homes so that the rich might keep their Italian paintings. If the looters were ravaging the rich homes, I couldn't blame them. Now the soldiers were eager to shoot the looters. The five men jumped on their steeds and followed Officer Piedmont out of the stable. I tried not to imagine what might befall any innocent who came across their warpath tonight. When the main corridor was clear of the soldiers and the stablehands had both gone to clean stalls, I slipped out of the barn through the front gate, which in their hurry the soldiers had left unlocked.

Ming met me at my tent. "Where did you go?" he asked.

By the sound of concern in his voice and the genuine look in his eyes, I knew that my earlier misgivings about Ming's integrity were unfounded. For some reason, he was intent on looking after my welfare with no malevolence.

"I went to the soldiers' stable to look for my horse."

Ming nodded. "Any luck?"

I shook my head. "Why are you awake?" I asked.

Ming shrugged. "The tent is full and my uncle . . . makes a loud noise." Ming squeezed his eyebrows and tapped his lips.

I could tell he was trying to remember the correct English word. He squeezed his nose between his fingertips and inhaled to produce a strange sound in his throat. I caught on finally. "Your uncle snores?"

Ming smiled and nodded quickly. "Yes, he snores. Very loud."

"Well, you can take my bedroll," I offered, pulling up the tent flap.

Ming backed away. "No, I do not want to sleep with you. Someone would see me here and there would be trouble."

"Fine. But the tent will be empty." I grabbed Trader's lead line and looped it around my waist like a belt, then closed the tent flap and headed down the path.

Ming caught up to me. "You are still searching for your horse?"

"What else can I do?" The question was painful as truth often is. Without Trader, I had no hope of providing for my family. My only other option was to marry Frank, if he'd even still have me. And how could I think this after the night I'd spent with Sarah?

"They say that the soldiers are hunting for looters tonight. I think you should stay at the camp until sunrise," Ming cautioned.

"If they're hunting for looters, then the soldiers will be distracted. They won't see me slip behind them." I smiled and shook his hand. "Don't worry, I'll keep my enemy in sight."

"I should go with you."

"No, I'll be fine. Stay here."

When Ming finally nodded, I felt a pang of fear. He joked that he'd rather spend the night with his snoring uncle than risk being hunted by the soldiers, then he wished me luck and turned to head back to the Chinese camp. I couldn't blame him, but somehow it felt like he was deserting me.

There were several soldiers out tonight, more than I had seen in the past two nights combined, and I had to keep my ears constantly alert for the sound of hooves. The dynamiting had stopped, for the time being, and I wondered if this meant that the fire might be close to finished. Smoke still blew up from a few spots on the horizon, but I couldn't tell in the waning moonlight which streets were charred and which were left to burn.

I came up Van Ness with my eyes stinging from the smoldering ash. Half the street was just as it had been a week ago while the other half had been flattened with dynamite. I paused near a fence plastered with billboards. I remembered the billboard I had seen advertising Yosemite Falls and the tranquil hikes through Yosemite valley. "I could go there after all of this," I said, loudly and to no one but the cold night.

Suddenly, the sound of hooves striking the pavement made me sliver up against the fence. I searched the dark street but saw no horse. My heart was beating in my chest as I wished for some hiding place to escape. Suddenly the rider appeared, directly in front of me.

I gasped and sank to the ground, covering my head with my arms as I saw the glint of gunmetal. But the gun wasn't aimed at me. I heard a man yell and quickly spotted the victim—a young man, similar in build to Frank, but with a shock of red hair. He was closer than a hundred yards from me, and I wondered that I hadn't seen him before. From behind the red-haired man, another soldier on horseback appeared. The two soldiers were joined by a third, and soon the red-haired man was surrounded.

I would have believed him a looter, except that he carried no bag. The man traveled as light as I did, with only the clothes on his back. Still the soldier's gun was aimed at him. The red-haired man's eyes were white with fear, and before the soldiers could ask him to explain his presence, he tried to run. I couldn't tell which of the three guns fired first, but all three soldiers took a shot at the man. He was lost before he had taken two steps across the street. The man sank to the ground and the three soldiers rushed in to see the damage they had caused.

Knowing this would be my only time for escape, I turned away from this scene of the dying man and tore down the street, blind to anything but the cobblestones under my feet. After two blocks, I turned off Van Ness, heading west, and collided directly into the flank of a standing horse. The horse sidestepped quickly and the rider yelled so loudly that I froze in place. The next moment, I dropped to the ground and wrapped my arms over my head. My heart was pounding in my ears. If I were to die, I would die a coward with my eyes closed to the horrible flash of the bullet's firing.

"Pull back your hands so I can see you," the gruff voice ordered.

Reluctantly, I uncovered my face, but kept my eyes closed. "Yes, sir." I whispered. "Please don't shoot," I was ready to beg for anything rather than let him gun me down as the red-haired man had been taken.

"You're the girl with the wagon?" the voice asked with surprise.

Was the soldier not going to shoot? I opened my eyes. "Yes," I faltered and tried again. "Yes, I had a wagon. But the army took it. Now I have none." In fact, I had nothing to offer in exchange for my life, save the clothes I now wore and the hidden jade on my necklace. "I have nothing."

"And is that your excuse for looting?" he asked. His horse tossed his head and stomped his feet as another rider, another soldier, approached.

"No, I—" I struggled to not let my voice screech with this answer. "I'm not looting at all."

The soldier, who had me cornered, waved the other rider away and faced me calmly. "What if I don't believe you?"

The gruff voice sounded suddenly familiar and I squinted at the man. A shiver of recognition raced up my spine as I saw Officer Piedmont's face in the dim light. The gun that I had used to shoot Midge was now pointed at me. I coughed and struggled to breathe. After a moment, I found my voice and answered, "Then you will shoot me." My voice carried a strange impartial tone to my fate. I guessed the officer would think I was a looter no matter what I said, but I wanted to defend myself. "I'm no looter. I'm trying to find the man who stole my horse. Though you can shoot me and call me a looter. No one will know the difference except me."

He laughed. "Yes, you're right about that."

I felt a second chill travel up my spine. How could he laugh? "Fine, then if you want to shoot me, get it done with." I was shaking from the cold or perhaps from fear. I couldn't tell which, but it stung my eyes and tasted like a salt lump in my throat.

Officer Piedmont laughed scornfully. "This is the wrong night to be looking for a horse thief." He kicked his spurs into his horse's belly and the horse lunged toward me. I tried to scramble away, but the officer caught my arm. He swung me over the back of his saddle and then threatened, "Now, girl, don't let go. That would be stupid."

I clutched the back of saddle blankets and tried to find a seat on the horse's rump as we set off at a gallop. We turned back onto Van Ness and headed away from the scene of the murdered red-haired man. I thought Officer Piedmont either had ridden Van Ness enough times to memorize every bit of rubble in the street, or he was too crazy to be cautious. We flew down the avenue at a speed that made my head cloud, and I thought I might be going to hell still alive, barely clinging to Officer Piedmont's death steed.

Officer Piedmont only slowed his horse when a group of his men approached us. The other horses whinnied to each other, and I heard the soldiers talk of the looters they had found and shot. I felt nauseous and was thankful that Officer Piedmont didn't offer me up as another looter to sacrifice. He didn't even mention me to the other soldiers, and I don't know that they even saw me in the dim light.

Officer Piedmont rode directly toward the Presidio and did not stop when the other soldiers at the gate waved at him. He slung me off his horse just past the gates and then caught my arm so I wouldn't try to run away.

"What you did tonight should have cost you your life," Officer Piedmont began. "If your horse is gone, I'm sorry, but you might thank me now for the next breath of air you take. I doubt very much that you will be so lucky the next time you venture out at night. Remember, we have a shoot-to-kill order for all looters."

He let go of my arm and rode away instantly. I sank down to the ground and finally let myself cry. Maybe I had wanted to die, but God wasn't in the business of granting wishes of late. I stumbled back to my empty tent and wet the green silk pillow with more tears. After I'd cried as much as I could, I tossed the pillow outside the tent, hoping someone would steal it, and fell into a dreamless sleep wrapped in the army's wool blanket.

Chapter 7
April 21, 1906

When I crawled out of the tent, I found the green pillow, wet with morning dew, and clutched it to my chest. The sun was just rising over the hills beyond the bay, and there was a clear view of the city for the first time in days. Smoke curled up in just two locations, seemingly as innocent as a couple of chimney stacks. By breakfast time, everyone was talking about the end of the inferno, but no one was ready to believe it would truly burn itself out. The fire had consumed so much and it was folly to trust in any hope that it was finally satiated. Who would have guessed that a fire could burn for three days in a city such as ours surrounded by water? I stood in line for breakfast and listened to my tent neighbors talk. Everyone had known someone who had died, and everyone had lost their home and all possessions except what they had dragged to the evacuation camp. Yet, this morning, most spirits were high. The fog lifted early and the sun was shining on a charred city, but the survivors now knew there was an end in sight and rebirth would begin soon.

I returned to the tent and happily ate a thick slice of sourdough layered with butter and drank a bitter mug of hot coffee. There is something powerful about waking up the day after you should have died that makes even bitter coffee quite palatable. After finishing the coffee, I set about clearing out the tent. As I rolled up the bedroll and picked up the army blankets, I noticed a small metal box in the back corner of the tent. I guessed that Sarah must have left the box by accident and wondered what was inside. Unfortunately, there was a lock. If I knew that I would never see Sarah again, I'd simply break the latch. But nothing was known for certain. I packed Sarah's pillow and the locked metal box inside the army blanket and tied everything together with Trader's lead line.

Ming came to my tent and gave a warm hug. "You are alive!"

"You were worried I might not be?"

"Yes," he replied seriously. "You should not have gone out last night. We heard the soldiers' report—ten looters shot."

"Only ten?"

Ming gave me a reproachful look. "I am happy the number was not eleven."

"You worry too much, Ming." I wasn't going to let him know how narrowly I had escaped last night. I didn't want to think about the harrowing ride with Officer Piedmont again.

"Where are you going?" Ming asked, pointing to the sack that I had carried out of the tent.

"To join my family. The other evacuation camp." The sack felt too light—an uneasy reminder of how little burden my possessions made. Trader was the only one I missed. I tried to convince myself I was lucky to be traveling light.

"Do you have to leave now?" Ming frowned. He seemed upset that I was going. Maybe he was lonely.

"Will you come with me?" I hadn't thought about asking him to come, but it was only logical. He didn't seem happy here. There were few reasons he should leave the Presidio, except that I wanted his company. I thought he would fit in well with my family. Charlie and Wes could use a role model. And my mother, for all her faults, never turned down someone in need. "I'd like you to meet my family. You could stay with us for a while."

He seemed to consider my suggestion, then glanced over his shoulder at the grassy rise that separated the Chinese from the others. "No, I think I will stay."

I didn't have any arguments to convince him to come with me. Maybe he was thinking that he would be segregated at the next camp as well. I was sad to leave him. "We'll meet again, I know." I pulled my jade necklace out from under my shirt and traced the dragon imprint, thinking of Papa. Papa would not want me to leave Ming alone, but I couldn't force his decision. "Somehow."

Ming smiled sadly. "Maybe . . ." He sighed heavily. "Your family is waiting. Go safely." He turned and headed up the grassy knoll toward his side of the camp.

I shouldered the sack and gave one last look at the tent. Although I had slept only two nights in that tent, those nights had forever changed me. Before I reached the main thoroughfare leading south out of the Presidio, I heard a whistle and saw a group gathering around a fireman. The tall fireman was barking orders, challenging any able-bodied person to step up to volunteer. They were recruiting hands to help stamp out the last remaining blaze. By the fireman's description, the last front was close—only a quarter mile east—and volunteers were urgently needed. To the east, one trail of smoke coiled up to the sky, rising like the snake imprinted on Ming's jade. Without second thought, I ran to join the group. I pushed my way to the front so I could hear what our orders would be and felt a nudge at my side.

Ming whispered, "What about your family? They are waiting for you, no?"

"My father would want me to help."

Ming nodded. "Mine as well. Then, we are together again," he said, holding out his hand. "Partners?"

I shook his hand and smiled. He was the only person I could trust here. We set off with the group, some carrying brooms, wet gunnysacks, or empty buckets. A priest who joined the motley volunteer crew gave us a blessing as the fireman led us through the streets at a quick jog. I noticed that we were losing people along the way because of the fireman's quick pace. By the time we reached the last burning strip of the city, only half of our volunteer group remained. Fortunately, there were other firefighters and volunteers already enlisted. Ming and I quickly caught on with the plan. Buckets of dirt were being slung at the flames, while brooms and gunnysacks were used to stamp out the embers. We joined the bucket chain and passed countless dirt-filled buckets.

My hands were bleeding after the first hour and by the second hour, the numbers in our bucket brigade had shrunk to half. The old priest was our official timekeeper, with his pocket watch swinging from a gold chain as he walked down the volunteer lines rambling prayers and encouragement. After three hours of back-wrenching work, someone at the front of our bucket chain gave out a cry of victory. "We did it! The fire's out!"

The broom and sack teams were still finding occasional embers, but the main blaze had been reduced to a smoldering campfire.

"God has heard our prayers and changed the wind's direction," the priest ranted.

I doubted that God had heard anything. Yes, the wind had changed direction that morning. The fire had turned back on itself, and with no fuel remaining and only ashes and metal in its back path, the blaze lost its strength. But everyone on that city block knew that the wind could have changed again and restarted the fire.

All of the volunteers and the firemen started clapping when it was clear that only tendrils of smoke remained. Ming looked at me and dropped the bucket in his hands. He gave me a hug and shouted, "We did it! We killed the fire!"

He was only echoing the battle cry that the other volunteers had started; yet in Ming's Chinese accent, the words were even more poignant. Ming had been in our city for only a few weeks. He had been stripped of every comfort—from the language he knew to the people he had loved. Everything he had cherished was gone now, and somehow he had saved his spirit. I started crying then, tears that would have embarrassed me, except that everyone seemed to be crying. The priest was crying too. The firemen informed us that the other fires in the city had already been extinguished. This block of smoldering ash was truly the end of the nightmare. San Francisco had finished burning.

After a while, the firemen recruited the volunteers to line up on the side of the street for a picture. A journalist from one of the newspapers wanted a photograph of the last hurrah against San Francisco's worst inferno. I stood next to Ming and posed with a broom. After the photo, I turned to Ming and asked, "Want to be my business partner?"

Ming raised one eyebrow. "What business?"

"I'm going to get my wagon back from the army and get a horse team. Mr. Douglas—Sarah's father—promised he'd buy the horses in exchange for helping his family. I'm going to run the same delivery line that my father had. But I need a partner." I stuck out my hand. "In this together?"

Ming eyed my hand as he considered my suggestion. I was scared that he would turn me down. The only possessions I now owned were in the sack tied over my shoulder, and everything in my business plan depended on someone else keeping their word to me, but it all seemed possible. Finally, he shook my hand and nodded. "Before, I would not have wanted to be partners with a woman, but now . . . I understand things differently now."

"A woman wouldn't have a wagon team and a delivery business in this town before, either. Everything is different now." I wasn't certain that everything would be different enough to allow a Chinese man and a woman to run a delivery service together, but I knew I had to take the chance.

I arranged to meet Ming at the Chinese camp in three days so we could finalize our plans for the start of our business. A wagon team would be needed immediately, and our delivery service could be in business as soon as the city rebuilding began. We said our goodbyes and I set off toward Golden Gate Park while Ming turned back to the Presidio. This was one parting I was certain would not signal the end of a friendship.

As I walked toward the park, the news of the end of the inferno traveled with me, or so it seemed. In the areas that the fire had not reached, people gathered on the streets and talked in excited voices about the end of the great disaster. People everywhere were making plans for the evening. It was to be a somber celebration. I could not listen to the news of any celebration, however somber. My thoughts were with Papa, and I desperately wanted to see my brothers and sisters. I wanted to pick up Wesley and feel his little arms hug my neck and listen to Caroline's chatter. Maybe I would have to listen more closely to Caroline's chatter now.

No one could argue that her dreams were mere coincidence. Too much had come to pass.

I kept to the shoreline and had a view of the ocean on my way into the park. Just as I came to the path that cut away from the ocean, I spotted Frank making his way up from the rocky beach. He paused and lifted his hand to shield the bright sunlight. "Bette? Is that you?"

I quickly closed the distance between us and hugged him. Maybe I hadn't realized how tired my body was, but in his strong grip, I finally felt every muscle cave with exhaustion. He held me tightly and I knew I was safe in his hold.

"What happened?" The concern in his voice was almost palpable. "I've never seen you so weak. Are you sick?" Frank set me down on a rock seat. His arms still held me and I shivered despite the warm breeze from the ocean. Frank continued, "I thought you would be back yesterday, and when you didn't return, I didn't know what to think. Caroline woke up screaming your name and we all thought the worst."

"I'm tired." I thought I felt fine, but seeing Frank again released all the emotions of the past few days. I wondered what Caroline had dreamed of this time. I would not want her dreams, nor did I want to know my future. One day was enough to struggle with.

"I've never seen you like this. You must be sick."

"Well, it's good to see you too, Frank. Do I really look that bad?"

He grinned. "You stink too."

I tried laughing, but I started crying instead. Frank didn't make me explain myself or ask any more questions. He just held me and waited. We had been through too much. I wanted it all to be over—to have burned out with the last blaze and be normal again. But our lives were still wrecked. When I finally tried to stand on my own, my knees shook and Frank had to catch my arm.

"I know you want to see your family . . . but will you stay here with me a moment longer?"

I sat down on the rocky ledge again. "You're changed, Frank. You look older, wiser."

"Neither. But I do feel changed."

Yes, he was still only seventeen years old. And the past few days had aged us both by the same degree. Still, there was something different in Frank's eyes.

"When I last saw you . . ." Frank shook his head. "When you found me on the ocean I was wandering toward death. I had made up my mind to kill myself, and I can't even tell you exactly why. Then I saw you. Bette, after you left me I thought it was a mirage and that I hadn't seen you at all. But I went directly to the park and found my mother with your family, exactly as you said. Then I knew I wouldn't kill myself. Caroline was the one to reassure me that you would return. Her dream last night . . ." He shuddered and let his words drift. Frank squeezed his arms tighter. "It almost changed my conviction."

I looked up at him and saw tears bead in his eyes. He didn't brush them away, and the drops slid down his cheeks. Whiskers had settled on his chin and above his lips, and I realized that was why he looked older. The light fuzz had darkened. Frank leaned close and kissed my forehead. I nestled closer to him, feeling at ease for the first time in days. Somehow, we would work things out. I still had Frank to depend on.

"Now the tide's brought you back to me. And I don't want to let go of you again." Frank gazed at the rising ocean swells. "I went down to the water today to ask . . . if you were still alive. The tide was coming in. Just as it was when you last found me."

Frank kissed my lips. I hadn't expected this and immediately pushed away from him. His words had lulled me into a sense of safety that my mind was too tired to analyze, but now I understood his intentions. I stood up, no longer weak or unsteady on my feet. "Frank, the tide did not bring me back here. I walked on my own tired feet. I've got to tell my family I'm back." I turned and headed quickly down the path. Frank had not given up. That he expected to have me forever was as obvious as it was painful. I wanted him for a brother and he wanted me as a lover. He wouldn't listen to me.

Wes shouted my name and gave a loud hooting call as soon as I came up to the tent. He dropped his toy soldier and ran for me, jumping into my arms so fast that I had to catch myself so we wouldn't both topple to the ground. Charlie was at my side in the next moment, and the excited noise of the two boys awakened the rest of the family to my arrival. Caroline and Mary appeared next, with Mrs. McCain and Mother last.

The campsite had changed since I'd left two days earlier. They had fashioned a stove outside the tent, and soup was brewing in the kettle. Next to Mother's cedar chest, which served as the table, they had added three chairs and a wicker basket. The smell of onions and ham was delicious. I doubted the taste would live up to the smell. All of the food was army handout, and if the bread was any indication of the military's standards, I assumed the ham would be close to inedible.

Frank arrived at the tent but didn't look at me. Caroline excitedly pointed out my arrival to him, and he explained that our paths had crossed just a few minutes earlier. Mother and Mrs. McCain nodded their heads in approval. I felt nauseous when I saw their nods. I knew just by their eyes that they were scheming again. Our families would join. It made sense. If Frank and I married, Mrs. McCain would move in with our family and we would all be under one roof—assuming we could rebuild a house on one of the lots where our two families had lived only days ago. As much as I loved my family and wanted to look out for their welfare, I felt this plan was impossible. Frank loved me, but I could not return those feelings.

"Where's Trader?" Wes asked.

Mother's gaze was on me just then, and I felt a surge of guilt. I had lost our family's potential livelihood on three separate occasions. I didn't even know what to hope for anymore. "A soldier took him."

Mother swatted a hand towel viciously at a fly that had landed on the soup kettle, but she didn't say a word. I hated her silence. Why couldn't she yell at me?

"Did you get a certificate for the horse?" Charlie inquired. "If they give certificates for wagons, they should do the same for horses, shouldn't they? I can hold onto the certificate." He fished a folded piece of paper out of his pocket and proudly displayed the wagon certificate.

"Thank you for keeping that, Charlie. It will be important later. Unlike the wagon, I didn't agree to let the soldier take Trader. He was stolen in the middle of the night. Someone saw a soldier take him, but no one in the army will admit to anything. I've searched for Trader everywhere."

Charlie scratched his head. "So we have a wagon and no horses?"

"Not exactly. We have a certificate for a wagon, which we can only hope the army will honor, and no horses."

Mrs. McCain spoke up finally, "Well, we have Guinness. If the army will provide a wagon in exchange for your certificate, we would only need to purchase one more horse."

I didn't like the sound of that plan. Frank would be my partner in that deal. "We'll see. We don't even know if the army will honor the certificate," I said, sighing. The weight of the uncertain future was more than I wanted. If only I had slipped into the boat with Sarah . . .

Mother scowled at me.

Mrs. McCain continued, "Yes, we don't know for sure, and you can't count on the army to honor certificates, I suppose. But if they do, then that will be our plan—to use Guinness and purchase—"

Frank interrupted his mother. "I would buy my own wagon."

"But why?" she asked, apparently startled by her son's thought. "What purpose is there in having two wagons?"

"Bette shouldn't work on the wagon."

I wondered if he was angry with me. Unfortunately, he was staring off at the path leading down to the ocean, and I couldn't read his thoughts.

"Oh!" Mrs. McCain exclaimed. "Of course, Bette won't work on the wagon, but you can own the wagon team jointly. And Frank, she could certainly help until you are married and begin having children. The wagon will be owned jointly."

My throat tightened with her words, and I couldn't force down the blush that was warming my neck. How could she bring up marriage now?

"I'd lose business if there was a woman working with me," Frank answered. "We'll have a one-horse wagon to start, and I'll take smaller jobs."

"There is no engagement," I said, fuming by this point and barely able to keep my voice level. I couldn't decide which angered me more, Frank's unwillingness to work with a woman or the fact that my marriage could be discussed as though I'd have no opinion on the matter.

Wes, who was standing closest to me, asked, "What is an engagement?"

Mary, who almost never answered any questions, replied, "An engagement is when a man makes a woman promise to be his servant. They marry and she leaves her family to work at his house."

Everyone was stunned into silence by Mary's clear answer. Apparently, she had been paying close attention to the nuns in the Children's Catholic Doctrine. Frank kicked at the dirt and looked over at me. I held his stare. What had happened to us?

After a moment, Wes folded his arms and said, "Then I agree with Bette. No engagement."

I placed my hand on Wesley's shoulder. "This is between Frank and me, Wes. But I'll take your opinion into consideration."

He nodded solemnly.

Mother then cowed all of the children into jobs preparing the late lunch. Frank went to fetch water, or some other excuse that I didn't hear. When he returned a few minutes later, with no water, he didn't look at me at all. He sat down on a stool at the edge of our tent lot and whittled on a piece of driftwood with his knife. I couldn't tell what he was making and didn't want to stare, so I helped with the meal and tried to ignore him. The soup was dished into mugs because we hadn't packed any bowls. The mugs worked just as well, and everyone ate their allotted salty ham porridge with the tin spoons that the army had given us.

Only the children chattered during the meal. Mary and Caroline served their doll first. They shared the one doll that I had brought out of the house and Caroline's pink blanket between them in a very civil manner. As it turned out, I had grabbed the doll that they both thought was the ugliest and neither was very attached to her. Charlie and Wes had plans to go exploring the beach after the meal, and Mother wasn't offering any restrictions against their plan. I avoided glancing at Mrs. McCain, Mother or Frank, and instead joined in the boys' plan to go down to the water as soon as we had finished the last dregs of the salty soup.

Frank watched me leave without saying a word. The boys led the way down the path, and I paused when we reached the rock where I had sat only hours ago with Frank. The tide was on its way out now, and the boys had their fun chasing the white foam as it ebbed on the sand. I scanned the beach for bits of abalone and clamshells and listened to the roar of the waves. Frank still had not asked me, at least directly, to marry him. Unfortunately, Mrs. McCain and Mother were right. Their scheme would be the best for our families. If Mr. Douglas lived up to his promise and got us a new horse, if the army gave us a wagon, and if we used Guinness, we'd be in business in no time. But there were a lot of ifs involved in that plan. And Frank had said he didn't want to work with me. I hated him for this, though maybe I didn't want to work with him either. Ming had reservations about working with a woman but had conceded to the venture. I didn't need Frank. Yet, it would be easier with his help.

Frank came down to the beach and the boys shouted hello to him. He saw me perched on a rock and approached slowly, as though he were scared.

"Hello, Bette."

I nodded at him. "We'll have a beautiful sunset in a few minutes."

He turned to look at the horizon, and then climbed up on the rock where I was sitting. I had set my collection of shells on the only other flat part of the rock, and he looked over them briefly, selected two and then pushed the others into a pile so he would have room to sit. He held two iridescent blue shells in his palm. "You have good taste."

"No, I just have good luck. At least, when it comes to finding seashells."

"Can I keep these two?" he asked.

I nodded and watched his fingers close over the shells. He slipped the blue shells in the pocket of his jacket and then laid his hand over mine. We both watched Charlie and Wes dragging a stick in the sand to make roads down to the water. As the waves crashed on the beach, their roads disappeared instantly. The boys shouted with excitement as the cold water bit at their bare feet, and they watched the destruction of their roads with as much pleasure as they had in marking the sand.

Frank cleared his throat. He had a mild cough that made me wonder if he wasn't catching something. It was probably just from all of the smoke that had been in the air for the past few days. Now that the fires were finally out, the ocean air would clean the city's stench. Frank started to speak and then fell into a fit of coughs, and I felt a pang of concern mix with a feeling of dread. His cough reminded me of Papa.

"Are you sick?" I asked.

"No. My throat is bothering me, but it's only all the ash in the air. Nothing to worry about."

"Mother has some herb tea that might help. I think we packed that in the chest. We can make tea before dinner."

"Thanks for your concern, but I'll be fine." Frank paused. "You know, at this point, I wouldn't be surprised if you'd rather push me off the rock into those waves than concern yourself with my health."

"You've only made me upset. We're still friends." I watched him for some sign of agreement, but he only stared at the ocean as if lost in thought. I added, "I hope, anyway."

"Yes." Frank squeezed my hand and then let go. "And thank you, for that." He coughed again and fell silent. The boys had spotted a young seal and were shouting hello to the creature. Charlie glanced up at the rock where Frank and I were sitting. He pointed out the seal excitedly. The creature was hauled out only a few hundred yards down the beach.

Charlie called, "May we go closer to see him?"

I nodded. "But be careful and don't go too near."

They dashed down the beach and, as soon as the seal saw them, he turned himself around and headed back into the waves. The boys didn't appear disappointed. They stayed at the far end of the beach, watching the seal skim along the waves.

Frank suddenly lifted my hand up to his lips and kissed my fingers. He kept his gaze out at the ocean and began, "Bette, I know my mother shouldn't have brought up marriage today. But you mentioned I seemed changed, and I think perhaps you are as well."

I shrugged. I didn't feel like a different person, just exhausted.

"I also think that an engagement has been on both of our minds, and I'm glad in a way that it is out in the open. I've thought about it a lot. We've been good friends for as long as either of us can remember. There's no one else that I'd want to marry except you. I've never felt brave enough to ask outright. I think I'm ready for your answer now."

I didn't say anything at first. I stared at Frank, trying to read his set face. Did he really love me? Sometimes I thought he did, other times I thought it was just friendship. How much would I hurt him by this? I didn't want to tell him no. I thought he'd never forgive me for that. Somehow, I had to make him stop asking. I hadn't changed enough to have fallen in love with my best friend. "Frank, please don't ask me this."

"Why not?"

I shook my head and watched the seal swimming out to sea. Two others joined this seal, and soon the three were splashing in the waves close to shore. My brothers were shouting in delight of this sight and I thought of Ming and how much he would like to see this. I didn't love Frank. I didn't love Ming. But they were both two friends I wanted to keep in my life. Then I thought of Sarah. Was she gone from my life?

"Why not?" Frank repeated. He kissed my hand. "Bette, I know you so well. I've known you for so long . . ." He smiled and I could tell by his sweaty palms just how nervous he was. "And I've always wanted you to be my wife. Remember that time when we fought because of that rumor that we were betrothed? I knew even then that I wanted you forever. We'll have a hard bit at first, but I know we can make it work. We're best friends and—"

"Frank, stop." I felt sorry for him. I could never love him as much as he loved me, and I refused to marry him.

"Bette, I . . ." My glare stopped his words. He swallowed hard. "I'll give you some time." Frank kissed my hand again and then jumped off the rock just missing the spray of a cresting wave. He gazed up at me, with the sweet brown eyes of the boy I remembered, though his body was a man's now. Without another word, he turned from me and headed back up the trail.

The sun was setting and wide streaks of purple and red filled the horizon. I guessed it was the remnants of smoke that still hung on the horizon that reflected the rays of light in stunning streaks. Charlie and Wes made their way over to my rock.

"Where did Frank go?" Charlie asked.

"Back to camp," I answered.

"Are you ready to head back? The seals are gone."

"I'll be along in a few minutes," I said. "I just want to see the sun set."

The boys nodded and jogged over to the rock path that led up to the park. I watched the sky darken and the rich tones of blue color the evening in dusk. After a while, I picked up the shells that I had gathered and chose my favorite one for Mother. I wasn't certain if she would ever forgive me for what I had to tell her tonight. Then I jumped off the rock and headed back to camp. When I had just reached the high point of the rock trail I heard a noise that made my knees weak and froze my legs in place. The blood seemed to drain from my head as I listened with dead certainty. It was a faint whinny that might have only been the wind whistling through the willows. But I knew instantly that it wasn't the wind. I ran blindly, fell on the rocks, and started running again. I had heard only one call, then silence. As I ran toward the sound, I heard it repeat in my ears, unmistakable.

The path opened up to a meadow, and in the dim light, I saw nothing. I continued running, away from the campground now, and on a path I had never taken. I reached the back side of the Conservatory Building and called for Trader. No answer. I continued running and reached the home of the park groundskeeper. I started to run past this home, when I froze in place. Suddenly the whinny came again.

Behind the groundskeeper's cottage, I saw four horses. I gave a weak call, and one horse lifted his head and flicked his ears at me. Trader. I ran toward him, calling his name over and over again, my words only a whisper. The gate of the paddock was locked with a heavy chain. Trader ran up to the gate and pushed his muzzle through the wood to find my hands. I let him smell my palms and his nostrils flared, then quivered. He pressed at the gate. "Sorry, boy," I started, breathless. "I don't have anything to offer. But I'm so happy to see you. You have no idea how happy."

His muzzle felt soft and warm, as I remembered it, and not as the cold muzzle that I had felt in my nightmares when I thought him dead. I climbed the gate and landed in the paddock. The other horses turned to watch me as I ran my hands over Trader's back and hugged his neck. A dog barked and I heard the door of the cottage open. I prepared myself to leap on Trader as soon as the paddock door opened. The groundskeeper couldn't hold my horse hostage.

An old woman appeared at the gate of the paddock with a lantern. She held the lantern up to shine a light on each horse until she reached Trader and saw me at his side. The dog growled at me, and I wondered if I shouldn't jump on Trader's back now rather than wait for the woman to open the paddock. I had expected a man to be my horse thief—not a woman. But if Ming was right and a soldier had taken Trader, it was possible that the woman had received the horse from the soldier.

"What are you up to in there?" the old woman asked.

"This is Trader, my horse." I choked on the words and had to clear my throat. I was so happy to have Trader by my side that I could barely think. "He was stolen from me two nights ago, and I've been searching for him. He called to me and I found him locked here."

"Well, I bought that horse yesterday." The old woman pulled the dog, which was still barking, away from the fence. "That gelding's mine now."

"You bought stolen property," I argued. "Whoever sold you this horse was a thief. Who was it?"

"The seller was certainly no thief, and I'd mind who you're calling that. He was an officer in the U.S. Army."

"What was his name?" I asked with a sickening realization that she didn't need to answer.

"Piedmont, I think." The woman shrugged. "Stolen property or not, he's mine now and I will ask that you come out of the paddock and leave my property now."

Dear Officer Piedmont. How much could I hate you? I started the letter silently and then shook my head and tried to ignore the taste of bile in my throat. Trader was at my side. It didn't matter who the woman had bought Trader from. I had found him and would take him back now. The old woman hollered at me to get out of the paddock and I ignored her. Then she threatened to shoot and I forced myself to look at her. The old woman had brought not only a lantern but also a gun with her. She set the barrel of the gun between the fence rails and angled the target on me. I closed my eyes. Maybe it would be easier if she did shoot me. I wouldn't leave Trader here.

"You don't understand. This is my horse." I hated the tears that were falling out of my eyes. "His name is Trader and he belongs to me." My voice faltered on the last words as the tears came freely now.

She adjusted the angle of the gun away from me. "I have papers to prove ownership."

"Your papers are worthless. He's my horse and I have witnesses who can prove he is stolen property."

A shout came from the side of the cottage, and we both turned to see who was coming up the path. I recognized the horse before I saw the rider. It was Guinness. Frank sat astride the horse and had his gun drawn. He cocked the gun and angled it at the old woman. "Take down your gun and unlock the gate. We have reports that you are in possession of stolen property."

By the light of the lantern, I watched the color drain from the woman's face. "Who are you?" Her gun was angled on Frank now.

"Deputy McCain," Frank answered promptly.

The old woman trembled. "I bought the horse. I have the papers."

"The horse was stolen from that young woman and your possession of him is a felony. We have orders from the mayor of the city to shoot all looters or any individuals found in possession of stolen property," Frank returned.

The woman relented at this and I knew right away that she had not bought him for much, if anything. Most likely, she was just boarding the stolen horses. She unlocked the paddock gate, muttering under her breath a string of cuss words, and then slid the gun off the railing. I jumped on Trader's back and nudged my heels into his sides. He trotted toward the open gate. I didn't breathe again until we had cleared the paddock gate and whisked by the old woman. Frank nodded at me, but kept his gun on the old woman.

Frank only joined me once we reached the main thoroughfare through the park and the gatekeeper's cottage had disappeared from view. I nodded at him. "You saved me back there. I don't know what to say but thank you."

Frank nodded.

"You were following me?"

"Well, I was worried that you had gone insane." He smiled. "I had been watching you from the cliffs and spied you head back to camp, then take off in the other direction running as if there was a madman following you." He paused. "Now I think it might be true that you are a little insane. How did you know where to find him?"

"I don't really know. I heard his call when I was leaving the beach. Don't ask me how, but I heard him."

"You couldn't have heard him over the noise of the waves. The gate-keeper's cottage is a half-mile inland."

"Yes, I couldn't have heard him . . . And yet I did. Here he is to prove it." I grabbed a fistful of Trader's black mane and let the strands slip through my fingers. "And I have no idea why that old woman believed your story. A deputy? You don't even have a badge."

Frank grinned. "I'd bet the woman knew the horse was stolen property. Or else my gun scared her."

"Speaking of which, since when do you carry a gun?" I had never seen a gun on Frank and wondered if he knew how to shoot.

"I found it." Frank laughed. "How do you like that? We take back your stolen horse using someone's stolen gun."

"Thank you again."

Frank nodded. "Consider it repayment for getting my mother out of our house. She told me what happened. I never did thank you for that."

I nodded. "Then our debts are settled."

It took a moment for Frank to nod his agreement. Our debts were settled, but there was something left that remained undecided. He wouldn't ask me tonight, but I knew it was still hanging on his mind. Why else had he been watching me?

Chapter 8

April 22, 1906

Golden Gate Park was the scene of a small celebration on Sunday morning as free newspapers were distributed. The paper declared the end of the city's most horrible episode. Rebirth would begin once the rubble was cleared and the casualties laid to rest. The news circulated that the evacuees would be recruited to help clear the city rubble and a few in the tent camp rejoiced that they could now return to their homes. Many more knew they had no home to return to. The tent camp would be our community for the next few months at least, and it was lucky that warm weather seemed to have come early.

After the newspapers had brightened spirits, one of the priests from St. Anthony's gathered a motley group together for Mass under a canopy of sycamore trees. In the midst of Father Donnely's "and pray for us sinners," the sun broke through the fog enough to bathe the congregation in golden light, and everyone gasped. We shook hands after the Mass and headed to the breakfast line.

Frank and I stood in line together, planning our day and joking with Charlie and Wes about the mold on the bread that the army served. When the subject of rebuilding a house for our two families to share came up, no one, not even Mrs. McCain, brought up the topic of an engagement between Frank and me. Since Papa had an insurance policy and Mr. McCain had a sizable savings, Mother and Mrs. McCain had decided to pool resources and build one house instead of two. We had no idea how long the rebuilding might take and knew that the park might be our home for longer than any of us wanted. Our spirits were indeed high, despite everything, and somehow, I thought, things would work out.

After breakfast, I sat down at the cedar chest by our tent with my notebook that I had left in Mother's trunk and a pen I'd bartered from a soldier. In exchange for my writing a letter to his wife, he had given me the pen. I had a true present with this ink pen and had never had one quite so nice. As soon as I had the pen in my hands, my first thought was to write a note to Sarah.

Frank found me writing. He sat down on the other side of the cedar chest. "Who's the letter for?"

In case someone came upon me, I hadn't put any name on the top line, just, "Dear—." I closed the notebook and capped the pen. "None of your business."

Frank smiled. "Now there's the old Bette that I remember. Come on, tell me, who's your beau?"

"You are." I winked at him.

Frank tried to grab for my notebook, but anticipating this, I stood up quickly and avoided him. "Come on, Bette. We can't have any secrets between us. There's no fun as it is. Tell me."

I decided that telling Frank would be easier than putting up with his attempts at finding out, and he'd attract the attention of my mother over it, which was the last thing I wanted. "It's a letter to Miss Douglas. She left her pillow and jewelry box. I was writing to tell her. But I don't know why I'm bothering. There's no way to send her the letter."

"We can try to post it at the Ferry Building."

"I don't even know her new address. She's somewhere in Berkeley, but who knows how many Douglases there are in Berkeley . . . No, I'll hold onto the letter for a while. I just wanted to write her while it was on my mind."

"It won't do any harm to try and send the letter. Maybe she'll get it, maybe she won't. At least if we try and send it, there's a chance she'll get it." Frank tapped his finger on the notebook. "Will you write a letter to Mr. Douglas for me as well? We can send them together."

I was reluctant to do this, but agreed on the condition that Frank not mention to anyone else that we had sent the letters at all. Frank dictated a letter to Mr. Douglas telling him that he had a horse team ready and would soon be securing a wagon. He wanted to be ready to run supplies for Douglas Imports. I thought Frank was rather brash in sending this letter, but he insisted it was the way of businessmen and I let it go. I finished my letter to Sarah, only mentioning the green pillow and neglecting the jewelry box or any of my feelings, on the chance that unknown eyes might review the letter before Sarah received it.

Frank then convinced me to accompany him down to the Ferry Building to post the letters. I wasn't eager for another trek through the city and tried to talk him out of it. Although I was curious to see how much was left of our waterfront, I didn't think Trader, or Guinness, were ready for another hard ride. Frank convinced me finally, promising that we'd take enough breaks to let the horses rest. I brought the newspaper with me, since it contained a list of all of the buildings and city blocks that had been destroyed and a map of the remains. The map might be useful in case we got lost in the wreckage. This was a strange thought—to be lost in your own city's rubble.

As soon as we left the borders of the park, Trader and Guinness both perked up. They behaved as if they were two colts begging for a run in the brisk morning air. Frank and I both had to fight to keep them at a trot. "And you were worried that they might need a rest," Frank teased.

I shook my head but didn't answer, focusing on keeping my hands steady on Trader. Without a saddle and with only a halter and lead line to serve as reins, he was a bit unwieldy. Although the smoke had dissipated, finally, the air still smelled of fire, and I wondered how long the stench of destruction would last. We were stopped twice by soldiers and asked to help clear the rubble. They would only let you leave after an hour's work, so it wasn't until well after noon that we made it to the Ferry Building.

Miraculously, the Ferry Building and a few other buildings and piers on the waterfront had been saved. Frank pointed to one of the boats that had been docked at the pier for over ten years. "Look, Mr. Ralph's old boat survived."

"Too bad. It could have burned and no one would have missed it." The boat was too decrepit to ever sail again and the owner of the boat had passed away years ago. Only rats and kids on the wharf ever climbed aboard the old vessel. Still, the sight brought a wave of nostalgia. "But I'm glad to see it's still there."

Frank nodded in agreement. "Of all the things that burned in this city—you wonder why that pile of old wood didn't even singe."

"The firemen were probably pumping water directly from the bay to soak the pier and the Ferry Building. Ralph's boat was just lucky."

Frank smiled. "Some of us are, I guess, regardless of our lot in life."

While I stayed with the horses, Frank headed inside the Ferry Building to post our letters and find out if any ships were sailing toward Berkeley. A few men passed by and tipped their hats to me. It seemed that everyone was in better spirits today. One of the men even smiled, as though he had a good story in his head or a girl he was on his way to see. We had survived, I thought. That was why he was smiling.

I sat down on the sidewalk and the horses hung their heads for me to scratch. Everything was covered in ash as though the city had been cremated. Near my sidewalk seat, someone had scribbled a poem:

> *The bricks have fallen*
> *Few trees remain*
> *But no one walks on*
> *With soul unchanged.*

After reading the poem twice, I started crying. The words were mundane and not very poetic, so I wasn't certain why I was crying. In fact, the whole scene was pathetic—one destitute and exhausted young woman sitting on a sidewalk covered in the gutter's filth and bawling at the sight of bad poetry scribbled in ashes.

I heard the porter's bell ring, signaling that a ship was about to set sail and realized I was crying for my father. Maybe these were his ashes. I used to go to the Ferry Building every afternoon with Papa. No other spot in the city had such a perfect view of the bay, and I used to love to come and watch the sailboats cut cross the water. I remembered how the smell of the saltwater blended with the smoke from the ships and the sweat of the men pouring out of the warehouses that bordered the piers. Telegraph Hill sat on the right and the brick warehouses covered the foot of the hill like ants trying to crawl up toward the big houses on the hill's crest. Most of the bricks survived the fire. And I survived the fire to come down to the wharf where my father once worked.

Papa had been cremated with the rest of the city. The ashes that remained had changed all those who walked the rubble-filled streets. I swept my hand over the ash to erase the poem and then wrote my father's name along with his dates of birth and death. Finally, I added one line of my own sad poetry, "We are changed knowing one touch of brightness."

With blackened fingers, I turned away from my father's tombstone inscription and read the newspaper article's exhaustive account of everything that had been destroyed. The journalist estimated that more than 25,000 buildings were lost, and the cost to the city was untold millions of dollars. They, however, did not yet have an accurate death toll. Someone said a thousand deaths had been counted and another said ten thousand deaths was closer to the truth. Did the final number really matter? Death was measured in single numbers—one life lost to a mother, father, sister, brother, daughter, son or friend.

Frank came out of the Ferry Building after a while. Fortunately, my tears had dried by then. He sauntered over to the horses and tipped his hat at me. "Afternoon, m'lady," Frank imitated a Cockney accent. "Care if I join your picnic there?"

I smiled and handed him half of the sweet roll I was snacking on. I had stashed the roll in my jacket in the breakfast line, and no one noticed when I took another for my plate. We were only rationed one roll apiece. But I felt half-starved from my days of roaming and knew one roll wouldn't fill my belly.

"Any ships sailing?" I asked.

"No. But I found a message board that listed all of the ships coming into port this afternoon. We're receiving supplies from all over the bay—Oakland, Martinez and Berkeley. They'll need some wagon teams to deliver all of the goods."

"And we have two horses that could pull a wagon." I was somewhat hesitant to tell him of the plan I had formulated last night. "I wonder if the army will honor my certificate for the wagon."

Frank didn't bring up his earlier prejudice against working with me. Instead he shrugged and said, "Maybe we could find my dad's wagon. Do you think the barn burned?"

"Yes. The barn burned to the ground. Completely." I shuddered at the thought of Mr. McCain's wagon carrying all of the dead bodies. I couldn't tell Frank about this, and what did it matter? He would never see his father's wagon again. "You're lucky you got the horses out when you did, I guess." Frank finished his bit of the roll and rubbed Guinness's muzzle. "After the earthquake, I just ran to the barn and got Guinness. I wanted to go for a ride—to get away from the house. I never thought the fire would follow my path."

"No one did." I shook my head. "Well, no one except Caroline. She had a dream about it a few weeks ago."

"Really? Why didn't you mention it?" Frank added, "Ah, no one would have believed it. But your sister sees things . . ."

"Who believes the nightmares of four-year-old girls?" I asked, standing up and dusting off my clothes. The ash had turned everything black. At least I was properly in mourning, I thought. I wanted to change the subject back to the delivery wagon. "Frank, I have a friend over at the Presidio that I want you to meet. His name is Ming and he wants to work in our delivery business. With three of us, and a two-horse team, we could really get a good business going."

"Ming?"

"Yes, he's Chinese." I almost added, *but he's smart and trustworthy.* Instead, I decided to forge ahead with my grand plan, hoping that Frank did not have the same prejudice against working with Chinese that he had against working with women, or if he did, I hoped that we would cure him of that quickly. "My idea is that we get the wagon from the army this week and take a loan for the other tack that we'll need. The sooner we have our wagon team down here waiting at the Ferry Building for all of the deliveries that the city is expecting, the sooner we'll be making more money than we've ever seen."

"Why do we need three people?" Frank asked.

"Ming needs our help as much as we need him," I started. "And you know we'll have more work than two can handle."

Frank interrupted me. "Now is not the time for us to give alms to the poor, Bette. We are the poor."

"Ming is strong and smart. A partnership with him is not charity." I wanted to slap Frank, but held still. I needed to convince him that this was the best plan. "We'll need as much help as we can get if there are as many deliveries coming as you say. All three of us will make a team." I jumped on Trader and looked down at Frank. "You're either with Ming and me, or you're on your own. And I want you to be with us. You know it will work."

"Bette, why is it that I've always gone along with your plans? Even if they are as stupid as buying ginger ale at the Palace Hotel?" He laughed, jumped astride Guinness, and then stuck out his hand. "Partners with a woman and a Chinaman . . . my father would cringe if he knew."

"None of us have fathers anymore," I argued. "But I think they will be proud of us, in the end." I shook his hand. "And, don't worry, Ming and I will go easy on you. Unless you can't carry your own load, and then you'll be kicked off the wagon and on your own."

He grinned mischievously, spun Guinness around, and took off at a fast trot down the street. I didn't have to give Trader much encouragement to follow. We raced through the streets and the city rubble blurred to a soft gray. I loved the feel of Trader's body, and the sense of freedom he gave me was inexplicable. Frank turned down the Embarcadero and headed us toward the last pier on the north side. He pulled Guinness up just before we reached the end of the pier and dismounted. We tied the horses and Frank started undressing. I glanced down the pier and back toward the empty street. No one was anywhere in sight. Frank was in his underwear and goose bumps covered his skin. "You're crazy," I said, shaking my head.

"Come on, we used to do this all the time."

"Yes, when we were eight years old and it was the middle of summer. Frank, the water will be freezing."

"Don't tell me cold water ever stopped you before."

I knew he was thinking of the time down by Pete's Fish Market. He had called me a sissy girl in front of a crowd of our school friends and I had pushed him off the pier into the frigid December waters. I had instantly felt bad for pushing him and tried to help him climb out of the water, but he only managed to pull me in with him. We had stumbled home, dripping wet and reeking of fish, only to both come down with the flu the next morning. Frank hadn't told our parents that it was my fault.

"It's not the cold water," I said, thinking about undressing in front of Frank. "It's just that someone might see."

"Maybe they'll take our picture." Frank grinned and peeled off his undershirt.

I felt my cheeks blush as he dropped his underpants. He laughed as I looked at him, shivering in the cold. "You're crazy," I repeated.

"So are you." Frank dove off the pier and splashed into the water. His head bobbed up from the surface after a second and his teeth started chattering. "Come on, Bette. The water's perfect." He laughed and dropped under the water again, swimming in a circle around the pier.

I scanned the pier and the side streets again. Confirming that no one was in sight, I undressed quickly. The air was cool on my skin, and I knew the water would be even colder, but it would feel good to be clean. The water could at least wash off the ashes. Frank watched me as I slipped off the last layer of clothing. He wasn't even pretending to allow me some modesty. When I finally stepped close to the pier, naked and shivering, he smiled up at me. "Quit staring, Frank. You could at least pretend to not be looking at me."

"Why shouldn't I look? You're all grown up, Bette, and something to be looked at for sure." He smiled as I tried to splash water at him. "Seems like we were just kids last week, you know." Frank backstroked out a few yards to give me space for a dive. "Are you coming in or do I have to dare you?"

I felt the water hit my skin and a shearing coldness ripped over my flesh. The ice water found every spot of blood and dirt and melted it off my skin. I swam over to Frank and grabbed his shoulders, pushing him under the waves. We splashed back and forth for a few minutes, trying to keep our blood flowing. Before long, we were both turning shades of blue. We struggled out of the water with numb fingers and chattering teeth. The sun had baked the wood pier and we stretched out on the warm planks to dry. Frank found my hand and held it in his. We were both staring up at the blue sky, cloudless for the first time in nearly a week. The sun was a perfect orange orb eyeing us from the western horizon.

"Bette," he started. Nothing followed for a minute.

I closed my eyes, knowing what he was about to ask. I wished that he might lose his nerve or hear my thoughts. Don't ask me, Frank.

"Bette, will you marry me?" His words were soft, just as if the waves that lapped against the pier had asked the question instead of Frank. "I just want your answer."

I squeezed his hand and then rolled onto my side to look at him. He was beautiful, I thought. Though as far as naked men, Frank was the first one I had seen, so I didn't have much for comparison. I loved his chest and the wide shoulders. I touched his cheeks, prickled with new whiskers, and then traced the jaw line down to his chin and along his neck to his Adam's apple. My fingers continued down his chest, past his belly button and then lower to his groin. I didn't feel between his legs. Frank shivered and I felt his muscles tighten. I climbed on top of him, draping my arms on both sides of his chest and letting my hips fall on his. He wrapped his arms around me.

"Your answer is no, isn't it?" he asked.

I couldn't answer. We both lay silent, letting the sun bake our naked skin. Frank's body was hard under me. His desire was obvious, but he never moved. I remembered lying with Sarah and feeling a similar need, but I couldn't tell Frank about this. He'd never understand.

I don't know how long Frank and I lay together. We fell asleep at some point. I woke first, brushed by a cool breeze, and listened to his even breathing. He slept so peacefully that I hated to wake him. After a few minutes, I rolled off and got dressed. Frank slept on, and I watched him with a mixture of love and sadness. Maybe I was wrong for not wanting to marry him. I waited for his chest to rise with each breath, seeing the muscles in his arms twitch as he dreamed of something. It occurred to me how different Frank and Sarah were. Sarah was soft, smooth and obviously feminine, and Frank was muscular, hairy and smelled of horses and dirt rather than sweet soaps. Frank loved me, but there was nothing he needed from me. He would always be there, but only if I was willing to let him take care of me. With Sarah, I didn't know how long she would want me in her life, if at all. Yet I knew I wanted to be there for her.

Frank opened his eyes slowly, rubbed his face and rolled on his side to watch me, saying nothing. Finally he asked, "You're thinking of someone, aren't you?"

I nodded. I couldn't lie to him.

"Are you in love with someone else?"

"No. I don't think so."

"Is it Ming?"

"Ming? No!" I laughed, surprised that Frank would think of this. Of course, he was the only man who I had mentioned. "I like Ming, but there's nothing between us . . . I picked him up on the side of the road the first night of the fire. My father helped move his family into Chinatown this past week. Ming has lost everything. Everyone in his family died." I paused, wishing suddenly that Frank could meet him. "For some reason, he reminds me of you, especially when he smiles. He's like another brother."

"So, he's not the reason you won't . . ." Frank left his sentence unfinished.

"No."

Frank nodded. He sat up and folded his knees up to his chest, then stared out toward the bay. "I love you. But you already know that I guess."

"I know." I didn't know what else to say to him. When Frank stood up, I turned away, not wanting to stare at his body. He dressed quickly while I kept my eyes pinned to the horizon. The setting sun had left a brilliant mix of pinks, oranges and purples above the ocean's edge.

Frank headed over to Guinness and I followed behind him. Before I'd untied the horses, his hand caught mine. "I won't know what to do when you marry someone else," he said, his voice gruff.

"Me marry someone? Frank, I'll be an old maid and you know it. I have my mother and the four kids to take care of. It's me who won't know what to do when *you* marry."

"She'll be pretty and make you jealous, but I'll still love you." He laughed and let go of my arm, then brushed my cheek with his palm. "And you'll know that forever."

I stepped toward him. Our faces were inches apart and I could feel his breath on me. He was waiting for me. I knew he would wait forever, if I only asked. I kissed him then, for loving me, and for forgiving me for not returning his love. I felt his hands brush over my arms as though he wanted to embrace me. Our lips held for a moment longer. When we let go of each other, his eyes were moist. Maybe this was our last kiss.

"I'll love you forever, as my brother and my closest friend. You know that."

"But never as your husband."

I didn't have to answer him. He turned away so I wouldn't see his tears. I had a moment of misgiving, but kept silent, thinking that my emotions were strained only because I was reluctant to disappoint my dearest friend.

Frank kept Guinness at a good pace heading back to the park. We had gone quite a few miles on bad roads and dusk settled before we were even halfway home to our tent city. As the sky darkened, I felt an uneasiness grip me. Every time Trader took an uncertain step or twitched his ears, I found myself glancing over my shoulder to check for any followers. Trader had no problem keeping up with Guinness, and the horses didn't act as though anything was awry. I didn't want to mention my uneasy feelings to Frank. We hadn't spoken since leaving the pier, save a few words to the horses. Frank didn't act mean or upset with me, but he scolded Guinness heartily when the horse tried to sidestep as he mounted him. Later, Frank kept his eyes focused on the path and sighed frequently. I knew he'd rather be alone than with me.

We passed city blocks where Frank and I used to run, passed the still standing steeple of St. Anthony Church, and then the smoking ruins of City Hall and the public records building. As we passed the public records building, or rather, where it used to stand, it occurred to me that my birth certificate was probably only a small bit of ash now. I could disappear and no one would have any record that I had lived at all.

Frank suddenly pulled Guinness to a halt and raised his hand for me to wait. He pointed down a side street that we were just passing. I squinted in the dim light and saw nothing. "What?"

He pointed again and I searched the darkness. Then I made out the body of a dead horse and shuddered immediately. Never in my life had I seen so many dead horses. It was unnerving. I realized quickly that he hadn't pointed to the dead horse but to the wagon behind the massive body. Apparently someone had abandoned the wagon when the horse could no longer pull it.

Frank dismounted and handed Guinness's reins to me. I jumped off Trader and led both of the horses to the side of the road. It seemed there were eyes watching us from everywhere and yet there was no sound. In fact, we hadn't passed anyone on the street for some time. What had been the bustling Market Street Plaza was more like a graveyard than a city center tonight.

After unhitching the dead horse, Frank maneuvered the wagon around the body. He managed to push the wagon over a pile of rubble and onto the main street. "Wheels are solid and the axle is smooth," he said, mostly to himself. "It's not a bad wagon and the previous owners don't seem to be in any hurry to get it back again."

"Still, it would be stealing," I argued.

"Take a look at the dead horse. He's been run nearly barefoot. The shoes are worn so thin."

I shook my head. The last thing I wanted was to take a closer look at the dead horse. "But the wagon still belongs to someone."

"Well, then we'll post a sign saying that we've found a wagon and it can be claimed if the owner can identify the horse that gave his life pulling it. Then I'll have a few words with whoever claims it about their poor treatment of horses."

I thought this was a good plan, and kept my reservations about taking the wagon to myself. It was stealing, no matter what Frank claimed. Ignoring my qualms, I decided that Frank was being practical. We needed a wagon, and I didn't trust that the army would ever make good on the certificate.

I backed the horses up to give Frank room to maneuver the wagon. Although it was designed for two horses, whoever had last used the wagon had apparently lost the second horse because an extra bridle, reins and hitch were tied to the front rail. The wagon was otherwise empty save a red blanket covering the floorboards.

I bridled Trader using the extra tack that had hung on the front of the wagon, while Frank tried to fit the extra hitch on Guinness. The bridle was too short. "It won't work." He handed the tack to me.

"Maybe we could just use one horse to pull the wagon. We'll have to go slow, but it could work until we find other reins."

Frank walked over to the dead horse and kneeled down to pull off this horse's bridle. I shuddered as I realized his plan.

"Frank, no. I don't think we should use that bridle on Guinness."

He didn't answer me.

"We don't need this wagon," I argued. The uneasiness that I had felt was growing, and my hands were shaking for no reason. I stuffed my hands in the pockets of my jacket and turned away from Frank. I couldn't watch him pull the bridle off the dead horse and instead tried to stand guard with the horses, keeping my eyes on the main road.

Suddenly, a gunshot pierced the air behind me. The horses side-stepped and tossed their heads, and I grabbed their reins to quiet them. I turned toward the direction I'd heard the gunshot, gazing past where Frank was crouched by the dead horse and down the dark side street. After a moment, I recognized a soldier on horseback approaching Frank. The soldier's eyes were on Frank. He ignored me. My gaze dropped to Frank as well. He was crouched by the dead horse as though he hadn't heard the gunshot at all.

"Frank?" I called his name out loud, despite the soldier's advance. At that same moment, I realized that Frank was not crouching by the dead horse at all. He had collapsed beside the horse. I dropped Trader's and Guinness's reins and ran toward Frank, not caring about the approaching soldier or his gun.

When I touched Frank he made no sound. His skin was warm and his mouth hung open as though he was gasping for air. Blood was soaking his shirt as I pulled open his jacket. He wasn't breathing. "Frank?" I called his name in a hoarse whisper, and then I screamed it. I looked up at the soldier and saw he was almost on top of us now.

Through eyes blurred with tears, I realized who he was, and swallowed down a smoldering fire of hatred. "Damn you, get back! Stand back!" I yelled.

He took a step back, recognizing my face or the anger on it. Frank was heavy in my arms as I slipped my hands under his armpits and drug his body across the street to the wagon. The soldier was intent on following me and was now making his way around the lurking body of the dead horse.

When he reached the wagon parked on the main road, I yelled at him again, "Stay back, I said. Stay away from us!"

I watched him dismount and slip his gun into the holster. He came toward me and I screamed again for him to stay back, but this time my choking sobs made my voice inaudible. The soldier was Piedmont, Officer Piedmont.

"Damn you." My voice was low, but the venom of my words made him slow his advance. "You shot an innocent, unarmed man. You gave him no warning." Piedmont's face was a dark mask. I couldn't see any sign of remorse. "What sort of beast does that?"

He had no reply and his lack of emotion pushed me over the edge. I collapsed with Frank, bawling into his bloodied coat. Somehow Piedmont took Frank's body out of my arms. He lifted the body up into the wagon silently, easing out of the way when I pushed his hands off Frank. I draped my body over Frank, ear to his chest, listening. The anger at Piedmont dissipated, replaced by the fear that I was losing Frank. His heartbeats came slow, then not at all. My ear was against his chest for over a minute, begging to hear another beat. After a silence that lasted too long, I finally admitted that he had left me. With my fists balled in Frank's clothing, the familiar scent of him enveloped me and I let my tears soak in with his blood. His death filled my body, nauseous and intoxicating.

Officer Piedmont was asking me something, but I didn't hear his words. All I heard was Frank's silence. The only sounds I cared about were the thumping of blood in Frank's heart and the whistle of breath in his lungs. The bullet had pierced through his chest and he had died too quickly. Too quickly even for me to say I loved him or that I was sorry I couldn't love him forever.

I don't know when I finally let go of Frank's body, but when I did,

Officer Piedmont was gone. Nothing made sense. Why had he shot Frank? Did he think he was a looter? Piedmont must have spotted Frank trying to take the tack off a dead horse. But how was that reason to kill him? My head was spinning with possible explanations. Maybe Piedmont had shot Frank by accident, or maybe he thought Frank was another looter he was hunting. But why had Officer Piedmont left so quickly—unless he realized that he had shot someone who hadn't deserved his bullet.

Somehow I managed to cover Frank's body with the red blanket folded up in the wagon. I finished hitching the horses, using Guiness's halter instead of the hitching bridle, and tied the reins to the halter rings. The big bridle would remain on the dead horse. I wouldn't touch it now. Once the horses were ready, I climbed in the wagon and slapped their reins. They took up pulling the wagon easily, as though Frank's weight were no burden at all. Yet the blanket-covered mound on the wagon floorboards was a weight I could hardly bear. Twice I pulled the horses to a stop and considered burying Frank in the rubble of a building. I knew this was not logical, but the thought of carrying his body back to Mrs. McCain and my family was horrible. How could I explain his death? It had been senseless. If only I had kept my eyes on Frank, I could have shouted a warning as soon as the soldier approached. Maybe that would have saved his life. This thought upbraided me until I was bloodied by my own mind's torment.

The moon was high overhead and circled with a ring of mist. We didn't pass anyone on Market Street. Again, I was struck with the thought that I was alone in a city filled with ghosts. The ghosts no longer frightened me. In fact, I knew many of them by name now. Traveling by way of the side streets to avoid any further contact with the military, we finally reached the front gates of the park. One of the soldiers guarding the evacuation camp raised his hand to stop me as I neared the guard station.

"Where did you get this wagon?" he asked.

"Officer Piedmont," I answered. "He took my wagon on loan on the eighteenth, and he gave me this wagon in exchange just this evening. I have a contract from the army for the wagon back at my campsite if you need to confirm this."

The guard sighed. "No. But I'll need to have your wagon and the horses registered. We've had some problems with thieving."

I waited as the soldier brought out black paint and a thin brush. He painted the number "06-888" on the wagon and gave me two metal tags for the horses with the same number. When all was done, he took my name and printed it in his registration book.

It was then that I told him there was another thing to add to his register. "Frank McCain, son of Jack and Emma McCain, born on the tenth of March 1890, died today, the twenty-second of April, 1906."

The guard squinted at me. "Were you his kin?"

I shook my head, "Not yet. We were engaged."

"I'm sorry. This disaster left a lot of widows, miss. You'll have company here." The guard nodded for me to pass through the gates and flipped through his book to pen in the details of Frank McCain. He didn't notice the tears streaking my face. The only company I longed for now was Frank's.

The horses trotted to the campsite and I was glad that no one was about. I jumped off the wagon seat, stiff from the long ride, and tied the reins to our makeshift hitch post at the side of the tent. I pulled back the tent flap and nudged my mother awake.

She knew something was wrong immediately and turned from me to Mrs. McCain. Mrs. McCain had awoken as soon as I had touched my mother, though she was on the opposite side of the tent.

"Where is Frank?" Mrs. McCain asked.

They say a mother's instincts are strong, and I knew that she understood he was dead without me saying anything. She started sobbing. Mother went to her and helped her out of the tent. My mother didn't cry. She held Mrs. McCain as she would Caroline or Mary when they cried.

Somehow I told them the story of finding the wagon and of the soldier mistaking Frank for a looter and shooting him. I assured Mrs. McCain that Frank had died quickly and that it seemed painless. I doubted if she heard me at all.

Mrs. McCain struggled against my mother's strong hold. "I must see him," she begged, between sobs. "Let me see him."

My mother cooed to her, treating her just like a child. Then Mother shot me a horrible look when I told Mrs. McCain that Frank's body was in the wagon. Then there was nothing anyone could do to keep Mrs. McCain from seeing Frank, and she finally broke out of Mother's arms and ran to the back of the wagon.

I stood next to her, staring at the red blanket, suddenly frozen. Her hands clutched the wood rails desperately. "Lift the blanket, Bette."

Pushing past my mother's arm, and ignoring her warnings to keep Mrs. McCain away from the body, I pulled the blanket back and exposed Frank's gray face. Mrs. McCain reached out to touch him, then seeing the blood on her hand, screamed. She collapsed on the ground at my side.

"How could you have done that?" Mother pulled the blanket up to cover Frank, and then knelt down to tend to Mrs. McCain.

"Is she all right?" I asked.

"How could you?" Mother didn't try to hide her anger now. Her face was twisted with it, and I wondered if she would blame me for Frank's death. Did she blame me for Papa's as well?

"Get the wagon out of her sight."

"She wanted to see him." My hands were shaking as I struggled to re-place the blanket over Frank while Mother tried to revive Mrs. McCain. With a splash of water, Mrs. McCain came back to us enough to begin wailing. Mother took her over to their makeshift table and sat with her as she bawled.

I started to fill a mug with water for Mrs. McCain, but Mother ripped the mug out of my hands and pointed at the wagon. "Take it away."

Fortunately, Mrs. McCain was too distraught to understand my mother. I did as I was told, glad that the wagon and not my arms would carry Frank's body. The horses willingly left the tent and followed my lead to the Red Cross tent. I approached the guard standing by the Red Cross flag and asked, "Sir, my friend has been shot dead by a soldier. His death has already been registered. Where do I take his body?"

A tall man with a stethoscope around his neck and a doctor's bag approached us. I guessed that he had heard me, because he immediately questioned, "You said someone was shot by a soldier?"

I nodded. "He was thought to be a looter, though he wasn't. The sol-dier shot him by mistake."

"Where is his body?" the doctor asked.

I pointed to the wagon.

The doctor turned to the guard then. "Call another guard and carry the body into the tent for evaluation." Turning back to me, the doctor continued, "He was shot without trial? When and by whom?"

"He was shot in the street only a few hours ago, by Officer Piedmont. He was shot without even a word of warning."

The doctor nodded. "Will you give your account of the event to my nurse?"

"Yes, sir," I answered, not certain that I wanted to repeat the story again. If I never remembered any detail from that night, I might sleep better later.

The doctor led me to another Red Cross tent, leaving my wagon and the horses to the care of the guard. I was hesitant to leave them but trusted the doctor. He left me in the care of his nurse, who saw to it that I recounted the event in detail. The nurse told me that the doctor had treated a number of gunshot wounds and was trying to make a case against the army for undue violence. When the nurse was finished with me, I left the tent and found my wagon, with the two horses. Frank's body had been carried away along with the red blanket. I was glad they hadn't left the blanket.

When I got back to the campsite, Mrs. McCain was gone, as were the children. Mother sat on an upturned fruit crate near the tent. She held a small box in her lap, and as I approached, she handed it to me quietly. It was the music box that the Lee family had given to my father. For a moment, I wasn't certain if I should open it. The song that it played would remind me of Papa.

"Where is everyone?"

"Mrs. McCain wanted to go down to the water. I made the children go with her. She shouldn't be alone." Mother brushed her fingertip along the length of the box. "Your father gave that to me the night before the quake. He made me promise not to open it until he'd passed . . . Open it."

I gingerly lifted the lid, and Mozart's tinned notes rushed out to greet me. Two slips of paper were folded in the box and under the paper were several gold coins. I handed the first note with Mother's name on it to her, then unfolded the second note with my name. Papa had an account at the Union Bank and he listed his account information. Below this, he had written:

My dearest Bette,

I won more than I ever imagined the day you were born. Perhaps I should have told you this years ago, but my thick head only now thought to tell you. I know you will take care of the children and Mother, and I'll also ask that you not devote your life solely to them. Somehow, make your own way. There's a gold coin for each of the children. Tell them each that I loved them dearly.

Papa

I folded the note, slipped it in my pocket, and then closed the music box to stop the song that was playing. I would give the children the coins and tell each one something that I remembered about our Papa. I handed the music box back to Mother. Maybe the music would ease her mind. She hadn't unfolded her note from Papa yet.

Mother didn't argue when I pulled a fruit crate next to hers and sat down. She patted my knee and then said, "I loved your father. He'd been so sick . . ." She dabbed a handerkerchief at her eyes. "I'm sorry about your Frank."

My Frank. He could have been my husband. Yet, not my lover. I had no way to describe exactly what I had lost—a friend, a brother, a partner. I might have married him and been happy. "I didn't think I'd lose him so soon."

"I didn't think I'd lose your father so soon either." She turned to embrace me. I couldn't remember the last time she'd hugged me, and I relaxed finally in her arms. When she released me, she whispered, "We'll miss them both. But us women always manage, somehow."

Chapter 9
October 1, 1906

Truthfully, I didn't expect to ever see Sarah again. Ming mentioned her name a few times during the first month that we worked together, wondering if she would come back to San Francisco. I knew he was hoping she wouldn't. Ming was worried that she would steal me away. Unfortunately, I hadn't heard anything from Sarah since we said goodbye at the Presidio boat dock and doubted she would remember we had ever met after six months' time. Ming wouldn't believe me when I told him that nothing would take me away from our business now anyway.

According to Mr. Douglas, who had come back to San Francisco only a few days after the fire to start on the reconstruction of his business, Sarah and Mrs. Douglas were staying with his son, Henry, in Berkeley. Sarah was studying music with a private tutor and had a trip to Europe planned. That was the only information Mr. Douglas gave me. He knew we had become friends in the short time we were together, and I suspected that was the only reason he mentioned her name to me at all. Otherwise, I only talked to Mr. Douglas about his supply orders. Every time I met Mr. Douglas, a pain in my chest reminded me how much I longed to see Sarah.

Ming was certain that I'd quit our delivery business if Sarah returned because he'd had a dream about it. I wasn't one to discount dreams, but I honestly believed that the delivery business was my life, and I had a family who depended on me. When I told him this, Ming only nodded and muttered something in Chinese that he refused to translate.

I had no idea if he understood my feelings for Sarah, and still couldn't understand them myself. I tried to talk to Ming more about Sarah, but he resorted to Chinese. I knew from his tone that he was being coarse, but I couldn't understand enough of his language. Ming had taught me only a little. I had begged him to teach me more of his language, but he stubbornly declined for several months. He said I was a slow learner and that he didn't have the patience to teach a girl. I reminded him that I was his partner, with a 60 percent share in the business, and that he could submit to teaching a girl a few phrases each week. Finally, he relented and I began learning Chinese numbers and simple nouns. I thought I caught on rather quickly despite his harsh teaching style.

As far as the delivery business, Ming and I got on well as partners. Getting the business started hadn't been easy. Fortunately, we had little competition. Few of the delivery men that ran the old supply lines could return to business right after the fire because of the wagon and horse shortage. With few wagons or horses available to run the deliveries and a huge increase in the number of orders, there was plenty of business, but Papa's old clients were reluctant to work with a woman and a Chinese man. It didn't take long for necessity to overcome their prejudice, and Ming and I were soon working split shifts on the wagon. We purchased an extra horse to give the other two a break. Trader was still my favorite, but I found a growing attachment to Guinness.

Ming was most fond of Yosemite, the new horse we bought. Mr. Douglas kept his promise to provide the funds for another horse as repayment for my helping his family. Although we already had a full wagon team with the two geldings, there were enough delivery orders to run the horses twelve hours a day, and I knew we'd overwork the team if we kept up with our orders. By taking on a third horse, we could give each one a half-day break at least every other day. I took Mr. Douglas up on his offer when I had the opportunity to buy a five-year old mare. The man who I bought her from said she'd been named Yosemite because she had been found shortly after birth, in Yosemite Valley, stone cold and presumed dead. Apparently they had revived her with warm honey and cow's milk, and then raised her on a ranch near Yosemite as a cow wrangler. She didn't take to the cows well, so they'd decided to sell her in San Francisco for a profit. Unfortunately, Yosemite didn't take to the wagon hitch easily either, and I threatened to sell her more times than I could count.

Yosemite was a spitfire with a flaxen mane and tail and a dark gold coat. Ming thought she was beautiful and had nicknamed her Yo-yo. The city had a shortage of horses and every steed was sold at premium prices. While the market was high, I thought we might sell Yosemite and keep the other two horses that were already well-broke to the wagon. But Ming got so depressed at this suggestion that I knew we were stuck with her. Yosemite could never edge up on Trader in my heart, though she was at least as strong as the geldings and had a stronger spirit. I let Ming keep her as his favorite. And I thought it must be good luck to keep a horse named Yosemite. Most of the billboard advertisements for the Yosemite Valley vacations had burned in the fire, but every now and again I'd pass Van Ness and see one of the signs. More than ever, I thought I might actually get there someday. Anything could happen.

Ming spent most of his time with my family, though he never really said he was moving in with us. My mother fiercely argued the addition, but Mrs. McCain quieted her with, "Well, we really might need a man around the house, at least until your Charlie gets older."

I had learned that my mother did, in fact, have a voice. She seemed to become downright noisy after Papa's death, and I wondered for several months how different my childhood might have been if she had talked as much before the disaster as she did afterward. At times, I almost wished she were quiet again. Mother and I failed to see eye to eye on many things, but I had discovered that she would often consider my side of an argument. We formed a sort of disgruntled partnership. Both of us understood the other's value for the family. Neither of us had any desire to become friends.

Our stint in the Park Tent City, as Charlie dubbed it, lasted five months. During that period, our house was rebuilt with the money from

Papa's insurance policy, and Mrs. McCain chipped in her savings as well. There were too many ghosts lingering in the rubble of the old McCain house for us to build there. No one argued that Mrs. McCain wouldn't move in with our family.

After losing Frank, Mrs. McCain became taciturn and moody. She seemed to be only a shell of the old Mrs. McCain I remembered coming to tea with my mother. I didn't really blame her. I was moody as well. Mrs. McCain clung to our house and rarely ventured out for anything. Mother enjoyed her company and the two had a growing business of sewing pillows and garments. Half the city seemed to be in need of new pillows, and Mother and Mrs. McCain had too many orders to fill. Little Mary and Caroline helped out with some of the pattern cutting, and Wesley had an apt hand for the sewing machine. Charlie had jumped at the offer to help Ming and me with the horses and was saved from Mother's sewing class.

When I finally saw Sarah again, I didn't know what to say. Ming and I were loading an order at the pier and I heard someone call my name. As soon as I looked up, Sarah's face filled my eyes. My tongue froze. In fact, I thought I wouldn't be able to say anything at all.

Sarah waved and called to me again, "Bette, wait."

Ming muttered something in Chinese and then kicked the wagon siderails.

"What's wrong?"

Ming crossed his arms and watched Sarah's approach. "Will you run off to play with her? We have work to do."

"I'll just say hello." I smiled at Sarah and returned her wave. My heart was thumping loud and I could barely believe it really was her. I turned back to Ming, "She'll see we have work to do."

As I started out of the wagon, Ming grumbled something again in Chinese. I landed on the sidewalk and smiled up at him. In my best Chinese, I said, "Don't worry, old friend. I love you as well."

Sarah hugged me as soon as we met. Her skin was smooth and she smelled like summer—wild grasses and sun-warmed earth.

"It's so lucky to see you here! I just got off the boat."

Sarah held my hands too long after releasing me from the hug and I felt my cheeks warm with a blush. I stepped back from her. "I didn't think you'd come back."

She arched one eyebrow. "What do you mean? I live here." Sarah caught my hand again and squeezed it, then noticing her father down the street, hailed him excitedly. "Oh, here's my father coming to see you too. He's told me so many tales of your little wagon business running the supplies for the city. He's proud of you."

I watched Sarah's father approach, feeling a lump form in my throat. Suddenly nervous, I wished Mr. Douglas would find an excuse to leave us alone. Mr. Douglas paused to speak with his driver, twenty feet from our wagon. Mrs. Douglas stepped into an automobile parked near the Ferry Building's west entrance. Sarah's hand still held mine. If it weren't for the sensations in my right hand where her skin touched my palm and the feel of her fingertips on the inside of my wrist, I thought the whole scene might be a dream.

Sarah squinted at me. "What's wrong?"

"Nothing, I'm . . . it's good to see you."

She nodded. "I've wished so many times for an excuse to come see you, but Mother makes me keep a busy social calendar, and with my studies . . ."

"Well, I'm glad you're here. I didn't think you would remember me."

"You're very strange, Bette. Ah, how could I forget?"

I shrugged. "But why are you here? You're studying in Berkeley now, isn't that right? And your father's contractor hasn't finished with the house yet."

"Father wanted to show the construction to Mother and me. He said you've been a great help moving supplies up to the house. I heard the windows are stained glass imported from Spain." She stepped a few feet away from me as Mr. Douglas approached. In a louder voice, she continued, "Father has been talking of the house so much for the past month that we just had to see it."

"Yes, I suppose I've been boring my wife and daughter. Bette, you'll agree with me, though, that the house is really looking quite well, though McKnight is dawdling with the finer points. Contractors! I think they just push for more money with each extension."

"The house will be grand, soon enough. I especially like the stained glass windows."

Sarah winked at me. Mr. Douglas waved to Ming who was still in the wagon. "How do, Ming?"

"Fine, sir," he replied. Ming addressed Sarah for the first time, "It's good to see you again, Sarah. You have missed many changes in our city." Ming rarely referred to San Francisco possessively. Maybe he realized how much of his own sweat had rebuilt the city.

Sarah nodded. "I trust there have been no changes that you or Bette can't update me on this evening." Turning to face me, she continued, "Would you both consider having dinner with my family tonight?"

Ming quickly declined the invitation. I was upset with his curt attitude, but knew why he wouldn't want to spend the evening with the Douglas family. He was still sensitive to my feelings toward Sarah. I wondered myself, if Sarah had asked me to leave now, would I even consider it? I was obliged to Ming and my family.

"Well, I'll accept the dinner invitation, if you don't mind taking one guest rather than two," I answered, avoiding Ming's eyes. "And thank you for thinking to invite us. It would be an honor."

Sarah was pleased with this. Her father gave me directions to meet their family at pier nine that evening at seven. The family had planned on keeping their yacht docked at the San Francisco pier for a few days and would take dinner on the yacht with a few other invited guests.

Once we parted with the Douglases, I realized that I didn't ask who else would be at the dinner and worried that I'd be sorely underdressed for any occasion involving dinner with Nob Hill socialites. Maybe Ming was smart to decline. I wondered what Frank's answer would have been. Would he have accepted the invite?

After finishing our last deliveries for the day, we took the horses to the stable and bedded them in for the night. The new stable was located in the same place as the old one. In fact, many buildings were rebuilt in the same manner as before the quake. New storefronts looked nearly identical to the previous burned down ones, and the houses slowly appearing on the charred lots were similar to those that had stood on the same lot before. I thought this strange, imagining that people would have wanted to rebuild the city in a completely new fashion, but Ming thought it perfectly normal. He claimed that people liked consistency and tradition more than something different and new.

When the horses were fed and bedded for the night, Ming and I walked home silently. He was upset that I was going to see Sarah, but I knew he wouldn't bring up the subject. I washed up and changed to the new dress Mother had sewn for church—the only thing I owned that was clean. Since working with Papa on the wagon, I had taken to wearing riding pants nearly all the time and had forgotten the awkwardness of a dress. I never looked forward to the Sunday Mass when I was required to fit myself into the trappings that Mother had carefully sewn. I also wondered what Sarah would think of me in a dress. She had seen me once in a skirt at the ice rink and thereafter only in riding pants. Still, I knew I was more presentable for dinner with her family in a dress. I clasped the jade necklace chain, only ever removing it for bathing, and thought of Papa. He would have been proud to hear of my invitation to eat with the Douglas family.

My mother and Mrs. McCain both raised their eyebrows when I appeared in the kitchen wearing a dress. "Where are you off to?" Mrs. McCain asked. "There's no Friday Mass."

Ming answered for me. "She has an appointment with Mr. Douglas and his family."

"Oh, the business," Mrs. McCain said, nodding. "Shouldn't you accompany her, Ming?"

"No," I answered. "Ming declined the invitation because he wasn't feeling well this afternoon. I'll have no trouble going alone. Mr. Douglas is always more than fair in business with our family."

"Yes, but a woman can't really deal business with men. Ming should go with you."

My mother interrupted, "Bette will take care of things."

Mrs. McCain bit her lip at this and the discussion ended. After finding my coat, I slipped out of the house as the children were gathering around the table. Caroline smiled at me and asked, "Are you going to see your beau?"

"No, I have no beau," I corrected her. "I have a business meeting and I must look fine for it."

"Business?" She crinkled her nose. "Wagon business? Why do you need a pretty dress for that?"

Ming lifted Caroline up in the air and started to tell her a story about Yosemite and wild horses running through California. I slipped out then, with the smell of hot sausage and Mother's apple struedel following me out of the kitchen. Leaving the warmth of a comfortable family meal wasn't easy, and the thought of seeing Sarah had my stomach in knots.

The pier was only a few blocks from our house, and I made my way there quickly. A sailor directed me to the Douglas yacht and, as I approached their dock, the sound of a harp's melody caught my ear. A group of a dozen people or so were crowded on the yacht's deck, with Sarah at the center with her harp. One of the servants saw me waiting at the edge of the boat and approached me to help me board the boat. As soon as he offered his hand, I recognized the old butler, and smiled with relief. It was nice to see someone familiar.

Sarah flashed her eyes in my direction, but continued playing her harp. A man with a violin took up the tune she had started, and the duo continued playing for a few minutes. Finally the crowd clapped and Sarah curtsied while the violinist took his bow. Sarah came over to greet me and I felt my skin burn as she clasped my hand. I was certain my cheeks were red, and I wished I could control my emotions better. How familiar Sarah's hand felt and yet how foreign all of this seemed. I could hardly fathom how I had felt so close to her during the quake. Her world was fancy dresses, fine music and dinner parties with the city's elite while mine was wagons, horses and heavy crates.

I submitted to a round of introductions, trying to meet the gaze of each person Sarah introduced. She started each time with, "This is my dear friend, Bette, who saved my mother and me from perishing in the horrible fire, and this is—"

I didn't catch half of the names, but everyone seemed to greet me warmly, which surprised me. I soon learned that the violinist was the same man whom I had met at the ice rink where Frank and I had skated so long ago. It took me a moment to remember his name—Darren. Frank had mentioned that his mother was a concert violinist, and I guessed he had made her proud with his own talents. Darren was again Sarah's date. Once I realized this, I felt acutely out of place, though really I had been out of place since my first step aboard the yacht. The fact that Sarah had a date did not really surprise me. Yet, I was more affected than I thought I would be when the man took Sarah's hand and pulled her away from me.

Darren had approached Sarah and asked her to accompany him to the bar, just after Sarah had introduced me to one of her father's business contractors, Mr. McKnight. I was familiar with him owing to our business interactions. He had immediately started up a conversation about horses with me. Sarah gave one look back at me as Darren pulled her arm. She slipped away, and I tried to do my part in discussing the various attributes of horses for a carriage team versus a wagon team with Mr. McKnight, though I couldn't care a horse's ass about any of it as soon as Sarah was out of earshot.

The dinner passed painfully. Mr. Douglas chatted about business with Mr. McKnight and Mr. Packard, who had said less than one word when we were introduced. I guessed that he had forgotten about our meeting on the day of the quake, and probably that was for the best. I sat next to Mrs. McKnight and the new Mrs. Packard. Mr. Packard had finally given up on his bachelor days and settled in with one particular woman a week after the quake. Maybe he had been as changed by the experience as we all were, I thought. Sarah sat between her mother and Darren's mother, the concert violinist. Darren's father was on the other end of the table. I didn't know the other couples at the party and didn't care to make their acquaintance. I spent the dinner trying to avoid Mrs. Douglas's attention. She was at the head of the table ordering the help around like a queen bee, and every time I saw her, I thought of eating rum chocolates with her as we tried to entice her to leave the doomed mansion. Her sanity had now returned, and she was in complete control of the dinner party.

Although the food looked delicious on my plate, I couldn't taste anything. Only the sensations of hot and cold reached my tongue, and the soup was lukewarm along with the salad. Plenty of wine passed round, and I had more than two glasses, which left my head feeling better, despite the food. I couldn't ignore the arm that Darren kept so close to Sarah's chair, but I found myself chatting with Mrs. McKnight easily after the wine hit my bloodstream. Mrs. McKnight was the daughter of some famous railroad magnate, though I forgot the magnate's name as soon as she mentioned it. I guessed that it was the railroad money and fame that had bought the McKnights an invitation to the Douglas yacht, rather than the husband's contracting abilities.

After dinner, there was a short concert by Sarah and again, Darren joined in. I wanted to stuff a napkin in his violin. The more he played, the more I realized how much I hated the violin's sharp notes and decided that if I never again heard a violin, it wouldn't be a great loss.

The McKnights stood to leave shortly after the concert ended, and I asked for my coat then as well. Sarah noticed that the butler had brought my coat and excused herself from Darren's side. She whispered something to her father, and he smiled at me and then nodded to Sarah.

Sarah was soon at my side, and the butler helped her with a coat. He stepped us both off the yacht, though Sarah argued this wasn't necessary. When I felt the familiar wood pier under my feet, my head finally seemed to clear. I looked at Sarah and felt a rush of excitement. I had longed to be alone with her all evening.

She pointed to the end of the pier and I followed her. Once we had passed the Douglas yacht and the noise from the party had dissipated, I turned to Sarah. "I've missed you. It's good to see you again."

"I'm sorry to put you through that dinner." Sarah motioned to the yacht. "Family oblidgations . . ." We reached the end of the pier and Sarah sat down, seeming to relax now that we were far enough away that the guests wouldn't see or hear us. "I knew you would hate it, but I wanted you to come tonight anyway." Sarah pulled my hand. "Sit down with me."

I sat down at the edge of the pier, letting my feet swing over the edge. We were silent for a few minutes, listening to the dark waves lap against the wood poles.

"Are you happy working with Ming?" Sarah asked.

"Mostly," I said. "He's easy to get along with, and my family likes him as well. The work keeps me too busy to really think about anything else."

"For now . . ." Sarah brushed her hand over the blue linen fabric of my dress. "You are more fitted for pants, I think. What will you do when you marry and give up your work? Still wear the riding pants?"

"I don't think I'll ever marry." I remembered that the last time I had thought about marriage I was with Frank on a different pier, and though six months had passed, it seemed like only yesterday that he'd been shot.

"You want to be alone forever?" Sarah asked.

I shook my head. "I have my family to take care of . . . and Ming is good company. But Ming will find a girl and marry soon, I guess. My brothers and sisters will grow up, and then I will be an old aunt for their children." I forced a smile. "I haven't thought about marriage for a long time now."

"You know, Darren and I aren't engaged," Sarah said. "You remember him from the ice rink?"

I nodded. "He skated with Frank."

"And Frank beat him in their race. I remember that night well!" Sarah grinned. "Darren's ego was badly damaged. He always thinks he can do everything better than others, especially someone from the waterfront." She paused. Quickly, she tried to restate her comment with, "I mean, it's just that he didn't think that someone from the waterfront would skate—"

"You don't need to explain," I stopped her short. Of course Darren would think that he could have outdone Frank. For the aristocrats on Nob Hill, Frank and I were nothing but rats from the waterfront. I shook my head, wondering again how two women from such different worlds could ever form a lasting friendship. Sarah couldn't hide her blush. She apologized, but I shook my head and told her I understood the remark was nothing.

"By the way, how is Frank?" Sarah asked, trying to change the subject. "I'm surprised you are working on the wagon with Ming instead of Frank."

"Ming is a good partner," I answered. I didn't want to talk about Frank's death at that moment. I never wanted to talk about it. My head was swimming and I knew I had drunk too much wine. I felt Sarah's hand touch my shoulder, and I realized I was crying.

"What's wrong?"

"Nothing." I shook my head. "Frank was killed by a soldier. The soldier thought he was a looter. But he wasn't. The soldier shot him in the back." I paused, hearing the gunshot again in my head. Whenever

I thought of Frank, I heard this awful noise. Every memory of him had somehow become connected to the sound of the gunshot. "He had no warning. The soldier said nothing. He just pulled out his gun." I wiped my eyes. I couldn't stop the tears now and didn't try. Sarah hugged my body tight, just as I used to hug Caroline when she had a bad dream. Caroline's bad dreams had all stopped now. I wished that the soldier's gun had been only in a bad dream and that Sarah's comforting could now wake me. I don't know how long I cried or what made me finally stop. Sarah let me go finally. She kissed my forehead.

"I'm sorry. You must miss him terribly." Sarah squeezed my hand. "That soldier should be brought to trial, you know."

I shook my head. "It's done now."

She sighed. Only the sound of the waves lapping against the pier disturbed our quiet night. Sarah hugged me. "You know, I thought you were too tough to cry. I'm glad you let yourself feel this. It's a horrible thing that I can hardly imagine—to see your friend die . . ."

My tears had left a wet spot of the fabric, turning the light blue linen to a dark navy. "It's the damned dress."

Sarah hugged me again. "It's a nice dress, though." She pointed to a harbor seal that had just popped his head up from the waves a few feet away. "Look. He's grinning at us. See? He approves that we are together. It could work, you know."

"What do you mean by that?"

Sarah shrugged. "I'm not engaged to Darren, but he's asked me twice now. I won't say yes."

I stared at her, trying to read the emotions that she wasn't explaining. Would Miss Douglas now be my friend? When she had stayed away for six months and sent no letter? We were too different, I thought, to be close. It was chance that we happened to ever be together, and the disaster had only placed us together temporarily. Once the city was rebuilt, positions and class would return. I could feel the divisions forming already. Sarah was the daughter of one of the city's richest men, and I spent my days hauling crates and sweating like a horse.

The only correspondence Sarah and I had kept since our brief time together was through Mr. Douglas, and he'd given few details. I wondered if she knew more about me. She never sent a reply to the letter I had sent, so I assumed it hadn't reached her. With no idea of where she was staying in Berkeley, I didn't try to post another. It was stupid to think she could care about me, I reasoned. Sarah was from Nob Hill and would marry someone like the violinist and have no need for a friend from the waterfront. Maybe Darren hadn't met her standards, but eventually, she would find a man who would. As much as I suddenly dreamed of being Sarah's companion, this was a foolish thought.

"Will you not ask me why I won't accept his engagement?" Sarah asked.

"I'm thinking that you don't like the violin?"

Sarah grinned and then covered her hand over her mouth. "Please do tell him that, I dare you!"

With a straight face, I continued. "And I'd wager that you prefer women over men when it comes to sleeping company. You know, men snore. And I have it on authority that you enjoy kissing women."

"On whose authority?" Sarah gasped, feigning shock.

"Furthermore, I have an item of yours that proves you may have a soft spot for female friends." I pulled the silver jewelry box out of my coat pocket and handed it to Sarah. This was the box that she had left in our tent, along with her green silk pillow. I had kept the pillow with no intention of returning it, unless she asked. This was my one reminder of our time together.

Sarah opened the box and found a postcard picture of a famous female actress. I knew the actress—seeing her a few times on billboards near the theater. She was a beautiful woman who dressed in men's clothing. The woman had signed the picture.

"You had this all along? Oh! I thought I had lost it and I was so sad. Of all my silly possessions!" Sarah held out the card and then smiled. "You know, my mother met this woman when she was in New York. They became good friends." Sarah paused, as if she was trying to clarify her thoughts. "My mother prefers men. Still, the actress gave this card to my mother. I found it in her desk once and begged my mother for it. She told me I could keep it and even promised a trip to New York to see the woman on stage. Isn't she gorgeous?"

"She's pretty. But I don't know about her suit." I smiled. "I think I prefer women in dresses."

Sarah shook her head. "Thank you for returning the jewelry box." She set the card inside the box before closing the lid. After a moment, she continued, "You know, I might have to marry some stupid boy eventually, but I would much prefer you as my companion."

"Companion?" I grinned. "Is that what we would call ourselves?"

"Why not?"

"Sarah, you can't have me as your companion. Women like you are supposed to marry and have position in life, right? What would your mother think?"

"We'll give her rum chocolates until she agrees." Sarah smiled and pointed at the jewelry box. "And she'll understand a woman who prefers riding pants to dresses."

I doubted this. It was one thing for her mother to appreciate the theatrics of a woman who dressed as a man in a play, and an entirely different thing for her to let her daughter avoid marriage to spend her days with a rough woman from the waterfront. "She would think you were insane." I sighed.

"You would bet against us," Sarah said softly. "Wouldn't you? I can tell by the way you sigh. You think it would never work, regardless of our families. But why not? We won't marry and we'll live together in some nice flat—maybe on Russian Hill. There are some artist flats there."

"Do you really think we could both not marry?" I shook my head. "Our families would never allow it."

She shrugged. "Other women live together and so could we." Sarah pointed to the jewelry box. "And some of those women become famous actresses. I know my father thinks highly of you. My mother would understand."

I wanted to believe her confidence, but I knew Sarah wasn't accustomed to being practical. She had never, not even for one day, really taken care of herself. The closest she had come to self-reliance were the few days after the quake. I thought back to this and remembered lying with her in the tent. Neither of us could say that what we felt then would last, but I realized suddenly that I didn't care about any reluctant thoughts tonight. If she could believe that being with me was possible, we could both be bohemians and ignore our separate realities. My responsibilities would catch up with me tomorrow, but tonight Sarah was in my world. "Will you stay with me tonight?" I asked, trying to keep my voice unruffled. "I don't know how much longer I can wait to have you back in San Francisco."

"You will wait for me, I know." Sarah kissed me once, then pulled away and grinned shyly. "I like kissing you."

"Why is that?"

"Your lips are soft compared to . . . a man's lips. And you don't push me." Sarah sighed. "I can't stay with you tonight. I have to stay on the boat with my family."

I couldn't argue. "And what if you disappear for another six months? How will I know if you are ever coming back?"

"Don't be silly, Bette. You know I will come back here. This is my home." She paused and kissed me again. "And I wouldn't leave my dear friend."

I shook my head and turned away.

"You don't believe me yet, I see. Well, then I suppose I will have to prove myself."

"Maybe."

She cleared her throat and straightened her back. "So. We will start as friends. In due time, I will convince you that I aim to be much more than your acquaintance." Sarah took my hand and gave a brisk shake. "How do, Bette?"

I smiled. "Fine, Miss Douglas. How do, yourself?"

She nodded. "Well, thank you. I've never thought of myself as a suitor, but I'd like to try for you."

"I'm harsh on suitors."

"So am I." Sarah raised her eyebrow. "And as for our plan—and I've thought some on this already—I'd like to learn to drive a buggy. If you act as my driving instructor, we will have an excuse to become better acquainted."

"You want to drive a buggy?"

"Yes. Would you act as my teacher? My father has already purchased a horse and buggy for me, and I will convince him that you should teach me. It would be proper to learn from another woman. Driving lessons—don't you think that will be a good excuse?"

"Perhaps." I decided not to conceal my doubt on this. "You may find the violin more pleasant than a carriage ride and request a change of subject—or at least instructor. Women and the wealthy are often finicky, I've heard."

"You've heard? And from what source, I wonder?"

I shook my head. Where could I start? Before I had met Sarah on the ice rink, I had known her only as a spoiled impetuous daughter of a wealthy importer. Everyone said she was stunning, but no one had ever given her attitude a good review. After a few long days with her, I had seen nothing of the spoiled girl that people complained her to be. I saw only a beautiful woman whom I would willingly take as a lifelong friend.

"Well," Sarah began in an indignant tone, "women are not as fickle as their reputation proclaims. And my income is not as secured as you might think. I don't believe I can be held to any reputation that I did not earn."

"And," I stood up and stretched my hand out for Sarah to take. "We'll see what your reputation becomes, soon enough."

"Is that a challenge, Bette?"

I laughed and clasped her hand. "Maybe. Yes."

Publications from Spinsters Ink

P.O. Box 242
Midway, Florida 32343
Phone: 800 301-6860
www.spinstersink.com

DISORDERLY ATTACHMENTS by Jennifer L. Jordan. 5th Kristin Ashe Mystery. Kris investigates whether a mansion someone wants to convert into condos is haunted.   ISBN 1-883523-74-5 $14.95

VERA'S STILL POINT by Ruth Perkinson. Vera is reminded of exactly what it is that she has been missing in life.
                                        ISBN 1-883523-73-7 $14.95

OUTRAGEOUS by Sheila Ortiz-Taylor. Arden Benbow, a motor-cycle riding, lesbian Latina poet from LA is hired to teach poetry in a small liberal arts college in northwest Florida.
                                        ISBN 1-883523-72-9 $14.95

UNBREAKABLE by Blayne Cooper. The bonds of love and friend-ship can be as strong as steel. But are they unbreakable?
                                        ISBN 1-883523-76-1 $14.95

ALL BETS OFF by Jaime Clevenger. Bette Lawrence is about to find out how hard life can be for someone of low society standing in the 1900s.   ISBN 1-883523-71-0 $14.95

UNBEARABLE LOSSES by Jennifer L. Jordan. 4th in the Kristin Ashe Mystery series. Two elderly sisters have hired Kris to discover who is pilfering from their award-winning holiday display.
                                        ISBN 1-883523-68-0 $14.95

FRENCH POSTCARDS by Jane Merchant. When Elinor moves to France with her husband and two children, she never expects that her life is about to be changed forever.
ISBN 1-883523-67-2 $14.95

EXISTING SOLUTIONS by Jennifer L. Jordan. 2nd book in the Kristin Ashe Mystery series. When Kris is hired to find an activist's biological father, things get complicated when she finds herself falling for her client.
ISBN 1-883523-69-9 $14.95

A SAFE PLACE TO SLEEP by Jennifer L. Jordan. 1st in the Kristin Ashe Mystery series. Kris is approached by well known lesbian Destiny Greaves with an unusual request. One that will lead Kris to hunt for her own missing childhood pieces.
ISBN 1-883523-70-2 $14.95

THE SECRET KEEPING by Francine Saint Marie. The Secret Keeping is a high stakes, girl-gets-girl romance, where the moral of the story is that money can buy you love if it's invested wisely.
ISBN: 1-883523-77-X $14.95

WOMEN'S STUDIES by Julia Watts. With humor and heart, Women's Studies follows one school year in the lives of these three young women and shows that in college, one,s extracurricular activities are often much more educational that what goes on in the classroom.
ISBN: 1-883523-75-3 $14.95

A POEM FOR WHAT'S HER NAME by Dani O'Connor. Professor Dani O'Connor had pretty much resigned herself to the fact that there was no such thing as a complete woman. Then out of nowhere, along comes a woman who blows Dani's theory right out of the water.
ISBN: 1-883523-78-8 $14.95